REAPED

(Wages of Sin #1)

GRACEN MILLER
TINA CARREIRO

Time and Tide Books
www.timeandtidepublishing.com

Time and Tide Publishing, LLC
7040 Seminole Pratt Whitney Rd. Suite 25-109
Loxahatchee, FL 33470
www.timeandtidepublishing.com

REAPED
Edited by Amanda Wimer
Proofread by Charity Chimni
Interior formatted and designed by Gracen Miller

Cover art designed by Tina Carreiro at Tincar Creations
Couple: copyright © bigstockphoto.com by Valua Vitaly
Wings: copyright © by Jessica Dueck – StarsColdNight

Look for us online at:
www.tinacarreiro.com
www.gracen-miller.com

ISBN-13: 978-0-9903057-1-2
ISBN-13: 978-0-9903057-2-9 (Print)

DEDICATION

For my readers—because you're awesome and would probably follow me into Hell, skipping while wearing a smile and guzzling the Kool-Aid. Love y'all! ~ Gracen

For my readers—you guys rock! You devour everything I write and embrace all my wickedness. I love you guys to pieces! ~ Tina

ONE

Tossed out of my home like garbage.

Threads of despair seeded Solas' hesitancy as a misting rain drenched her. This uncertainty was new to her and not a welcome feeling. With all of her reaper power gone, thanks to the loss of her wings, where would she go? How would she survive as a human? They were fragile creatures, and she'd been powerful all of her existence.

The wind swirled about her as if she were the element's single-minded mission, whipping hair into her face and obscuring her vision. The edges of her jacket lifted with the breeze as she twisted her hair and tossed the strands over her shoulder.

Hunching into her coat to escape the drizzle, she perched on the edge of the building's roof and surveyed the crowded city street below. She tugged the leather tighter about her shivering form, the material drew snug against her shoulder blades, and she winced. The stylish garment failed at providing warmth.

Angel wings hacked off and in their place, mounds of scabbed flesh. Tears blurred her vision. She'd never seen Father so angry as when she'd refused to slay her assignment. At His instruction, the Lamb of God had sheared her wings from her back with his sword. Still throbbing the pain was unlike anything she could've guessed, and her brother had kicked her out of Heaven. Almost literally. After a hard nudge of his foot to her hip, she'd free-fallen from the streets of gold to the grimy, wet asphalt of mankind littered with cigarette butts, excrement, and God only knew what else.

For millennia she'd served Father as an angel of death. And not until she'd defied her maker had she discovered she alone could grant the one slated to die a stay of execution. Refusing to assassinate her mark, granted him clemency. She'd been ostracized, cast out of the only family she understood... but *he* was safe. *And I am terrifyingly human.*

None of her family would aid her. Not that she could blame them. They feared their father too much.

What am I to do now?

Nowhere to go, powers stripped, wings hacked off, the once self-healing body she had taken for granted was all she had, and it was damaged. And she ached all over. Is this what it was like to be mortal? To feel so much? If this was what humanity endured, she was ill-equipped to survive.

Probably already have an angel of death shadowing me. She shivered. From the cold, not from any fancy that a reaper haunted her back.

Running her hands along the arms of her leather jacket, she conceded that the chances of imminent death were slim. A quick demise would negate her punishment.

So that brought her full circle... *how do I proceed?*

Solas spied him, the man she should've murdered because her father wished it. Ryan Sinclair. Such a common name for an uncommon man.

Nothing noteworthy about his intelligence or his skill level. An average human, working a dead-end job as a stock crew at the supermarket down the street. Above average in looks— even for a mortal—but it was his soul that sang to her. Pure. Not unmarked by sin, but without malice of any fashion. He cared for his fellow man, begrudged no one their good fortune, but he was no saint either. Ryan was not a virgin, and he was a liar. She'd heard him tell a co-worker that his father was a fallen angel. He was not a Nephilim. She would've sensed it.

Inconceivable for him to attain such virtue in this messed up world unless he held paranormal kin, but even those weren't pure of heart.

It was not that she didn't want to obey God and kill Ryan. She physically could not bring herself to do the act. The injustice would be in following His orders and ridding humanity of what it needed, someone with values, compassion, and a willingness to aid those who suffered.

She jumped from the three-story building. Mid-fall, she remembered her wings were gone. To soften her drop she twisted to adjust her mark, bounced off an awning, then hit the pavement with her feet and barrel rolled, catching the curb with her shoulder.

The hard knock didn't hurt as much as the tender flesh did where her wings had been. Hot tears cooled against her cheeks. She knocked them aside with the back of her hands, furious at her body's unfamiliar display of weakness.

So many new and undesirable things to learn about this frail physique. Sustenance would be required, as well as clothing and—

"Are you okay?" Ryan knelt in front of her, while others strolled quickly past. Some casting curious looks while offering no aid.

Solas blinked at the man responsible for her fall from a world of safety, warmth, and acceptance. The very one she'd defied her father for and refused to kill. Not that he was to blame. She'd made the choice to disobey. That he offered help while the rest of humanity dismissed her further proved she'd made the right choice to save him.

His emerald gaze swept over her as if he attempted to locate injuries in the shadows.

"I'm fine." Her voice sounded gritty, unused. Looking everywhere but at him, she allowed him to assist her into a sitting position. The warmth of his palms bled through her jacket, and she resisted curling into his chest to seek more of his heat. Clamping her chattering teeth together, her head ached from the effort to withstand the pain of her injuries and the cold seeping into her body.

"Take it slow. You might've broken something."

She'd shattered enough bones during her tenure as a reaper and based on all the screaming her victims had done, somehow she suspected she'd be hurting a lot more right now if she had fractured something.

Ryan cupped her chin, his touch gentle, and he carefully tilted her head back, then to the side. "Only a few minor scratches, nothing major enough to go to the ER."

"I'm fine," she repeated when she was forced to glance at his face. Her breath hitched and burned in her chest as she stared at the man she'd fallen a little in love with before she refused to do her father's bidding.

No, no, I'm not in love with him. I respect him and value his life, but love is for humans, not a weakness immortals suffer.

Even in the dim lighting she could make out the sharpness of his green gaze as he perused her body. Cool, assessing consideration, like the examination of a physician. "No wonder you fell. The boots are sexy but not serviceable for this weather."

Before tonight she'd always dressed for style, never with a care for the elements because the weather hadn't been a factor. Thanks to receiving the boot from her homeland, her wardrobe would require an upgrade.

"Please tell me you're from out of town. Otherwise..." Words ceased, and he gaped at her face. Solas got the feeling he was just now looking at her as a man, rather than in a clinical nature.

She held her breath, waiting for him to complete his sentence. When he didn't so much as blink, she prodded, "Otherwise?"

He cleared his throat. "Where are you from?"

"Not here." She clenched her molars to stop her teeth from chattering. "Is it always this cold?"

"It's only supposed to go as low as fifty." Unfamiliar with the normal temperatures for the southern Alabama city in late fall, she guessed by his comment that fifty wasn't all that cool. "A girl like you shouldn't be out here this late."

Knuckles slid across her cheek, and his fingers brushed her hair over her shoulder. Goosebumps owned her flesh, but had nothing to do with the climate.

"A girl like me?"

"Pretty." The word was clipped like the syllables disgusted him. "Makes you a target for the unsavory."

"I can take care of myself." Could she? With her wings shaved off, whatever talents she remained in possession of were unknown. Before, she had walked among humanity without being seen. Her sudden visibility weakened her, making her wary. With her wings gone, she was at a severe disadvantage. Had she retained her aptitude to fight? Did she even maintain possession of her blade? So many unanswered questions lingered in her mind.

He snorted. She bit her cheek to keep from grinning. A fool could understand he had no faith in her ability to defend herself.

"You live around here?" Ryan stood, a quick, fluid move, and offered his hand.

She wanted to accept his offer, but touch was in short supply in Heaven. The way he'd touched her moments before had been too intimate, and she worried she'd be unable to withstand much more without revealing her respect for him, which would also expose her as a fallen reaper. Even having

5

lost most, if not all of her power, that secret would still mark her for the unsavory paranormal creatures that hated Father.

"No, I don't live nearby."

Where did homeless people live? On buses? Under bridges? On benches? She had no idea, indicating, once more, she was ill-prepared for this humanity gig.

Forgive me, Father—catching Ryan's green gaze halted her silent prayer. No, she forgave her creator for His rash decision to punish her and for wanting this good man dead.

Whatever he saw on her face, delivered a rush of compassion to his features, softening the cautious creases about his eyes. He shrugged out of his jacket and placed the garment around her shoulders. "Your boyfriend kick you out?"

"S-something like that." If he only knew, he'd be calling her a freak and shunning her. Defying Father was an unforgiveable offense. "Ryan..." She halted. She wasn't supposed to know his name. What would he think about her knowing?

"Ryan your boyfriend?"

"No." Confused she gaped at him. *Ryan is him...* but she wouldn't correct his error.

He threw his arm around her shoulders. "Come on, you can stay with me tonight. At least take a shower and get warm. It'll give you a night to plan your future. No frisky stuff. I promise."

Uncertain what 'frisky' he implied, she nodded, assured of his good intentions by his boyish smile and by the man she'd come to know as she'd watched him and plotted his death.

TWO

$\mathcal{S}$omething was off with the woman at Loki's side, and it had nothing to do with the wounded vibe coming off her. At first he'd been suspicious when she called him by one of his human identities, Ryan. He'd hoped her answer would've been yes when he asked if Ryan was her boyfriend. Keeping an eye on her would be essential and was why he threw his arm around her and offered to let her bunk down at his home for the night. Couldn't let her leave until he confirmed she wasn't a threat.

Not human, his instincts had warned from the moment he touched her cheek. Which meant imminent threat for him. If the wrong person discovered his identity, he would be in grave danger.

At least that was his gut feeling. But contradictory to his gut, her warm skin told a different story. Mortals were always warm to the touch; immortals of any kind were cold. His ability to tell was like a self-preservation mechanism. Had one of the other gods figured out a way to fool him? Tricking the trickster... poetic, but frightening.

Even more frightening was that he was attracted to not just the woman, but also the idea of protecting her. The novel feeling annoyed him. Heroics weren't one of his virtues. The fragility of her bones beneath his palm soothed him, reminded him he could divest her of life as easily as he picked her up from the pavement.

Her boots clacked against the sidewalk, heralding their approach. Too noisy, like a human. She peered at the world with wary hesitation and a jaded curl to her upper lip. Only the world-weary carried that particular expression. The jaded twist to the corners of her mouth validated his reasoning. What an enigma. One moment she seemed young and innocent and the next cynical. Against his better judgment, he was intrigued and compelled to discover her story. Almost as alluring, was her familiar scent. He caught just a hint of her smell every time the cool breeze whipped through her hair, but it was enough for him to flip through memories in an attempt to locate her in his past. The scent was comforting, almost like it had followed him in the shadows of his day-to-day life.

Too curious for his own good. That could be problematic if she were a wolf in sheep's clothing.

They took a left onto Wilmont Street. She flinched when he cupped her elbow. That was another thing, her obvious dislike of touch. Most supernatural creatures detested closeness, but he'd met a few humans over the years with the same issues.

"There." He pointed at a window on the top floor of a building. Gazing upward, she followed the direction of his finger. Were her ears pointed? "That's where I live."

"Maybe this isn't a good idea."

About time she questioned the wisdom of following a strange man to his apartment. "It's the best option you have."

Black eyes studied him. Unusual, she could withstand his stare, when mortals innately cowed to his superiority.

She couldn't be human. Petite in build, she held her spine straight and her shoulders squared, not the typical slouch mortals traditionally wore.

"Your choice…" He didn't even know her name. "The cold, wet streets or a warm shower and a place to lay your head."

She bit her bottom lip and lust poured through him, shocking him with the sudden tightness of his pants. "I'll accept the offer of a shower, but…" Furtive glances down the street as if she expected someone to pounce from the shadows. "I'll think about the place to lay my head."

8

Guessing she had no real concept of what he meant with the offer was one more reason to believe she wasn't mortal. Not to mention the odd inflections in her voice, as if talking was new to her. Or English might not be her native tongue.

What would she think if he offered *his* bed with him in it? He guessed that depended on if she were human or not. "Follow me."

In silence, she trailed him up the stairs and into his loft. Her arms were wrapped around her middle when she entered his place. Loki waited until she breached the doorway before nudging it shut with his toe. A slight clicking, audible only to him, verified the magical locks reengaged as they always did when he returned home.

He waited, watching her, as she peered about his home. Her inky black hair fell to her waist. Visions of his hand wrapped in those tresses, yanking her head back as he fucked her hard from behind flashed through his psyche. The sudden tightness in his jeans had him shifting his stance for a more comfortable position.

Better to redirect his thoughts. "May I take your coat? And mine?" She swiveled to face him. "I'll hang it to dry while you shower."

A slight nod, as he lifted his jacket off her. She shrugged out of her impractical garment that would offer little to no warmth. She winced as the leather slid across her back.

"Are you injured?"

Her gaze ripped to him. "I—I think my... shoulder hit the pavement harder than I realized when I fell."

Lie. He let it slide.

He stepped toward her as she held her jacket to him. "What's your name?" He draped the garment over a chair. "Huh? Oh... Scarlet."

Another lie. He drew close enough to run a finger along her jaw. Still warm, indicating humanity, yet everything about her suggested otherwise. "Interesting. I would've pegged you more as an angel." Although he wouldn't mind catching Scarlet Fever. "A fallen angel preferably."

'Scarlet' stiffened. "Is that a pickup line?"

He shrugged.

"It's atrocious."

Loki chuckled. And she was hiding something.

She blinked. Loki tossed her a cheeky grin and motioned her to follow him down the hall where he gave her a quick run through of his bathroom, showing her the location of the towels and washcloths. He withdrew a robe from the closet and placed it on top of the counter. "For after the bath. Toss your clothes on the floor in the hall, and I'll dry them for you."

Scarlet nodded, staring at the robe as if it were see-through lingerie rather than a fluffy, cotton housecoat that would hide any curves she possessed.

"Take as long as you need. You'll find me in the living room when you're finished." Loki vacated the room, shutting the door with a heavy click behind him and trying his damnedest not to visualize her naked with water coursing over her wet body.

He waited just down from the bathroom until all her clothes were tossed into the hall. Scooping them off the floor, he traversed to the laundry room. The rattle of the pipes indicated the shower had been turned on. Everything she owned was black. As black as her hair and eyes. Even her skin was the color of dark cream. The woman was a knockout and invited impure thoughts, but something about her hinted of innocence. Loki wanted to bury his cock so far inside her all that purity would be invalidated with a single stroke.

Frustrated by his thoughts and unusual attraction to a woman of unknown origins, he threw her shirt and jacket into the dryer and searched her pant pockets. Nada but lint. Must've removed any items shoved in them since she hadn't been carrying a purse. Odd for any woman not to have a handbag.

After tossing the last of her clothing in the dryer, he retraced his steps and stopped at the bathroom door, trying to convince himself not to peek inside. It was wrong to snoop, but—ah, hell, when had he ever nourished a conscience?

The well-oiled hinges were silent when he pushed open the door. Steam wafted through the open doorway and swirled about him, her scent assaulting him once more. Maybe she took the same path as he did every day? Why couldn't he place the delicious smell of her skin? Shaking his head, he returned his focus to the task at hand.

No personal items on the sink counter, the toilet lid, floor or anywhere else that he could see. Not a chance she'd been kicked out of her apartment—by a boyfriend, parent, or landlord—without at least one personal item. At the least, she should be carrying a driver's license and some cash or change.

A hiss from the shower startled him, reminding him that a very naked, beautiful woman used his shower. Tempted to join her, he caught his reflection in the mirror. His glowing purple eyes detailed his lack of humanity and derailed libido. If she had his exterior melting away without his awareness, she represented bigger troubles than he'd originally suspected.

With noiseless tread, he exited the bathroom and leaned against the sheetrock opposite the bathroom door. With his patience thin, he waited for her to depart the stall. As soon as she walked out that door, he promised he'd get to the bottom of her peculiarity. By any means necessary. Afterward, he'd ditch her corpse where no human would unearth it for years to come.

He hadn't spent these long eons avoiding gods to be trapped by a slip of a woman—mortal or otherwise. If she was a trap, he had to give his enemies an A for effort because he wanted to fuck her more than he wanted to kill her. Her lush, red lips were designed to wrap around a hard cock. Loki could easily envision her bent over at the waist, his hand fisted in her fuck-me-hair, as he drove into her mouth hard enough to make her gag. Just before he came, he'd swipe the contents off the table, shove her facedown over the tabletop, and... he'd take a moment to admire her fleshy ass tilted upward for his inspection. With no warning, he'd drive into her tight pussy. Of course her cunt would be tight. That was the way he liked them. Hot, wet, and virgin tight. Defiling the innocent was his favorite pastime. Afterward, he—

The click of the doorknob's mechanism signaled her exodus from the bathroom. Loki straightened, his gut clenching tight with anticipation. Steam preceded her like a celebrity's entourage. Wet, towel-dried hair hung limp down her body, stray locks clinging to her cheek and neck. The terrycloth robe hid her delectable curves, and he knew what he'd find beneath the soft material would be visually erotic. He was certain of it.

Her black eyes met his for a moment before she glanced away and swallowed. Why'd he make her nervous?

Loki reacted. Grabbing her, he jerked her close, then spun her and slammed her back against the wall. A sharp cry fell from her lips as his hand clamped around her throat. No way had he harmed her. He hadn't used enough strength to hurt her. Not yet, anyway. So her yelp must have been because she was startled by his abrupt violence.

"What the fuck are you?"

Eyes wide, her arms limp at her side, she made no move to resist his hold. Mouth working open and closed, she finally croaked out, "What?"

Thumb pad swishing back and forth against the erratic pulse in her throat, he struggled against dipping his head and licking the rapid tap. He leaned closer. Instead of his closeness intimidating her as he'd thought it would, her breath stuttered to a sudden stop, before continuing much too fast. Her dark gaze centered on his lips. Did she want him to kiss her? Fuck him. He wanted to accommodate her wishes badly.

He squeezed her throat a fraction, just enough to garner her full attention. "Scarlet's *not* your name. Who are you?"

Remaining mute, she licked her lips.

"More important, *what* the fuck are you?"

Just above a whisper, her voice trembled. "The same as any other woman."

He severely doubted that. She was anything but similar to her gender. But the way she said it, with such a sad note in her voice, coupled with the woebegone expression—for a moment she looked lost, weary, and a touch terrified—and he almost believed her.

Loki shifted his hand to her nape, snagging a handful of hair between his fingers and anchoring his palm flat against the wall. Holding her gaze, he lifted his other hand and speared his fingers beneath the fabric over her collarbone. The satiny smoothness of her flesh against his fingertips confirmed his suspicion... she wasn't human. No adult human was as soft as a newborn baby.

He skimmed his touch downward between her breasts and realized she held her breath, while making no effort to stop his investigation. His digits descended, creating a valley where material was disturbed by a slim view of flesh. The knot on the sash offered no resistance, and the robe parted. A thin swatch of black pubic hair covered the entrance to where he wanted to plunder.

Itching to plunge his fingers inside her to determine if she was wet, Loki denied his baser desires and raised his focus back to her face. Her stare locked on his mouth.

"What would you lose if I fucked you right now?" Because he was a few scant breaths away from acting upon that proclivity.

"I've... I—" She shook her head. "You're not invited inside me."

Loki scowled. What the hell type of answer was that? "Did you think I was asking?"

A frown creased her forehead. "Shouldn't you be?"

"Oh, for the love of all that's holy, don't pretend you're a twenty-something virgin." There were too few maidens for his tastes. She looked wide-eyed and too innocent for his peace of mind, escalating his irritation. "Enough bullshit."

Roughly, he jerked the robe over her shoulders, and she cried out as he yanked it down her back. What the fuck? That was twice she'd reacted with pain. Unshed tears glittered in her eyes, and she bit her bottom lip until it turned white. Using her hair, he snatched her forward and spun her about, ignoring her yelp. Loki shoved her face-first against the wall. With her cheek pressed against the sheetrock, he restrained her by her nape.

"Stop." The whimper at the back of her throat almost undid him.

Loki had never been a pussy, his survival required the use of his bastard skills almost twenty-four seven. "Shut up," he growled against her ear.

The chit reacted, affixing her palms to the wall on either side of her head and rearing back only a fraction. He clamped his fingers tight on her neck until she submitted against the wall of her own accord. Tears slid down the cheek he could see. She could cry all she wanted. He wouldn't risk his safety for her comfort.

Loki scanned down her backside.

Fan-fucking-tastic ass. Round, fleshy, just what a real man needed to grip as he rammed into her tight hole and fucked her anally. His cock twitched just thinking about plunging into that dark depth.

He shoved her hair aside and lost the ability to breathe.

"*Fuck. Me.*" Someone had done a bang-up job on her. The motherfucker! He ran a fingertip down the center of where a wing had recently resided. A sob ripped from her, signifying his touch hurt. He withdrew his finger. "You're fallen." Which also meant she *was* a virgin. His dick hardened to the point he probably bore the imprint of his zipper.

"Not exactly."

Loki released her. "Give me your real name, and explain the 'not exactly' part."

She pushed away from the sheetrock and faced him, her gaze wary as she took particular care not to touch the wall. "My name is Solas. I had no desire to leave my homeland, but was ejected from Heaven."

"Why?"

"I refused to kill"—she looked away—"someone."

"You're a reaper?"

"Was."

"Who was your target?" When she didn't immediately respond, he pinched her chin with his thumb and forefinger and forced her to meet his gaze. "I asked *who*."

"Ryan Sinclair. You," she clarified.

Ah... now he understood, and her eyes dilated as if she fully comprehended for once. They hadn't told her his real identity. If they had, she'd surely have swung her sword. When she'd refused to kill him, her pious parent had kicked her out of her abode, probably hoping after a few days of witnessing the cruelty of humanity firsthand she'd kill him to get back in His good graces. It was no surprise she seemed lost and lonely. A reaper would have no real-world knowledge of how to fend for oneself.

"Ryan Sinclair is an alias. My real name is Loki."

She blinked, thoughtful for so long he wondered what information she had on him. "*The* Loki?"

He nodded.

"I thought you were trapped somewhere with venom being dripped on you slowly. You're the cause of the earthquakes with your shudders of pain."

He offered her a salacious grin. "There are many myths about me. All of them unflattering. Few authentic. I'm what keeps the more powerful of the gods from absolute human domination."

"You're the trickster demi-god—"

"I'm a god."

"—that turns humanity away from salvation."

Loki shook his head. "No." But he wouldn't get into it with her. "Your wings won't grow back the way they're seared off. I can fix them so they'll grow back—"

"Yes!"

"—but it'll be very painful."

"I'm lost without them." Solas had no reason to trust him, and he couldn't figure out why she would. "Anything to have them once more."

"Why do you trust me?"

She wedged a lock of hair behind an ear. "The same reason I refused to terminate you. I sense no evil within you. That's unheard of in my line of work."

Loki wrapped his fingers around her nape and pulled her naked body flush with his. "First, I will make you scream in pain as I fix your wings. Afterward, I will bend you over the table and fuck you until you scream with an orgasm, ridding you of your virginity."

"I should protest."

"Yes, but it wouldn't matter. If you want your wings, the outcome will be the same." Loki yanked her head back by her hair and kissed her, thrusting his tongue between her lips when she gasped. She tasted better than he'd have guessed, better than God's vintage of celestial virgins. He ripped his mouth off hers. "Come, before I fuck you first."

THREE

$\mathcal{L}$oki watched her like he would devour her in a millisecond. Shivering beneath his stare, she failed to generate the energy to care. It was weird, but she'd watched him for so long she felt like she knew the man. And she'd always been sinfully attracted to him. Deciding she'd die on Earth either way, at least this way she'd go out with some sexual experience and more than one sin under her belt.

"Lean over the table." His abrupt command caused her core to clench in an unfamiliar way and moisture to leak from her channel.

Bent over naked would be too embarrassing. "Let me get the robe—"

He caught her hand, halting her retreat. "Clothing is not optional. I can't fix your wings if they're covered. Besides, I want you naked with your glorious ass exposed for my pleasure." He palmed her ass.

At the contact, gooseflesh paraded across her skin, and she gulped at the intimacy he expected.

"That just made you wetter, didn't it?"

Strangely, it had, but she did not understand why. Or if her reaction was normal.

He grinned knowingly. "I cannot wait to teach you the fine line between pleasure and pain."

That sounded daunting, but she'd do anything to get her wings back. Even sell her soul.

The dark wooden table was glossed with a high shine. Solas flattened her palms on the top and slowly bent forward over the round furniture.

"Nice… slow-motion method has my cock itching to pound that pussy."

The things he said to her. So crude, yet arousing. The cool surface caused her nipples to crinkle into aching, hard beads.

Loki came around to her head, grasped her hands, and tied the sash to her robe around her wrists, then tied the other end to the table leg. "Try to get free."

Solas squirmed and yanked. The material held. "Is that necessary?"

"Yes." Blunt and to the point. "When I scrape the cauterized wound, you'll try to fight me."

Okay, that worried her. *Anything for my wings.* But she couldn't suppress the anxiety that tickled down her spine.

He strode to the other side. "Spread your legs."

That would leave her intimately exposed to his view, but she followed his instructions and soon realized the position only tightened the restraints on her hands. Snug fetters went around her ankles, but she could not identify the material by texture and had no idea when he'd acquired more restraints. He secured them to the legs of the table, as well.

"Too tight?" His fingers trailed up the backside of a leg.

Warmed by his care, she fought against her brain shutting down from his simple touch. "I—I don't th-think so."

A finger penetrated her pussy. Solas jerked, but the restraints held her in place.

"Mmm… tight. And wet. The only way a pussy should ever be." His finger exited her body, and slid back and forth across her clitoris.

Solas moaned, and he thrust his thumb into her opening, pumping it as his fingertip continued to stimulate her clit. Seconds ticked off the clock. The world fell away until her only focal point was the pleasure surging from between her thighs.

"Getting wetter." His thumb sank all the way inside her, and his pad slid across her nub with the right pressure at the right angle and she shattered, crying out at the catastrophic hedonism deluging her body.

When she found her voice, she rasped out, "What was that?"

Loki chuckled. "A climax, gorgeous. You like?"

"Yes." Why had Father forbidden them from experiencing pleasure that profound? "Are you sure my wings will grow back?"

"It's a little late for mistrust now, don't you think?" His palm cupped a butt cheek, and he nipped the tender flesh. A hiss parted her lips at the slight sting. Loki licked the abused spot and slid his hand down the back of her leg. "You're trussed up for my delight, Solas, and fuck what a perfect view." He smacked her ass. "I'll fuck you like this afterward while your wings rejuvenate. Feel me." His jeans scraped the back of her legs as he swiftly rose and pressed his cock against her backside.

The hard length of him scrubbed along the delicate curve of her core. Sheesh, that felt good, made her throb where he rocked. How much better would it feel with him inside her?

He leaned over her and pressed his lips against her ear. "I regret having to hurt you in this manner."

Gathering courage, Solas sucked in a breath. "Do it."

He bit her ear, sending pleasurable chill bumps along her body, and pushed off her. Staying wedged against her bottom, he kissed between her mutilated wings. Taught not to question Father's motives, she felt guilt cross-examining why He saw Loki as a threat. Father should've known she'd sense Loki's goodness, so why send her to kill—

The first scrape against her right wing jerked a scream from her. That hurt worse than she'd anticipated. Fiery talons of pain erupted along the edges of her wound and extended outward.

A fine bead of emotion emerged from Loki, but it was so slight she could just make it out. Regret. He held no desire to harm her regardless of her former mission.

Solas curled her fingers into her palms and clenched her teeth waiting for the next explosion of pain. When the agony came, it took every ounce of willpower not to cry out as she bit the inside of her cheek to hold back the shriek.

Slow and methodical, Loki worked against her right injury. Convinced he'd never complete the job, she whimpered. She felt Loki stiffen against her, and she was thankful her face was hidden beneath her hair.

Heat hit her wing. Not in pain, rather soothing like Heaven's bliss. The heat disappeared, and Loki leaned over her left shoulder. He brushed her hair out of her face and licked the tears off her cheek.

"Your wing already peaks through. Feathers as black as your hair."

She wheezed when he skimmed his finger along the beginning tufts of her re-growing wing. They'd always been extra sensitive.

"Are you ready for me to fix the left wing?"

No, but she could endure the agony for what she'd gain. She nodded. "Please heal me, Loki." She wouldn't be whole again until she recovered both her wings.

Solas held her breath through the next wave of suffering. Nausea rolled from her belly, and she sagged against the table, allowing the anguish to overtake her. These were new experiences, and she'd never felt weaker or more disoriented.

"Done," Loki announced as the comforting warmth touched her back again. "You did amazingly well." He licked the delicate flesh between her wings. More of that remarkable, comforting heat poured along her skin.

"What are you doing?" Her voice sounded low and throaty. "It feels incredible."

"It's my healing magic." Loki shifted, and cool air hit her backside.

In a perplexing way, his presence reassured her, and she missed him. The metal clicking of a zipper giving free sounded loudly in the quiet kitchen. Solas' breath hitched as she realized he freed his cock to take her. A moment later, his jean clad thighs crowded against the back of hers. Was he so impatient he'd take her fully clothed?

Unsure how she felt about that, she dismissed her wariness as he ran the head of his cock through her intimate folds. He focused on rubbing the crown back and forth across her clitoris. Belly cramping, she moaned as another climax approached.

Loki slid downward, and she anticipated the rub back up against her clit when he slammed to the hilt inside her pussy instead. She yelped at the unexpected pain. Panting, she throbbed around his foreign length buried deep. Solas went to say something, but his fingers curled in the hair on her nape and pulled her head back to the point of discomfort.

"That's the last of the pain, Solas. The next scream you make will be in pleasure, with my dick so far inside you, you'll think we've become one." He flexed his hips, pulling almost all the way out before sliding back to the hilt inside her. "Did that hurt?"

Solas attempted to shake her head, but the hand in her hair immobilized her. A "no" squeaked out past dry lips. Loki set a slow, deep rhythm. Giving her time to adjust? She'd witnessed humanity copulate. This leisurely pace wasn't what she'd expected from him.

With the burning pain of his sudden entry dissolved, the movement of his cock was very different. Aside from the odd sensation of having a hard object moving inside her, she liked the feeling. Enjoyed how she felt both depraved and erotic.

This was what humanity vied for, fought wars against, and sinned to have. Sex was dirty, raw, and the way he heated her flesh just thrusting into her was fantastic.

"Hear how wet you are for me, Solas?"

"Yes." The slippery noises weren't loud, but they were audible over their pants.

"Your pussy feels so fucking good around my cock." To emphasis his point, he moaned as he thrust into her. "That's it. Squeeze that cunt around me."

His hand exited her hair and curled around the front of her throat, and his thrusts altered. From languid to brutal, giving her everything he had. Eyes going wide, her mouth parted. No idea what she'd intended to say, a groan exited in its place when his other arm curled around her hip and his fingers located her clit.

"Fuck," he groaned against her ear. Using the pads of two fingers, he rubbed. Hard. Almost too hard. She whimpered. His gruff voice sounded harsh. "Come for me *now*, reaper."

As if he held the trigger to her release, she climaxed with a low-grade scream, and the slapping noise of his hips meeting her flesh grew even more frantic. The stroke of Loki's fingers increased. Solas whimpered and tried to squirm away as the pleasure turned intense, too much to handle.

"You're at my mercy, Solas." He readjusted the texture of his touch on her clit, using his thumb and forefinger to rub and pinch along the sides. "I'm not ready to come yet."

Being a demi-god, unlike her, he could control his release. Loki pulled all the way out of her, and she felt empty, but achy from her first time. He slammed back in, and she cried out at the mixed pleasure and pain.

FOUR

*L*oki wrapped his fingers back in her hair and lifted his torso off her body. He watched as his cock exited her, streaked in her virgin blood, only to ram back into her tight, wet cunt without mercy. Solas' sounds of pleasure conveyed what she liked. And so far she'd enjoyed everything, except his initial entry as he broke her maidenhead.

Solas was the first angel he'd fucked. Her pussy tighter than any human he'd ever enjoyed.

He shoved into her, and the way she throbbed around his dick hinted she was close to coming. He pinched her clit hard to abolish her forthcoming release. She whimpered her frustration, and Loki grinned.

He might keep her awhile. An angelic fuck-buddy would be fun. What better slap in the face to her creator? Perverse entertainment for Loki. He released her clit. "Don't come, yet."

"I'm so close."

"I know, angel, I know." He let go of her hair, and his other hand left her clitoris. Half grown, her wings were glorious, as sable as her hair and glossy. He kissed one and licked the strands of the other.

She shivered. "That's like touching my clit."

He hardened his voice. "Don't come."

"Then stop."

Loki chuckled as he spread her butt-cheeks. "I should fuck this too."

Solas shook her head as he circled her puckered hole with his thumb, pushed just enough that the tip of his thumb disappeared. She grunted and jerked against the restraints.

He withdrew from her pussy and shoved two fingers inside her wet heat. As he pressed back inside her warm sheath, he pushed a wet finger into her ass.

She gasped. "That burns."

"Only for a moment." He pushed deep into her ass as he buried himself to the hilt inside her pussy.

Her back arched a fraction, the restraints allowing nothing further. Her wings vibrated as she buried her face into the wood. He fucked her slow with his finger up her ass and his dick in her pussy. Once her whimpers came non-stop, he added the second finger. Anal muscles clamped down on him, and a breath hissed between her teeth.

"Do you want to come, Solas?"

"Yes. Yes. God, yes."

She groaned as he reached around and deftly located her clit. He pinched hard, and she jerked. Loki increased the speed of his thrusts into her body. Watching both his digits and his cock penetrate her had his balls tightening and his head throbbing to release inside her. He'd pop both her cherries and flip off her creator while doing it.

For you, you bastard, he sent the thought to Solas' maker, but to her he said, "Come, right now." One swipe of his thumb across her exposed clit and she came around his fingers and cock.

Loki threw back his head, joining her as he groaned his release. A few more pumps, and he collapsed over her back, and a moment later a sizzling burn trickled down his spine. Proof her father had gotten his message and the motherfucker disliked it.

Release her. The words were shot into his head like a megaphone. If the decibel level was meant to intimidate, it'd missed wide of the mark.

One's cast-offs are another man's gain. The smugness of his mental voice was clear. Her creator's burn grew blistering hot, but since Solas' architect couldn't harm him further without being in Loki's presence, there wasn't much else He could do.

Loki chuckled against her nape. Her scent was refreshing in the diseased landscape of humanity.

"What's funny?" Her voice sounded raw.

"Your father is displeased I defiled you." He kissed the back of her neck and nuzzled the delicate spot behind her ear. Had he corrupted her? He sure liked the idea of it.

She tensed. "He'll come for me. Kill me."

"No." Neither. He'd protect her from her father.

Solas relaxed again, and he liked that she trusted him to keep her safe. "You've given me the courage to die with pride."

She didn't trust him, but had accepted her fate. That infuriated him.

"You're safe here, Solas. It's magically protected." Loki clenched his teeth. "I will *not* allow Him to harm you."

"You can't stop Father." She sounded so forlorn, and that caused a pang in his chest. "He owns me."

"Not anymore." Reluctantly, Loki withdrew from her and was pleased to witness her shiver. Did she miss his closeness? When he was finished with her, she'd be addicted to him.

He released her from her restraints and carefully rolled her to her back so she wouldn't injure her newly reformed wings. Loki clasped her face between his palms and stared straight into her black eyes. "He threw you away. I claimed you. That makes you *mine*."

A tiny frown plowed across her forehead. "Why would you want Father's discarded garbage?"

He could give her many reasons. To piss off her maker at the top of his list. But that would ultimately be a lie. He wanted her. Her innocence was refreshing in the jaded world in which he resided. It couldn't get any simpler than that. He wanted to teach her many things. Most of them deviant and what some would consider amoral.

"You're not garbage." He released a cheek and cupped a breast. Toying with the nipple between his fingers, he watched her face. A thin starburst of silver pierced her pupil. "You like that?"

Solas ran her fingertip along his jaw. "Very much."

The breathy quality to her voice almost undid his resistance. She'd be sore from his brutal fucking, not that he regretted taking her the way he had. He lowered his head to her breast, cupping the underside with his palm and holding it motionless so he could tongue the rigid nipple.

A sigh escaped her parted lips but turned into a ragged groan as he suckled. Her fingers plunged into his hair, holding him close. Loki shifted between the mounds until she undulated beneath him, pressing her dripping pussy against his belly.

He caught a nipple with his teeth and rolled it between them.

"Loki!"

"I think I shall give you another orgasm." Just so he could watch her face as she came this time. Would the stars bursting in her pupils expand along with her pleasure?

She made a small whimpering sound. "Why do humans call it that when it should be called a 'shattering'?"

Loki chuckled and lifted his head to get a better gander of her face. Perfect features, a seductress denied her purpose in life. Until now.

"Is that what it feels like?" He trailed a finger down her belly to frolic through her intimate curls. "That you're shattering?"

"Yes." The word wasn't much more than a whisper as he speared a finger into her channel, coated in her juices and his semen.

"Then I cannot wait to watch you *shatter*." Loki shifted quickly and replaced his finger with his mouth.

She jerked when his mouth touched her and moaned when he thrust his tongue into her. He used his thumbs to spread her so he could fuck her with his tongue easier. Hips flexing beneath his mouth, she wound her fingers in his hair, holding him to her.

"Put your legs over my shoulders." As she followed his instructions, he hooked his finger on either side of her clitoris and pulled the hood back, and kissed the exposed nub. "Good girl." He stabbed his tongue into her and twirled it around. Withdrew. A slow drag upward. Solas moaned and writhed on the table as his tongue moved over her clit.

He was so fucking keeping *his* discarded reaper. The nerve of her father for kicking her out. Instead of evading his enemy, maybe it was time he went after her maker.

Loki centered his tongue over her clitoris and swirled. He looked up along her body and discovered she'd risen on an elbow to watch him. Her hand still anchored on the back of his head. Catching the tiny nub between his teeth, he sucked and laved, sucked and laved... she *shattered*. All worry vanished from her face, softening her features. Her pouty lips parted, and she cried out as her body shook with her climax. The starburst in her pupils expanded and overtook all the blackness.

Nearing the end of her orgasm, he rolled his shoulders, and her legs slid down his arms, her knees wedging in the hook of his elbows. Loki jerked her to the edge of the table. Standing, he impaled her with his upward momentum. Solas' head fell back, her eyes wide as a startled cry exited her lungs.

He locked gazes with her as he thrust. There was no need to ask if he hurt her with his abrupt penetration. The bliss painting her face provided all the evidence he required to know she was unharmed.

"Tell me you are mine." He hooked one of her legs around his hip, the other still suspended over his elbow.

"Yours." No hesitation on her part. He liked that.

"I can do as I please with you."

"Yes."

"Say it."

"Do as you please with me, Loki—"

"I own you."

"—never stop making me shatter."

"I own you. Say it."

Her breath hitched. "You want—"

Loki drove balls deep inside her, quickening his thrusts and increasing the depth of his penetration. She gasped, and then moaned as he released her leg from his hip and used his thumb against her clitoris.

"Say I own you."

"I give myself to you," she blurted. "I give myself to you." She ground down against his cock.

"Do you know what that means?"

"I'm your… property." Her eyes went wide, her mouth lax, and she came. Hard. Crying out as her pussy squeezed his shaft, milking him.

"No." Loki buried deep inside her, groaning his release as he spilled into her. "My wife."

Together they'd make her father pay for casting her out.

Loki kissed her, and her mutter against his lips sounded more like confusion than a proclamation. "Husband?"

FIVE

Solas groaned as a ray of sunlight blasted her in the face. She turned her head to get away from the brightness, but got a face full of sheets instead. Blinking, she realized she was naked with only the bedding draped across her lower half. She shifted to roll onto her back, but stopped when the various aches and pains of her body protested movement. She lay there a long moment, recounting the last twenty-four hours.

It wasn't bad enough she'd been kicked out of Heaven, but she'd given her virginity to her father's nemesis—Loki. He was the reason for the discomfort between her thighs. Running on adrenaline, endorphins, and gratefulness, she'd committed extremely poor decisions and all for a set of new wings. Sick to her stomach, she speculated if this was how humans felt when they made bad choices?

Her black wings flattened over the bed like a blanket. They were worth the sacrifice of her virginity, and she was indebted to him for their return. Loki wanted more than she could give and claimed they were married. How much more would she pay before she escaped him?

The mix of emotions flooding her was alien and not to her liking. How could she be thankful toward the man that had also tricked her into pawning her chastity? Had he tricked her or taken advantage of her? He'd vowed to return her wings and promised to fuck her too, she'd known what she was getting into before she made the deal. She hadn't planned to bind herself to him in matrimony, and that *had* to be some form of trickery, because in a sane moment she'd never have agreed to that.

A bang jerked her into a seated position. The racket seemed to come from the other side of the penthouse. Time to face the male responsible for her fall.

She tested her wings, flapping them up and down, and rotating them backward and forward. They felt good, as solid as before the Lamb of God chopped them off. On mental command, they slid easily into her body, disappearing from view.

After tossing the covers aside, she exited the bed and rummaged through Loki's closet for something to wear. Silk button-up shirts in a variety of colors caught her attention. Cool and soft against her fingertips, she suspected they'd feel dreamy against her skin. She selected a red one and sighed as she slid it on... *decadent!*

She rolled the long sleeves to a more manageable length. The garment barely covered her bottom, but she'd have to live with the indecent display. Not like he hadn't seen it all, anyway. Up close and personal no less.

The visual of his head between her thighs and his mouth on her privates slashed through her head. Heat burned her cheeks. Just the memory made her throb at the apex of her legs. Quickly, she shoved the recollection aside. With no idea what she'd say to Loki when she found him, she was determined to settle their affairs. She'd politely thank him for taking care of her last night, and then she'd depart his company.

It is the sane thing to do. Safest, too.

Last night, I agreed he owns me. What a fool she'd been! Letting the trickster trick her into giving away her freedom for nothing more than a climax.

Solas found Loki in the kitchen, placing food on the table. The very table he'd taken her on last night. He paused for a long heartbeat before setting the plate down.

His perusal did funny things to her, left her squirming while igniting a fire between her legs she'd been sure would've been quenched last night.

Loki wore only jeans that rode low on his hips. Muscles delineated physical strength, but it was his demigod strength that was the most impressive. Mussed dark hair and scruff shadowing his jaw, she didn't think he could get any sexier. This appearance wasn't similar to the one he'd worn at any time since stalking him... short blond hair and reedy physique. Many angels could alter their appearance, so it wasn't a bombshell that he possessed the capability.

"This the real you?" She made a circling motion about her face and then pointed at him.

"Yeah."

"Better."

A devilish grin tugged at his lips. His green eyes were the one constant until they fizzled with a touch of purple as they skimmed her exposed legs. If she'd seen that two years ago when she first stalked him, she'd have known he wasn't the human Ryan Sinclair she'd been ordered to kill. Had she known, she'd probably have reaped him as she'd been ordered.

"That shirt looks much better on you than it ever did on me."

His words startled her back to the present. Uncomfortable beneath his scrutiny, she fiddled with the collar and looked about his kitchen, anything to keep from making eye contact. "I have no idea where my clothes are."

"You need new ones. Sit." His palm touched her lower back.

When had he approached? He guided her toward a chair. After she settled into the seat, she ran her fingertip along the top of the table. She'd lost everything and regained her life while strapped to the glossy wood.

"Table brings back fond memories, huh?"

Stunned by his forthrightness, she shot a glance at him. His hawkish gaze seemed to gauge her mood.

Solas swallowed past the sudden lump in her throat. "I'm unsure if they're fond—"

"You're sure, but in the morning light, you're second guessing everything."

"I've made unwise choices lately."

He flashed her a grin, and his voice held a note of something she couldn't identify. "Regret not murdering me for your daddy now?"

"It's what I've done for millennia without question. Instead, I disregard his commands and give you my chastity." Recognizing the volatile buzz surrounding him, she held his penetrating stare and still gave him the truth. "I repeat: Unwise choices."

Running his finger across his bottom lip, Loki nodded and perused the enormous selection of fare. Without warning, his foot connected with the leg of her chair, and he shoved her away from the table with a screech of wood against tile. He knocked her off balance when he caught her hips and jerked her to the edge of the seat, as he went to his knees. She tried to adjust her position but was diverted when he buried his face between her legs.

His tongue licked through her folds, and she arched her back, crying out at the insane pleasure. Nothing should feel this good. It was no wonder Father forbid indulging in sexual activity.

Loki wrapped his hands around her thighs, adjusted her to his satisfaction, and immobilized her into position against his face. As he swiped his tongue through her, she trembled each time he connected with her clit. She buried her hand in his dark-brown hair to anchor him to her, while tilting her head against the back of the chair and losing herself in the erotic sensation of his tongue.

Solas rocked her hips against him in a quest to reach the *shattering* she must have. She coveted them as surely as she ever had manna, more than she ever had Father's approval. Her belly cramped as her loins pulsated, and she gladly anticipated the cataclysmic release.

Loki moved away from her flesh, and she groaned at the death of her climax. He dragged his mouth across the inside of her thigh, smearing her juices all over her skin. She waited for him to get back to business. When he didn't, she lifted her head from the chair and looked at him.

A smile chock full of depravity appeared on his lips. "I own you, Solas. The sooner you admit that, the easier this relationship will become."

Her jaw dropped, and she dragged in a breath to flay him with her tongue, but he shifted upward and cut off anything she'd have said with his mouth on hers. His tongue speared inside and laved against hers. Solas gripped the chair to keep from pulling him closer.

Their kiss ended, and he dragged his mouth across hers in a feather-light caress, continuing onward across her cheek and to her ear. He whispered, "We have a deal. You are mine. I won't allow you to renege."

He moved away, striding across the kitchen to the counter. Solas worked at reorienting her libido as he poured two mugs of dark liquid.

"A deal with the devil," she mumbled beneath her breath. What had she been thinking? She'd hoped she hadn't made the pact she feared she had.

"I'm certainly no angel." He plunked sugar into one mug and flashed her a depraved grin. "Fallen or otherwise." He crossed the room again and set the mugs on the table. "Coffee with lots of cream and sugar. I didn't know how you liked it, but I surmised you're the sweet tooth type."

Solas didn't eat human food and had never tasted coffee, so she said nothing, just stared at him and ignored the mug.

As he sat back in his seat, he crossed his ankle over his opposite knee. "Have at it." He motioned to the table and sipped his coffee. Black by the looks of it.

She scanned the fare, recognizing a couple of things. "I don't know what some of this is."

"You've been reaping humanity for how long?"

"I watch mortals die, not eat."

SIX

Solas amused Loki. Last night she'd been unsure of herself and desperate to get her wings back any way she could, willing to pay any price he asked. This morning, she was grumpy and belligerent but still very much his.

He liked the rumpled look. Hair mussed from sex and sleep. And the way she smelled, a mixture of him and her, nearly undid him. His cock jumped at the memories of being inside her. That she wore his shirt did nothing to lessen his growing arousal.

He attempted to divert his attention away from his escalating libido and pointed at food choices, identifying each. "Bacon, ham, grits, eggs, waffles, pancakes, peaches, strawberries, toast, oatmeal, and biscuits. I didn't know what you liked." Maybe he'd gone a little overboard.

She picked up a fork and ran her fingertips over the tines. "I… don't eat."

With the regrowth of her wings, her immortality should've returned, which meant her need for sustenance departed. "Is there something else you'd like to do?"

A flicker of her angel prisms burst through her eyes. "Stab you in the heart with this." She indicated the fork with a serene smile.

Goddamn it to hell, but he adored her sass. "That's impolite after my benevolent hospitality."

She snorted. "Your hospitality benefited only you."

"If you truly believe I'm the only one who benefited, I could remove your wings again." He flicked imaginary crumbs off the table and watched her out of the corner of his eye.

Solas tensed, and her jaw clenched. "You wouldn't."

No, he wouldn't, no one deserved to be butchered and lamed in that manner. Spurned from her family and home, her father had kicked her into the cruel mortal world. Without him accidentally bumping into her last night, she would've died. Of that he was sure.

The reminder of the vulnerability on her face last night did crazy things to his protective instincts, instincts he hadn't realized he had until she fell at his feet. If he could get his hands on her maker, he would avenge the suffering wrought upon her.

Giving himself a mental shake, he caught her wary glance at the door. Was she planning to make a go for the door? He'd catch her if she tried. Not to defile her like her father had, but to keep her right where she belonged. Safe and with him.

"For the record, Solas, I'm not a good man." God forbid he ever become one of the holy rollers. "I've slayed more than one of your pious angel brethren, and I'll happily murder any others He sends my way. You should've killed me while you had the chance." The irony was that she out of all her predecessors could've succeeded. He hadn't even been aware she stalked him, which made her extra special in reaping talents. "I like to party, drink too much, and raise a lot of hell. I love to fuck. A lot. I'll use every orifice on your body to quench my insatiable lust." She made to rise. "Sit," he instructed, his voice growing dark. She eyed him for a long moment, weighing her options he suspected. Whatever she saw in his eyes caused her to sit primly on the edge of her seat, her gaze cautious... or was that excitement? Either way, remaining seated was the best choice she'd made since entering the room.

"I'll dominate you, force you to submit, and otherwise debauch you any way I can before I release you. You want to know the bitch of it all?" She said nothing, just gaped. Loki pushed out of the chair and stood over her. "The bitch of it all is, you'll love every goddamn second of it, and I'll make you come until you think you really will *shatter* when you climax."

Solas shook her head, and Loki caught her chin between his fingers halting the movement.

So naïve. He hadn't met a woman yet that wasn't trainable in the arts of sex. He couldn't wait. Could not fucking wait to begin with Solas, only he couldn't decide where to start first.

"You sold yourself to me for the regeneration of your wings and an orgasm. I won't keep you indefinitely, angel." He ran a fingertip along her jaw. "It would be unfair to enforce the contract to the letter of the law. You'd have said anything at that moment. So I'll keep you with me for a time, teach you the dark ways of men, and only when I've ruined you beyond redemption will I release you from our bargain. Do we have an understanding?"

"I think I might hate you."

Loki laughed. "You wish you did, but I recognize that look in your eyes. Right now you're curious what I'll teach you first... and if you'll like it. I promise by the time I'm finished teaching you the ways of pleasure, I'll have your body so trained you'll quiver in need from a feather-light caress."

Solas crossed her arms beneath her breasts and leveled him with an incensed glare. "Your arrogance is—I'd say amazing, but that's inaccurate. Atrocious is more like it."

"Can't be arrogance if it's true."

She knocked his hand aside. In return, he gripped her chin tighter and forced her head back so her undivided attention landed on him. "Listen carefully. I give you one warning only because you don't know my ways. The next time you touch me like that, I'll punish you."

With defiance shining from her black eyes, she leaned back, disconnecting his hold. "Nothing's stopping me from killing you, trickster."

Her voice might've been impersonal, but her gaze had his cock jerking in his pants. If she lowered her focus, no way she'd miss his erection.

"It's Loki, and if you wanted me dead, you wouldn't be threatening me. Not that you're a match for me." He waved a finger at her. "God, remember?"

"I forgot, pity the delusional angel."

He almost laughed at her sarcasm. "Better reapers than you have tried to snuff me."

In the next breath, she had him against the wall with her forearm to his throat. "I realize crushing your windpipe won't harm you, but never underestimate me, Loki. I'm sent in when all others fail."

Good to know, but he couldn't resist prodding her. "And yet you failed, too."

"Unwise choices." And they were back to that again. She lowered her arm and stared up at him. "Let's not pretend for one moment I'm here for any reason other than I chose to be."

"Another unwise choice, Solas?"

"I'm getting good at them."

"How human of you."

Mutiny blazed from her stare, and she angled her chin a notch higher. Damned if that wasn't one of the pious angel glares he'd become accustomed to throughout his life. Hers had the opposite effect on him. Instead of driving his spear into her, he wanted to drive his cock into her body.

"So you're choosing to stay with me?" He fingered her hair, relishing the cool silkiness of the locks.

She executed a dismissive one-shoulder shrug. "I can't return to Heaven."

"Unless you kill me." Not that he would stand by and allow her to gut him, but he was curious what she'd say.

The dry smile failed to touch her eyes. "There *is* that."

"But…"

"Is your arrogance so huge you haven't considered that my creator planned my fall and… the rest?"

"Wouldn't it be foolish of you to warn me if it was?" He hadn't considered the possibility, but his mind swam with opportunities now.

She pursed her lips as she considered his question. "I've never known a reaper to possess freewill before. It's plausible I might not remember our agreement."

"Or you could be lying to me."

Solas nodded.

Loki braced a hand on the wall next to her head. "Or you could be lying to yourself, wishing that were the outcome."

She took the bait. "I know I like the way you kiss me"—she took his hand and guided it to her pussy—"here."

Wet heat warmed his palm as she kept her hand over his, holding his in place. Loki almost swallowed his tongue.

"That's good to know." He strummed the fingers of his other hand through her sable locks and hoped he sounded calmer than he felt. "Have you ever given yourself pleasure before?"

Black eyebrows pulled together. "As in make myself… *shatter*?"

"Yes."

"No." As if the word wasn't enough, she shook her head. "Of course not. If Father found out, He would've—I don't even know, but it would've been terrible."

"Welcome to adulthood, where you can do any goddamn thing you want without parental consequences." He swung her into his arms, and she squealed at her sudden reposition. "And welcome to your first lesson."

Impatience riding him hard, his strides ate up the space between kitchen and bedroom as he carried Solas down the hall. Had he ever been this eager to train someone? He couldn't recall a time when he had been.

In the bedroom, he kicked the door shut and slowly lowered her to the floor, her body scrubbing against his. The shirt hiked up, and he palmed her bare bottom, slipping his digits through the crack. He ran his hands up her back and cupped her face. She stared at his mouth, and he knew she wanted him to kiss her. He didn't give her what she wanted, but instead lowered his head and licked along her neck.

He released the top button on the shirt and kissed the exposed flesh. A scrape of his teeth between her breasts, a lick to her ribs, and she shivered in his arms. As he went to his knees before her, he kissed her belly button, and reached the final button on the shirt. He unfastened the shirt, and the silky material parted. Only her erect nipples kept the fabric from separating completely.

What a fucking view! Perfection, just like the angel she was. She gazed at him as he licked the flesh between thigh and pussy. Her fingers dove into his hair, hugging him near. Ignoring her silent direction, he placed open mouth kisses along her abdomen just above her cunt, leaving a wet trail to her other thigh.

"Loki…" As she whispered his name, she attempted to navigate his head between her thighs, widening her stance to grant easier access. Goddamn, to think she'd been a virgin less than twenty-four hours ago. He liked her innate sexuality and that she was eager to express what she wanted. That made her very trainable.

Loki captured her hand and kissed her palm before guiding it between her legs. A slow breath pushed past her lips as he steered her fingers through her folds. Watching those digits slip through her wetness was the hottest thing he'd seen in a long time.

"Feel how soft and wet you are, angel? This here"—he guided her fingertip in, circling her clitoris—"is what you like for me to kiss." He sat back on his haunches, releasing his grip on her hand. "Make yourself *shatter* while I watch."

SEVEN

$\mathcal{L}$oki led Solas down the street, his palm on the small of her back. His possessiveness toward her churned inside his gut, making him queasy with his suspicion of her. None were as pure as she seemed to be. It didn't matter she'd been a virgin until he took it, because virginity didn't equate to purity. Neither did it matter she was an angel, because there were good and bad among all factions of the supernatural world regardless what her parent would have mortals believe. She was also a reaper, and reapers slayed on command. They slaughtered innocents, the devout, men, women, and even children without question. Their conviction rested in the belief that their parent knew what was best.

Sanctimonious fucker.

The ends of her raven hair brushed against the back of his hand, causing his fingers to flex with the need to coil inside her locks. Normally he didn't feel possessive over the women he took. Solas was the exception or maybe the feeling had to do with the fact he'd come so hard he'd thought he saw her maker. Sex with her had damn sure been cataclysmic enough for her father to make an appearance and attempt to reclaim her. That had to count toward something.

"Where are we going, Loki?"

As they strolled down the street, he watched her wide-eyed gaze bounce around like a child watching a ball in a toy store. Awe filled her features, as if she tasted the world differently now that she'd been reborn. Maybe his magic allowed her to see the reality of the world, instead of viewing it through her father's self-righteous eyes.

Whatever put that glaze of astonishment on her face, her innocence hardened his cock. He stopped on the sidewalk to adjust and mentally talk his dick into behaving.

"You need a wardrobe, angel." Not that he minded what little she wore, but society frowned upon indecency. Neither could he deny that for some insane reason something about her wearing his shirt had him wanting to pound on his chest like a goddamn caveman. Ridiculous, but why fight his unusual reaction? "As fuckable as you look in those boots and my shirt, you'll need more for your stay. There's a boutique up the street."

"Boutique?" Her bottom lip slid under her teeth in an insecure way he hadn't seen yet. As she fiddled with the jacket Loki loaned her, a piece of paper fell from the pocket and blew up the street. Solas chased it until a woman stepped on the folded paper.

The woman bent to retrieve it and held it out for Solas, wearing a pleasant and open smile. "Here you go, miss."

Loki watched as Solas reached back as if to grab for her wings. "You can see me?"

The question resulted in the lady's open expression growing wary, and she backed up, staring at Solas as if she might bite.

I kind of hope she does.

It was an expression Loki knew well, since that's how most mortals reacted to him if he didn't use his magic on them. With long strides, Loki caught up with Solas and placed his hand on her lower back again. Her tense stance slackened, and she seemed to lean back into his touch. More absurd chest pounding flashed through his head, but he liked that she found comfort in his presence.

"Thank you." He accepted the paper from the woman who made a 'cuckoo' sound before beating a hasty retreat, glancing back once she made it across the street.

"She could see me." Eyes as black as his heart slammed into his gaze. "How? I don't understand." The back of the jacket she wore pushed out, and Loki knew she tried to expand her wings. He almost pitied her for being so naïve, but he knew her father had hidden much from her. Keeping His minions uninformed guaranteed He remained in charge with little opposition.

"You're changed now, angel."

"But my wings..." Her hand slid under the jacket, and he watched the impression of her fingers play with a feather.

Loki slid a single finger down her cheek, tracing the contour of her delicate jaw, and tilted her face until their eyes locked. "Your wings are mine, Solas. I made them, not your father. With your wings, your powers should've returned, but you're visible to the world now."

With a gasp, she backed away from him. "Father forgive me... what have I done?"

Oh for fuck's sake, did he have to listen to this? He thought they were past her regret. Irritated, Loki wrapped his hand around her wrist and yanked her back into his space. "Don't even think about it, reaper. You try to flee, and I'll rip your goddamn wings off."

"You're an evil bastard. How could I have been so wrong about you?"

"Now you're getting it." Loki palmed her back and tugged her against his chest. On contact, her lips parted and her eyes dilated. Despite her wariness, she was attracted to him, and it pleased him that she remained aroused by his mere touch. He could use that against her for his benefit. "We'll discuss this later, but first let's finish our task so I can get you back home and violate you more."

"You're disgusting. I'll never allow you to violate me again."

Damn if his cock wasn't hard again with her declaration. Calling her bluff, he sent her a smirk because there was no way she'd manage resisting him. Not with the way she responded to him physically. She was too innocent to ignore her body's desires. Maybe he should heed her point about *Him* planning her fall. Would she fuck him to death? My god, he could only hope. *If I'm going to go...*

They were a block away from the boutique when his spine tingled with an unwanted energy. More reapers approached. Loki halted their progress in front of an alley and eyed Solas. She peered about with that innocent, fuckable look on her face. Was she playing him? Could she be as good a reaper as she claimed? He moved his hand away from the comfort of her back and gripped her upper arm. She gave him a cautious look. Grinding his teeth, he turned and led her into the alley to engage her siblings head-on.

"Why are we going into the alley? I thought you said the boutique was that way?"

"Don't fuck with me, reaper."

"Loki—"

"Is this the plan? It's actually perfect if you ask me." He pushed her back against the wall as the tingle down his spine increased and heat settled in his pelvic bone. "How else would you take down a god but with a woman? Just like that whole apple thing, that didn't go well, now did it? Seems your father is taking notes from the opposing team."

A frown grooved along her forehead. "I don't know what you're talking about."

Almost convinced by her confused expression, he doubted his intuition. She seemed harmless enough, and reapers offered no contest to his skill so he didn't worry about engaging her kin.

He opened his mouth to speak, but the wind swirled and that damn heat in his spine spread across his back and flamed along his skin. Noting Solas' startled expression, coupled with the way the fine hairs on the back of his neck prickled, he knew the reapers had arrived and stood behind him.

"I-I had no idea." She had the decency to look put out and almost irritated. He wasn't buying it. For now, he'd let her little charade pass, but there'd be an accounting later. "It must be part of the change you talked about. I didn't feel them, and I should've."

The more she spoke, the more his indecision about her sincerity surfaced. But even Lucifer spoke convincing lies, and he was the same as Solas... a fallen angel.

"I'll deal with you later, wife." He released her and spun on the two reapers behind him. "Boys... you should have called. We could have had drinks, gotten laid—" They attacked in silence. A third reaper landed at the alley's entrance and headed straight for Solas. *Interesting.* Solas was obviously the focus of their attack, not him.

From the corner of his eye, Loki watched Solas as she easily fought off the reaper. She was indeed skilled, and hot as fuck when she brawled. The jacket kept her wings from expanding, giving the reaper she fought the advantage, pissing Loki off. If anyone hurt her, it'd be him and none other.

Disliking these mixed emotions swirling inside of him, he shrugged them aside and focused on the fight while knowing he'd have to face them after he killed the reapers.

Solas screeched. The sound echoed in the alley and bounced off the walls. The reaper had his blade to her throat, and Loki could smell her blood in the air. He turned his gaze back to the two he scuffled with. "Okay, boys, I'm done here."

Drawing on his power, he struck quickly with his magic, knocking them off their feet. Both hit the ground with a thud. With one potent yank, he de-winged them in unison. They screeched, shattering the glass windows of the business across the street and setting off shrilly alarms. Once their bodies vanished, he moved to Solas. Grabbing the reaper by the wings, he slammed him face-first into the wall next to his wife.

"You should be careful who you touch. Some don't share well with others."

"You're going down, Loki, demi-god of tricks… demi-god of mischief, of fire and deception. Of evil!"

Moron. *I am a god.*

Loki smashed the reaper's face into the brick wall and wrapped his hand tighter around one of the reaper's wings. He laughed and shook his head. "You poor soul. You have no idea which myth to hold onto, do you?"

"You and your fallen whore will die."

He heard Solas gasp and felt an odd pain punch him in his chest. Loki plucked a feather from the reaper and watched his foe's face contort in pain, delighting Loki with his discomfort. "You'll hold your tongue about my wife." Loki slid his gaze to Solas. "Go to our home." Even as he gave the command, he wasn't certain she would return to his penthouse instead of fleeing.

"But—"

"Now!" She flinched at his harsh tone, as she should because when he gave an order it was to be followed immediately. Instead of becoming intimidated as he expected, she narrowed her eyes on Loki, and her jaw tensed. His little angel's glare made it apparent she detested following his instructions. *Too bad, she'll have to get used to authority.*

With a sexy huff, she spun on her heels, pleasing him with her obedience. It was a sign of progress in their relationship.

Watching her retreat caused a tightening in his chest. He loathed the alien feeling, and was confused by the uneasiness it generated.

"Angel." She halted mid-stride, her back to him and ramrod straight as she waited for him to proceed. "Be careful. If you need me, yell and I'll come to you." Confused why he made the offer, he noted when she glanced over her shoulder she wore a bewildered expression. Why should he care if she made it safely home? "And don't you fucking dare flee or I'll chase you down and spank you."

Her eyebrows shot upward as if surprised by his threat of violence. She opened her mouth as if she'd speak, but then must've decided against whatever peppered her tongue because she shook her head and strode off, hips rolling and drawing his lusty stare.

Once she finally left his sight the heavy feeling in his chest dissipated, and he turned his full focus on the reaper in his grasp—*where my focus should've been all along instead of distracted by her.* "Why are you after Solas?"

Why had she been marked? They threw her out, so it wasn't like she'd left in a huff and threatened to build her own kingdom. Neither had she departed on an immature whim. She'd been kicked out *after* being mutilated, leaving no question all parties agreed to her ejection from Heaven.

"Go to Hell... demi-god of chaos."

Loki rolled his eyes. Seriously? That was the best slur the reaper could come up with? He should volunteer to teach them how to ridicule with style and effectiveness. There was talent in lacerating an enemy with words. "Good lord, doesn't He allow you to read modern text? Please, don't tell me you're still reading ancient scrolls and a book that's been rewritten a thousand times?"

"I'm saying nothing. You'll have to kill me."

"In due time. First, I'd like to hear you scream a little." Loki plucked a feather from the reaper's wing drawing a hiss of pain from him. *Music to my ears.* "She loves me"—he plucked another feather and watched it fall—"she loves me not." On the fifth feather, the reaper screamed in agonizing pain. "Ahh... she loves me." A deviant grin stretched Loki's mouth.

"Father wants her dead because you took her while she was in human form." The reaper blurted out, surprising Loki that he'd caved so easily.

Baffled by his words, Loki stared at the reaper. Why should it matter to anyone how he took Solas? Without warning, an emotion coming from the angel hit him, one so strong it nearly knocked him on his ass. His eyes watered as he tried to shake the reaper's confession away, while he questioned what he'd just felt. Not just hatred toward Solas for her rebellion, but... *Surely this is a trick.*

Pregnant. His wife was pregnant.

Reeling in surprise, he reflected on why they would hate her for becoming pregnant? Then again, Solas couldn't be with child on his first taking. Could she? How would even her creator know she was pregnant this soon? It wasn't plausible to know this quickly, was it?

Her wings had already started to regenerate when he spilled inside her. As a god, he could control whom he gave his fertilized seed to, and he rarely came inside a woman just to be safe. But with Solas, he'd felt a primal need to mark her as his with his semen, had even given her his magic to heal her wings because her cries of pain had torn at his black heart. *I will not dissect that momentary weakness.*

He thought back to when he took her, how her wet pussy felt fisting his dick, and an uncontrollable desire hardened his cock. His feelings for her were... odd, uncomfortable. Even confusing and disturbing.

"You were sent to tell us about the child?"

"I was sent to right a wrong." Loki's grip tightened on the reaper's neck, but the imbecile continued to talk, not bothering to temper his words. "Solas and the abomination must die. Will die."

Over my dead fucking body.

Loki glared at the reaper beneath his hold. That was *his* child and *his* wife the angel threatened. "Go tell your maker you've failed." He released his grip.

"You-you're not going to kill me?"

"No. Deliver my message, and tell Him I'm coming. I'm the creator now."

Now he'd have to convince Solas to march right up to those self-pretentious fucking pearly gates by his side and invade

Heaven. If she carried his child, and they entered the gates…
it'd be apocalyptic. They'd defy God and prove His power
wasn't "almighty." Solas had been banished. *He* had banished
her, and now… a child had been created from two damned
souls. Apocalyptic indeed.

Loki was positively gleeful over the outcome. Couldn't
have worked out better if he'd planned it himself.

EIGHT

$\mathcal{L}$oki's command had prickled Solas' tolerance, causing heat to suffuse her cheeks as fury swept through her. He expected her to cave to his demands simply because he uttered them. Like she was a submissive or a creature beneath him. Among fellow reapers, she'd been at the top of the food chain.

No reaper would talk to her the way he had. None would dare to dismiss her the way he had. They knew her rank, and her ability to reason. *He shames me with his command. That's how little he thinks of me.*

She'd rather crash to earth again without the aid of her wings than yield to his directives. A thousand different ways to kill him chased one another through her thoughts, making him beg for death at the top of the daydream, then he'd ruined that fantasy when he said, *"Be careful. If you need me, yell and I'll come to you."*

Confusion had slammed into her harder than her fury had. Why pretend to care when he kept her for the sole purpose of his own pleasure... fucking, and pissing off her father? And then he'd threatened her if she left him.

I was dead wrong about the purity of his heart. He's a narcissistic bastard through and through.

Knowing he'd underestimated her, she'd given him a casual shrug and sent her fellow reaper a sidelong glance, but Jares had kept his focus locked on Loki like he was the real threat. Imbeciles. Their deaths could be delivered before they knew she planned to reap either of them.

That Jares had moments before held his nice, shiny blade to her throat wasn't evidence of her skill… or lack thereof. Loki had come to her rescue right before she'd freed herself.

Imbecile, she mocked him again. He *so* miscalculated her skill, and she intended to use that blunder against him. She'd teach him, and it'd be the last lesson he learned.

Pride stung, she'd pretended compliance of his edict and had spun on the heels of her boots, adding an extra swing to her hips just in case Loki watched.

The whole way back 'home' she'd chastised her foolishness. She'd obviously fallen for a befuddlement spell. Nothing but the usage of clever magic made any sense. Otherwise, she wouldn't have mistaken his soul as moral or mortal. He'd since demonstrated the depth of his corruption. Because of him, she'd executed the worst mistake of her life and rebelled against her parent.

Loki must die. She would beg Father for forgiveness when she dumped the demi-god's body at her creator's feet.

When Loki entered his home a little while later, Solas waited in the kitchen, leaning against the table. Her wings were pulled tight against her back, safe, out of view, but ready for combat.

Loki paused, his gaze dropping to her mouth where she dragged the half-eaten cherry along her bottom lip. Too mushy against her palate, and weird tasting—definitely not the manna she loved—she grimaced as she swallowed and ditched the remainder of the atrocious fruit with a casual toss.

Purple sparkled against the backdrop of his green-eyed gaze, testifying to his magic or his mood. "Undress and get on your knees." She went with *mood.* In response to yet another command, she shook her head as he yanked his shirt up his body and over his head, tossing the garment aside. "I'm in no temperament for games, Solas."

Silent, she glowered at him, hoping he saw the derision she felt for him in her gaze.

"I saved you from the reapers. I deserve a blow job."

Solas snorted, a dark deprecating sound. "Your arrogance is shocking."

"His shiny sword rested on your throat. I saved you."

"Your ignorance is even more shocking. I had ahold of Jares' sword."

"So?"

So it meant she'd nulled her sibling's magic, like she did *all* paranormal creatures. That particular mojo was one of her most useful gifts as a reaper. Since she outranked her brother reaper that meant her powers were infinitely superior to his. "So it means the worst he could've done to me was given me what humans call a paper cut. I was about to take him out when you intervened."

She thought doubt flickered in his gaze, but in the end he grunted his disbelief. "Undress so I can teach you how to suck my dick."

They were back to that? In this, Loki wasn't any different from a mortal man.

Allowing her magic to fizzle through her veins, she knew the moment he noted the silver expanding from her pupils because his eyebrows elevated.

"I've decided I'm no longer taking commands from *anyone*." *That includes my father.* "I reject your offer of lessons to suck anything."

Jaw hardening, while the purple of Loki's eyes decimated what was left of the green, he said in a casual tone, "I warned you."

His long-legged strides ate up the space between them. As he reached for her, she reacted, jabbing her palm upward and connecting at the base of his nose. He stumbled back a step. His stunned expression detailed his incredulity that she'd attacked. As he glowered at her, while popping his jaw, her wings expanded, and she plucked two feathers.

"Plan to tickle me to death?"

She gave him a one-shoulder shrug. It was apparent his knowledge of reapers was mediocre at best. Proof none had ever come close to killing him and it also verified why she'd been called in after all the others before her failed.

"We're really going to do this?" He wiped his nose with his palm, smearing blood along his cheek. "Last chance… undress and submit or I'll spank you into submission afterward."

Adjusting her grip on the feathers, she mocked, "In your fantasies, trickster."

He surprised her with his quick footwork. Going into defensive mode, she dodged him step-for-step, but soon she understood her error. He'd effectively corralled her like cattle, boxing her into a corner. He backhanded her across the cheek, her teeth shredding the inside of her mouth. Blood pooled, and she choked on it.

As his fingers touched her throat and slid backward, she spit the blood in her mouth in his face. He recoiled enough she used her feathers on him, slashing along his chest, creating long, deep gouges into his skin. Wet work with her feathers was her specialty. Only on rare occasions did she utilize her sword.

She stepped back and steadied her balance a nanosecond before delivering a front kick beneath his chin. The blow caused his head to snap backward, and he stumbled. Staying on the offensive, she followed his retreat, and the moment he came to a dead stop against the table she swung her left hand, ramming the tip of the feather into him. The black plume wedged deep between his ribs, only the final inch of the shaft protruded. Even the downy barbs resided inside him. Dark-red blood oozed over the weapon.

Loki defended himself, smacking her openhanded across her other cheek when she went to jab the other quill into the opposite side of his chest. The blow was still hard enough Solas went careening, crashing against the opposite wall, the sudden halt jarring her teeth together.

Panting, she shook off the ache and ogled him, assessing his weakest points. Odd, but he hadn't used his magic on her yet, just stuck to human smacks. That made little sense when he fought for his life.

"I will pluck you like a goddamn pheasant." Using his forefinger and thumb, he gripped the slippery shaft and pulled it out slowly, grimacing as he freed it.

Exploiting his distraction, she went for him, at the last second by going up and over his head, slicing the vein across his throat. Too bad for her, he wasn't as distracted as she thought and caught her wing on her descent downward. Drawn up short with her flight abruptly ended, she slammed onto the table, her other wing caught beneath her.

There was an obvious crack of bone, and she screamed as her vision darkened. Biting her bottom lip, Solas staved off her body's need to shut down from the pain. Losing her senses while in the enemy's grasp could mean her life.

"Cry uncle?" Loki's voice sounded raspy, verifying she'd sliced his vocal chords with the slash she gave him.

Unfamiliar with what his request meant, her response was to kick toward his knee. In retaliation, he twisted the wing he held. The shriek burned her throat. Sudden darkness was her blessed savior from the pain. The only problem with that was she eventually woke up.

Solas had no idea how long she was out. Before opening her eyes, she attempted to evaluate her situation through her senses alone. Both wings broken, one severely. They ached so bad she could barely concentrate. Their sensitivity was amplified in all situations. Like when he'd stroked her wing last night, it'd felt like he'd applied his touch against her clit. There was anything but pleasure now. The hardness beneath her spine implied she remained on the table.

"I know you're awake."

She couldn't assess his temperament by his tone. A coward would avoid him as long as possible, but she was known for her bravery. She opened her eyes to find the demi-god leaning over her, his forehead wrinkled with... was that concern?

"Don't pretend you care if I'm injured," she whispered through the pain, fighting back the urge to vomit. All movement hurt, even breathing. "You broke my wings."

"I defended myself." He smoothed his palm over her cheek, and buried his fingers in her hair. His grip tightened, stinging her scalp. "I didn't want to hurt you. You *made* me do this." He managed to sound angry, regretful, and blaming all at the same time.

Yeah, she'd expected him to fight back. She'd also expected her mojo to null his magic like it did all other lesser paranormals. Loki's had been unaffected by her abilities. Panting, she stared at the ceiling, realizing she wouldn't win against him in hand-to-hand combat.

"Nifty trick with the feathers, but where's your sword, wife?" She hated that term because of the derogatory way he said it. "Afraid it'll out you? Confirm you're not as high up as you claim?" He uttered words in a language even she couldn't understand, and she knew all but the oldest of them. His wounds healed as she watched. Lucky bastard. It'd take time for her broken wings to regenerate. "I bet you're as new as your siblings in the alley. If you weren't, you'd already have killed me." A brief, satisfied smile curled his lips, giving him a devilish appearance. And it only made him hotter and more desirable, because apparently she liked arrogance. "I trust we won't repeat this insanity."

It was a statement, not a question. Arrogant bastard. Underestimating her again.

"Help me sit up." She elevated a hand toward him, but he cupped the back of her neck and lifted her. Pain stole her breath, and she knew she'd have to retract her wings before they could heal in their broken state, because they could only mend correctly inside her. But she dreaded the moment she must withdraw them because the pain would be worse than in this moment.

Legs dangling over the side of the table, she plucked a feather before pulling her wings into her body. She endured her pain in silence. Wetness hit her cheeks, and she lifted her fingers to determine the liquid.

"Tears." Loki confirmed her horror.

She'd only ever cried as a human, but he'd returned her wings, and given her power back. Confused she peered up at him, as he slid between her knees and used his thumbs to wipe the offensive wet-weakness from her cheeks.

"What are you doing?" he asked when she dragged the tip of the shaft of the feather she'd plucked along her tongue.

"There's an anti-inflammatory in the shaft." That was the truth, just not in this instance. There were many different oils in the shaft of her wings. Some were paralytics, others various venoms, even truth serums, and memory loss agents to name a few. She'd even reanimated a corpse once, but only long enough to ascertain the information she looked-for.

His dark-brown eyebrows elevated, and she realized his eyes had returned to their vibrant green. All hints of the demi-god inside his skin were once again cloaked beneath his human veneer.

Lowering her gaze to his chest, Solas flipped the quill through her fingers. A few minutes ago he'd worn the injuries she gave him. He looked no worse for the wear now. The evidence of her incompetence frustrated her. The trickster was nearly indestructible. *Maybe he is a god like he claims.* Nah, she decided a moment later. Father wouldn't lie about something as minor as Loki's godhood.

His palm cupped the back of her head, and he used her hair to tilt her head back. Contrary to their battle, his touch had turned gentle. "How bitter does your defeat taste?"

"Gloating is unattractive." *He won't be rejoicing for long.*

"I moderated my strength." Leaning forward, he wrapped his other arm around her shoulders and nuzzled his face against her neck. "Didn't want to damage you or our little package."

It was galling to think he'd defeated her using none of his magic. How much worse off would she be if he'd used his demi-god abilities? A shiver ran along her spine. She shoved the disturbing thoughts from her head. "You're not making sense. To what little package are you referring?"

He dragged his mouth along her skin to her jaw. Damn her, but her body reacted despite the aches of her recent defeat at his hands. Against her ear, he whispered, "You're pregnant, wife."

She went still. Even her heart skipped a few beats.

Only God could create. Despite the myth of Nephilim, to her knowledge, no angel had ever conceived. Only the fallen, those who'd lost their powers, had procreated. Terror slammed into her with all the potency of her fall to Earth.

This is bad. This is… "Blasphemous."

He chuckled, the sound vibrating along the shell of her ear and sending goose bumps to skitter along her skin. He leaned back and met her gaze. "No. It's a *miracle*."

More blasphemy! Father would never accept her back into Heaven now. She was ruined, damned, right along with the other fallen angels. Sadness fisted her heart with an actual physical throbbing. Needing some alone time to think, she pushed against his chest, but he tightened his grip on her shoulders. The hand on the back of her head relocated to her belly.

"Our baby." He rubbed his palm back and forth. "If we can create life together, imagine what else we can construct. What else we can *do* together. What we can *rule* together. We can wrestle Heaven from God's control. It'll be my wedding present to you."

Mind reeling, she shook her head. She had no aspirations to rule Heaven or to subdue her father.

The oil on her tongue was thick, and she swallowed some of the toxin so she could speak a little clearer. "I wanted none of this."

"Don't worry, wife, I'll protect you." He went to kiss her, and she turned her head aside. "Don't be that way, angel. I'm not angry that you tried to kill me. It kind of turned me on."

He rubbed his jean-covered cock against her pussy to prove his arousal, but he stilled when she said, "The oil from my wing isn't an anti-inflammatory. It is a toxin that'd kill you." She added pressure to his chest again, and he stepped away from her allowing her to slide to her feet.

"You were going to kill me with a kiss." A lopsided smile devastated her libido.

Why was the fool grinning? She gave him a noncommittal shrug, questioning her own sanity over the way she reacted to his panty-dropping grin. "You had it coming."

Laughter burst from his lips, a light chuckle at first that turned into a full-on belly laugh. "Once again, you *fail* at your job. Don't get me wrong, I'm thankful, but—"

Fueled by instinct, she reacted without thinking and stabbed the tip of the wing-shaft into his neck. Angered by his taunting, she was *done* with his attitude. A strangled gasp was the only response he had time for before the venom went to work on his nervous system. The pupils of his eyes dilated, and he dropped to his knees before careening to the left and sprawling to his back on the floor.

Solas knelt by his side, hoping he'd learn a valuable lesson this time, and she threw his words back at him. "How bitter does my success taste, *husband*?" Of course no response was expected. Not that he'd actually die. A pity, but... she blew out an agitated breath. It wasn't like she could kill the father of her child either. *If* she were really pregnant as he claimed. He hadn't become known as the trickster for no reason.

Either way, the remaining venom was just enough to paralyze him and knock him out for a few hours. Unless his metabolism worked faster than other paranormal creatures, she'd have a good four or five hours' head start before he woke up. She'd be long gone by then and thankfully wouldn't be subjected to his ridicule.

Future unsure, she required money in this human world to make a hasty getaway. That she carried a child had her questioning her own immortality.

Needing to stabilize her volatile emotions, she took a moment to internally focus her thoughts. Once clearheaded, she patted down the front pockets on his jeans and came up empty-handed. She rolled him to his side, grunting at his weight—*damn he's heavier than he looks*. In his back jean pocket, she hit the jackpot. She dug inside, coping a feel of his godlike ass before she yanked out his wallet.

She could feel his analysis *and* his anger, but she ignored him. One by one she flipped out his credentials, and several credit cards, each one hitting the hardwood with a dull thud. The entire lot of cards bore his human name, Ryan Sinclair. The bright-silver one hidden behind the others drew a sharp squeal of excitement from her. *A platinum card*. Nice. A human she'd watched stole someone's platinum card and had racked up excessive charges. That's when she'd learned credit cards had different limits. She could do some damage to Loki's pocketbook with the limit on this little gem.

Ironically it bore a different name. Loki Agod. She rolled her eyes at the absurdity of the name. But aliases didn't matter in this instance.

Giving him her attention, she held up the plastic wedged between her index and middle finger. "Retail therapy is just what I need to get over you."

Hostility glared from his purple irises. She straddled his waist and leaned forward to lick his mouth. The toxin on her tongue blackened his lips, and a painful groan sounded deep in his throat, the only evidence of the sting the poison created. Once dried, the venom would lose its potency. But she withheld that information for the sheer pleasure of tormenting him. Let him stew in his defeat believing he'd die. His arrogance could use the blow.

Too bad he's still supermodel hot.

"Don't be petulant. You have no one but yourself to blame." She ran her finger back and forth along his belly near the waistband of his jeans. The lack of his tension verified his paralysis thanks to the venom. Soon he'd be comatose. "I tricked you into thinking I wouldn't defeat you, and you fell for it. I would think you of all people would appreciate the irony… *trickster.*" She smacked him hard enough on the cheek her palm stung. "Thanks for my wings and the *shatterings.* Those were"—she shrugged—"nice enough."

She thought he tried to utter the word 'bitch', but her poison already affected his vocal chords. She pushed off his prone body and strode to the door.

A new wardrobe was in her near future, then she'd ditch his card, locate a new place to bed down at least three states away, and *then* she'd find a way to verify her pregnancy. Just because he claimed they'd created an offspring, did not mean she trusted him. Oh, no, despite those *shatterings*, trust was not a commodity he'd earned.

NINE

"*B*ithss…" Partial paralysis still marred Loki's speech. Uttering the word bitch, to hear it with his ears would've soothed him, but he could only slur the word like a drunk. Fury torpedoed through his system, and he knew if he could see his eyes, his anger would be reflected there. His rage was matched only by the painful erection in his pants, proving the depth of his deviance. She'd tried to kill him. Solas' actions thrilled him, aroused him even, yet the fear accompanied by a near death experience settled into the pit of his stomach adding to his confusion.

After he regained the use of his arms, he pulled himself across the floor into the bathroom. Struggling like some weak… *fuck!* Forced to such a low, ungodly like action—an action *she* forced upon him.

Loki clutched the counter and hauled himself to his feet. Placing his palms against the marble counter, he leaned forward, staring at himself in the waist-length mirror. Black coloring flowed beneath his skin, evidence of Solas' poison filling his veins. With his forefinger at his heart, he checked its beat, and then traced the black line to his neck to toy with the feather embedded in his flesh.

Many things swirled in his mind while his body absorbed the poison. She could have fucking killed him. No one had ever bested him. No one had ever gotten this close to him to try. And no one had ever made his blood boil like Solas had.

Or turned him on the way she did, even as she bragged about felling him.

Death was not a good look for him. After flicking the feather with his finger, he pinched the end and plucked it from his body. Unable to continue looking at his reflection, he spun and leaned back against the counter. Could she have spoken some truth when she claimed her maker sent her? Was she sent so that his lust would blind him long enough for her to kill him?

He shook his head to dislodge the thought. Impossible. He was immortal. What Solas did only stunned him, and he grudgingly admired her tenacity. She didn't have the power to kill him, but the fact she had the power to subdue him was scary enough. What if she could kill him? *No.* Loki ran his fingers along his forehead. He wouldn't entertain the thought a second longer. She'd pay for what she did to him, but not like he'd make someone else pay. No, his woman would pay in ways that had his cock dripping with need.

Now, how the fuck was he supposed to find her? She'd left him paralyzed on the floor hours ago, enough time to be in another state if she walked. If she was brave enough to take flight and alert her enemies of her location, then she could be dead or much further away from him. That thought sent a chill through him. If she was dead, so was his child—*if* she was pregnant. He wouldn't put it past her siblings or her father to lie.

Jerking his head toward the pinging sound coming from the living room, Loki moved his stronger leg forward and dragged the weaker behind him. He bet he looked like a fucking zombie with his staggered gait. *Fucking bitch.* He made a mental note to make sure Solas knew what it felt like to have aching, and useless, legs as he reached for his phone on the counter. Tracing his thumb over the messages, he tapped the text alert from the bank. His lips stretched into a grin as he read, *an unusual purchase was made at Kitty Kat's Boutique, please confirm by responding* ACCEPT. He clicked the link to the Boutique to open the Internet map. Directions and a phone number filled the display, making him almost giddy. Hunting down people used to take decades, but with today's technology… It figured his angel would choose his platinum card. He was glad she had because it was the only one that would alert him to a questionable purchase. If she'd known it would lead him right to her, she'd have probably rethought her choice in plastic. It was the only real card in his wallet, though. Either way she would've been caught.

After pressing the number to Kitty Kat's, the phone rang followed by a polite, young voice. "Kitty Kats, Amanda speaking."

"Hello lovely, this is Mr. Agod. My Kitten is in your store."

"Oh, yes, Mr. Agod."

"Shh… quiet, love. I want to surprise my wife. She wanted me to come shopping today, but I wasn't feeling well." Shifting the phone to his other hand, he shoved an arm inside his shirtsleeve and shrugged it over his shoulder.

"That's too bad."

"Yes, I thought so. I'm feeling better and want to come surprise her. If you can delay her, I'll make it worth your troubles."

"Your card is on hold, Mr. Agod. Without you here, I was waiting for the bank, but now I'll use it as an excuse to keep her here if I need to," Amanda whispered into the phone, her tone full of mischief. Humans were so gullible. He could be a serial killer for all she knew. He'd filled her head with silly romantic plans, and the simpleton readily agreed to aid him.

"Thank you, lovely." Ending the call, Loki tossed the phone on the bed and struggled to pull his dress pants up his legs. Loki morphed into the appearance he wanted. He wouldn't match the photo for Ryan Sinclair, but he looked more like himself than he'd ever allowed outside his penthouse in the past. Before ambling out the door, he glanced at his image in the mirror. His familiar green eyes, the set he was born with, stared back at him and hair as black as his heart, but clean cut like a businessman. It was dangerous to look so close to his original self, ancient enemies would notice if they saw him. Maybe it was the near-death experience, but there was a sudden need inside him to grasp onto something familiar—something real.

After walking a few safe blocks from his home, he called on one of his hidden powers. A power he rarely ever used because it left an atmospheric residue, like a supernatural footprint. Getting to Solas quickly was the only thing concerning him, and teleportation was the fastest route. He'd have to call for a car in case he needed it for the drive back. Solas would be in his possession by then, and the urgency of transportation gone. Standing with his back against the wall, he sucked the energy around him in like a magnet. The air charged, snapping and popping with arcs of light. Loki closed his eyes, his body humming with power before everything went silent.

***

When Loki opened his eyes, he stared at the storefront of Kitty Kat's Boutique. The power he'd used to teleport would delay his healing, and Solas' poison still thrummed just below his skin. The toxin itched, but he resisted scratching because he knew it wouldn't help. He would also have to be careful, or she'd detect his weakness. Once inside the medium-sized store, he manipulated the room. Humans wouldn't want to enter, and the one already in the store quickly shoved a dress back on the rack and left in haste. A woman walked to the front counter from the back as he approached.

"Amanda?"

"Yes." She met his gaze, but the magic had affected her, and he could perceive her need to flee.

"Mr. Agod?"

"Why don't you go take an extended lunch—"

"No, I couldn't. The store." But she glanced at the door with longing.

"I promise to take good care of the store. Here's a couple hundred dollars. Have a good lunch." Her decision came slowly, and he could almost see the struggle in her eyes as she fought against giving into his request. But she had little choice in the matter. The magic he used would prod her to go against her better judgment and succumb to his wishes.

"Thank you. Your wife is in the back dressing rooms." At the door, Amanda looped her purse over her shoulder and paused. "You swear to God you'll keep the store safe."

"Oh, I swear to Him." Her eyes narrowed, and Loki was sure the grin he wore held wicked intent. Amanda lowered her gaze, choosing not to challenge him, locking the door with her key from the outside as if it would stop him from getting out. Having used so much energy to human-proof the building and its surroundings, he longed for more time to heal. Full strength was needed when dealing with his wife, and many hours of orgasms—his of course, not hers because she deserved none. She'd beg his forgiveness for long, grueling hours before he relented and granted her permission to come.

Once in the back, he surveyed the dressing lounge. A cluster of full-length mirrors shaped in the form of half an octagon lined the wall at the end of the fitting room hall. More mirrors surrounded a platform he guessed was for a panoramic view of one's outfit. To the left of the platform, sitting against the back wall and facing the hall of the dressing rooms was a plush, red velvet, Victorian chaise lounge, framed in a deep mahogany wood. The chaise was impressive, very high-end. His angel had expensive taste to match his own. Not surprising given the fashionable attire she'd worn last night when he'd saved her.

As he walked toward the dressing rooms, he marveled at why she had a need for expensive, materialistic things. Didn't that go against her father's teachings?

Loki thumbed the material of a dress tossed over one door. Her taste may be more expensive than his, and he hoped she wasn't spending his money on an uptight garment like this. He liked a little flesh to show, or at the very least the assets to be visible.

"Amanda, is that you? I need you to tell me if I have this thing on right. I've worn nothing like this before."

Now this could be interesting. Loki unbuttoned the closure at his wrist and rolled up his shirtsleeve. He leaned against a stall and crossed his arms over his chest. From the noises coming from the last stall, Solas struggled with the item of clothing. It sounded as if she fell against the door, and then she spilled out into the hall.

"Good lord! What are you wearing?" Something was wrong with the stores ventilation system because he suddenly felt breathless.

"Loki!" Solas spun, narrowing her eyes as her gaze traveled his body, taking in his new look. His appearance may be different, but she'd recognized him all the same. Was the red taint staining her cheeks a sign of her guilt? She made no effort to shield her body from his view, and there was a shit ton of it on display. The emerald and black lingerie corset she wore, along with matching panties and, god help him, thigh-high stockings had his dick whacking his zipper, no doubt tenting his slacks.

Pulling himself from his relaxed position, he ambled toward her. His cock leaked just from the sight of her. Solas was a work of art dressed like his wet dream. "Wings out, angel."

She shook her head.

"*Now.*"

Indecision flashed through her eyes, and she glanced about. She seemed frightened, or at the least cautious. He'd thought he'd wanted fear from her, but some unnamable emotion shifted inside him, and her reaction tugged at his core. Two feathered arches appeared behind her, and the totality of her ethereal beauty burned through him. If she was part of some master plan, sent by her father to kill him, then he was surely a dead man. Every punishment he'd planned—everything he'd salivated doing to her in the name of penance for his suffering, evaporated at the sight of her.

"I should take what I gave you as punishment." It was a bluff because he knew he couldn't maim her that way. What was it about her that weakened him and had him chucking his no mercy rule?

Solas notched her chin in a defiant manner. "I'll fight you to my death before I allow you to take them."

"You'll lose."

"Maybe."

"You think I'm evil—"

"Deny you are."

He elevated an eyebrow, amusement tugging at one corner of his mouth. "I'm not."

Solas snorted. "Serial killers don't think they're evil either. Doesn't mean they're right."

"Judging by the number of kills, you're more comparable to a serial killer than me, angel."

She winced but didn't dispute his analogy.

"Your father evicted you for refusing to kill me. I saved you and returned these." He trailed his fingers along the top edge of a wing and watched as lust created silver starbursts in her eyes. "A gift out of the goodness of my heart. I could've left you shivering in the dirty streets like the castoff you were." Harsh words but the truth nonetheless. He'd offered her protection and made her whole. She repaid his good deed by attempting to murder him.

Anger flared in her eyes. "You got something out of that *gift*."

"Don't be bitter, angel. I cherish your virginity. Thank you for that gift. Don't forget I could've chosen to take pleasure and given none, but once again I demonstrated the type of god I am. Generous. Neither did I turn my god-power on you when you attacked me, even though I was within my right to protect myself." Loki executed a hard stroke to her feathers, and she shivered. "Use these on me again, and I *will* put welts on your naked ass with a power you've never seen and show no mercy."

"Minimize me or dismiss me again, and I *will* use them on you again."

At an impasse and unsure how to respond, his dick had no problems, and throbbed its demand to be inside her. "Your father unfairly labels me as evil, yet you slay at His command without questioning the innocence of your victims."

"Questioning His reasoning for wanting *you* dead is why I'm in my current predicament. Doesn't mean His request was unjust."

"All right. If I'm evil, what type of monster does that make you with the blood that stains your hands?"

She inhaled a sharp breath as if he'd physically struck her. Her eyelids drooped, and she turned her face aside. Had he hit a nerve?

Loki gripped her chin and forced her head around. Her lashes fluttered upward, her gaze hesitant as he scooted further into her personal space, hovering over her, with their lips inches from connecting. He stared into her dark, expressive eyes trying to decide what caused her shame. Did she feel guilt for taking lives? For refusing her father's order to take his?

"I don't care how much you've killed, there's no judgment from me." Solas was a reaper. She'd been born to kill. Delivering death was in her DNA, but the obvious remorse in her expression startled him and left him pondering who the real trickster was between them. "It's what you do from this point forward that I'll judge. All I ask is that you make your own judgment about me without letting your father's opinion flavor your decisions." He thought he'd gotten his point across. It was time to change the subject. "Do you plan to purchase everything on the chair?" Using his free hand, he motioned to the pile of garments stacked in the seat.

"I've never shopped before. Father gifted my clothes, but those I watched were happy when they shopped. Indulgence is a sin, but I couldn't resist trying on the prettier things. I only planned to buy necessities though."

"Shh…" He placed his finger over her full lips and glanced down at the way the corset shoved her breasts up, highlighting them. "You've chosen well."

"What? This isn't a necessity." Her brows drew together into a cute frown. "I'm not even sure I'm wearing it right, but it *is* pretty."

"Oh, I think it is very much a necessity. Did you try others similar to this on?"

"Like you will see me in them." Her lips thinned into a tight line, and he couldn't help but smile.

"Angel, let's not fight again. All is forgiven. We're starting over." Loki held out his arm and pulled up some reserved energy. "I should thank you for poisoning me." Solas stared at his forearm. Her eyes widened when she saw the black swirling underneath his skin and widened more when it disappeared.

"Why would you thank me?" She gaped, distrustful as if he'd attack any second, but he hoped he kept his emotions out of his eyes.

"You've made me immune to your poison." A lie he hoped she'd believe, because he feared being vulnerable in her presence was the gravest mistake he could make. He should protect his future and kill her, but the thought of hurting her sickened him. If he could mask his skin until the inky color dissipated, he'd pull the illusion off. Then he'd be strong again, and prepared to go another round when she engaged him once more, because they were both too strong-willed not to fight again.

Solas shook her head in denial. "It's not possible."

"What part of *god* are you not grasping, Solas?" He stepped closer, until his chest pressed her back into the mirror. "Take a feather from your wing and try again."

"No." Solas shook her head in an almost frantic rhythm. "I'm not in the mood for bloodshed."

"Do it!" At her defiant glare, Loki plucked a feather for her, ignoring the longing to kiss her and soothe away the ache when she winced. He shoved the feather between her fingers until she had no other choice but to grasp it. "Now, wife, end me."

"No. I will do it on my terms."

"Are you so weak that you must attack when I'm not prepared?"

"It *is* the smartest play."

"Admit it, Solas, you don't want me dead!" The changing stall's doors blew off their hinges and crashed against the walls as Loki's power exploded in the room. "Or are you afraid of my power?"

She peered over his shoulder, probably at the evidence of his magic. "I should kill you so I can have my freedom." The truth of her statement sucker punched him. His angel had never been free, had never made a choice... *except for the one that saved me and damned her.* Joy leapt through him as he realized the only time she'd held her ground it'd been because of him. "I was angry that you dismissed me because I have my pride, too, and I deserve to be respected the same as you. I'm angry, so angry with myself because I've been gullible, and tricked into trading one owner for another. At least I understood Father's motives, but with you I understand nothing."

Loki covered her mouth with his as he reached behind her and buried his fingers in the silky feathers, executing firm strokes to her wings, making her moan deep. Her pleasure vibrated through him.

"We own each other," he said against her mouth.

Did her words mean she was incapable of killing him? She was a reaper—*killing is her job*. Would she hesitate next time, or were her words coated with lies?

"Loki, have mercy, let me go." Solas wrapped her fingers in his shirt by the collar. Her eyes pleaded with him to release her, while she pulled him toward her by his clothes. As the scent of his woman wrapped around him all thoughts of her sucking him off vanished. Solas was aroused and wanted him, whether she admitted it or not. She was also insecure of her choices and uncertain of her future.

"We need to talk about this apparel." Loki touched his finger to the top of the corset between her breasts. "First, as lovely as this garment is, it needs to go." As he moved his finger downward, the fabric heated. Solas flinched, whimpering as the heat flamed against her skin. When Loki reached the end, the fabric parted and fell away from Solas' body. "Should we try that on your panties?"

"No, I think you burned me."

"There's not a mark left on you." Loki arched a brow, as a wicked, lopsided grin toyed with his lips. "Lose the panties, angel."

"Wha-what am I letting you do to me?" Her hands moved up to cup her breasts. Was she hiding from him? Or fondling herself in anticipation of what would come? "My flesh is weak."

"How sinfully mortal of you."

She blinked at him and nodded. "I'm broken."

"Then we are broken together. This," he shoved one of her hands aside and pinched a nipple between his thumb and finger, "is not the part you should guard, wife." Loki leaned down until his mouth was at her ear. He wrapped the fingers of his other hand around the arch of her wing and held her against the wall by the delicate structure. At his firm hold, she emitted a breathy gasp. "I have an urgent desire to lick your pussy until you scream. If you don't lose the panties, I'll burn them off you."

"Loki!" Her tongue swiped across her lips as her confused gaze settled on him. Her struggle was almost palpable, and he could *feel* her warring with herself, between her desire and her sins. "What if I don't want this?"

"Then I'll respect your wishes and won't lick your pussy." Loki fell to his knees in front of her and stroked the inside of her thigh with his fingers, coveting not just fucking her or her satiny skin, but yearning for the soul of the woman. He'd never gone to his knees before any creature and damn sure not for any *woman* regardless of their human or immortal designation. They went to their knees for him. With Solas, it felt right to bend his knee to her. It didn't mean he was weak, but simply that he'd elevated her above the others that'd come before her. He'd never been comfortable among the other gods, but Solas felt like... home. Following an eternity filled with constant conflict, he could suddenly look to the future with anticipation so long as she remained in his life.

After years of being persecuted, she was *his* gift, someone maybe he could eventually trust to have his back. He had to proceed carefully with her to earn her fragile trust. Once he had her trust, he'd have her heart too, and then nothing and no one could stop them. "If that's what you want, walk away, Solas."

There would be no manipulation this time, no magic, and no threats. He wanted her to want him as much as he burned for her. Although he yearned to punish her for how she'd incapacitated him, and he would punish her, he still would never *take* from her. Yielding her body to him would always be *her* choice.

As his mind spun with new ways to handle Solas, he stared into her black eyes and waited for her decision. When the flicker of silver appeared in her eyes and her hips rocked forward, he felt the weight of the universe lift from him. The feeling was both elating and upsetting. He worried he made the biggest mistake of his life dancing this deadly game with her, a match that could go either way, and one that could end in his death, while he'd do everything in his power to save her life. If she won, he'd die with a smile on his face.

Lifting her left leg, Solas looped it over his shoulder and dug her stocking covered heel into his back. The brazenness of the action had his erection throbbing so hard he felt each pulse at his temples.

"Burn them off, Loki." Her heel dug deeper, urging him forward until his lips brushed the emerald satin covering her warmth. He pressed his lips against the fabric and felt her wetness beneath the satin, smelled her alluring scent.

Pressing his finger against the tiny straps holding the fabric together, Loki burned them, and peeled down the front panel of her panties. After he yanked them free from between her thighs, he peered up at her, hoping she understood the significance of his position. He bowed to his wife, humbled himself before his partner, and his equal. The silver pulsing in her eyes detailed her desire, unraveling his control, and he buried his tongue inside her with no further foreplay.

"*Loki!*" She sagged lower, dropping more weight onto his shoulders, trusting him to support her.

Still weak, Loki wanted to move her to the chaise lounge. No, he *needed* to get her to the red velvet chair. The erotic picture in his mind of her naked body laid out for him over the antique curve of the arm had his tongue lapping at her clit with one raving need—to make her come fast and hard. Her fingers clawed at the back of his head and tugged his hair. "How do you do this to me?"

She panted as she cursed him beneath her breath. For being the bastard he was, for making her weak-willed, and for introducing her to the sins of the flesh. He grinned because what could he say when he excelled at everything she cursed him for.

Flattening his tongue, he raked it up her flesh and teased her clit with the tip. Solas went wild, rocking her hips against him until he was forced to hold her still beneath him, and then she pleaded with him to make her shatter. As he kept her teetering right on the edge, the strokes of his tongue grew bolder. She slid down the wall, adding more weight for him to carry. As much as he enjoyed this, he had to move soon or she'd realize the extent of his weakness.

After inserting two fingers inside her, he closed his mouth over her now sensitive clit and sucked. He felt her flesh harden under the tip of his tongue and knew she was ready to come for him. Why did her pleasure make him feel so good? With his free hand, he flattened his palm against her mound and pulled her skin tight, exposing her clit. He flicked the bud continuously with his tongue and worked his fingers inside her. Solas came without warning. Her nails dug into his scalp, and she held his face against her pussy, soaking him with her cream.

Loki stood before she could regain her composure and walked her to the chaise lounge. "Lie down." His tone sounded like gravel.

She cupped his cock and purred. "Do I get this now?"

Loki clenched his jaw and pointed to the lounge chair. When he was sure she wasn't looking at him, he dropped his guard and let his confusion mar his brows. What was wrong with him? He should fuck her, fuck her so hard he'd break furniture. But she expected that, didn't she? Without a word, he fell between her legs again and lapped at her juices as if he hadn't just gotten her off.

"Please, no more." She attempted to push his head away, but with a growl he dug into her core and licked her harder. "Please, Loki, take your pleasure."

Something in her tone made him understand what he needed to do—after he made her come again.

"Give me one more, angel." He worked her with his tongue, holding her hips to the chair to stop her wiggling. His cock pounded in his pants demanding release. With all the self-control he could manage, he lowered his zipper and released his engorged erection. As he tongued Solas, her throaty whimpers urging him on, he smoothed his thumb over the head of his cock and moaned at the sensation. His crown was wet with his precum.

Loki looked up just as Solas' gaze locked onto his hand at his cock. "Let me—"

"No." He batted at her hand as she reached for his dick. Convinced he'd lost his fucking mind, he slowed his tongue. "Wife?"

"Yes." When her silver gaze met his, he stabbed his tongue into her core, and then slid it up to her clit swirling on the bud. For reasons he couldn't explain, his excitement elevated as she watched him pleasure her. "Oh, right there."

Her back arched, but he held her down so their gazes could remain locked.

"Here?" Loki asked, flicking his tongue over the spot he knew she loved having licked. "I won't underestimate you again, angel." Something shifted in her gaze, and an unfamiliar emotion seemed to hang over them. "Just… shatter *for me*." Only ever for him because he'd never let her go.

As his words blew across her flesh, she came undone on his tongue. He'd never heard such a high-pitched sound, neither had the mirrors because they shattered into a million pieces, just like his angel.

Solas may be a reaper, but what he picked up from her in this moment was all female, the urge to please, and care for her man. Loki stood and dropped his pants. Wrapping his hand around his cock, he stroked himself with long and slow movements. "How were your shatterings? Were they... *nice enough?*"

She drew in a sharp breath, but ignored the question and scrambled to her knees on the couch. "Loki, no"—one leg slid to the floor—"Let me do it for you."

He held her gaze and shook his head. "You tried to kill me." Oh, taunting her with what she wanted, but couldn't have was much more exciting than he could ever have imagined. With his free hand, he unbuttoned his shirt, slid his fingers across his chest and down. Solas licked her lips when he reached his stomach. "You can watch me come, angel, but you can't make me come." Denying her the privilege of pleasing him would be her punishment.

"If I wanted you dead, you'd be dead," she said, setting him on fire with the way she watched him masturbate.

"And yet I live." Tightening his fist, he stroked faster.

"There wasn't enough toxin left in my feather to do more than paralyze you."

Good information to have, and he was surprised she admitted to it. Why'd she divulge the information? Didn't change anything, though. She *had* to be punished, if for no other reason than to remember he might forgive easily, but he would still punish her when she deserved it.

Her hands curled, and she looked distressed at the idea of him pleasing himself. His lips parted, and the air pulsed from his lungs. For someone who hadn't been touched much, or given a man pleasure with her mouth... she was literally shaking with her desire. She licked her lips and stared at his hand working his cock. Her breasts swayed with her motion, and her nipples puckered from her inky, long hair brushing over them. Beautiful black wings spread behind her, expanding past the ends of the couch. Pleading eyes met his, and her bottom lip tucked beneath her teeth.

"Jesus fuck, angel. You're stunning." *And I am a dead man.* Even if he saw the killing swing, he'd probably let her finish the job just to make her happy. Grabbing the base of his cock, he stilled his movements and squeezed. Loki was close, so close his cock dripped with the evidence. "Look what you do to me." Her gaze snapped to his fingers as they circled the silky fluid over the head of his cock. His chest heaved, and he pumped his shaft with a renewed fire.

Loki grunted, and Solas' eyes sparked with a silver flare. Black wings circled him, and yanked him toward her. "I want to help you! Please let me shatter you the way you did me."

When she bent to take him in her mouth, Loki threaded his fingers through her hair and yanked her head back hard enough to sting. She gasped at the rough treatment, even as her hand cupped his balls. The touch almost ruined his self-control.

"I said *no*." She was strong, fighting to take what she wanted, and it was the hottest thing he'd ever encountered. "This is your punishment." He tilted her head back and grunted as his cock filled with his seed.

"My punishment?" Her eyes glittered, and her jaw clenched. "I think not. My father is the *last* that'll ever have the power to punish me." Solas' wings swung between them like arms, knocking his hand from her head. "In that case I'm definitely taking what I want."

Before he could stop her, or maybe he gave in for a few curious moments to know what her mouth would feel like on him. Either way, lips plumped with desire closed over the head of his cock, then she sucked hard.

"Ah, *fuck*." A part of him wanted to let her continue, the part humbled by her willingness to suck him off after she had tried to kill him, but the other part of him wouldn't allow her this level of control. He grabbed the back of her wings and thrust his hips forward until the head of his cock scraped the back of her throat. A delightful experience that had his breath catching in his lungs, but when she gagged, he withdrew and rethreaded his fingers through her hair. "No, means no." Jerking her off the couch, he pushed her to her knees in front of him. "Since you're such an eager little angel, I will give you something for your efforts." Loki rubbed his cock over her lips, leaving the shiny evidence of his arousal, and then jerked his length with vigorous strokes. "Open your mouth, wife."

When she didn't hesitate, heat shot down his spine at the way she looked on her knees, with mouth wide open to receive him. His orgasm vibrated through him, drawing his sack tight. He stared into the silver eyes of his beauty and came on her tongue, harder and louder than he could ever remember coming. His chest heaved with his release, and he hissed as Solas licked the slit of his cock. She stared up at him as if waiting for him to say something. Praise her maybe? No, he bet she'd never received praise or ever expected it.

Swiping his thumb across the corner of her mouth, he held it up to her. "You missed some." Loki smiled. Before he could wipe his thumb clean, Solas leaned forward and sucked his pad.

An unconscious growl rumbled in his chest. He smoothed back her hair, shaking his head in awe at his leniency with her. Had she been anyone else that had attempted to kill him, he'd have ended her life the moment he found her in the boutique. Instead, he'd made her come twice, and then spilled inside her mouth, rewarding her for her violence. He thought he might be the one broken instead of her.

Loki used his finger beneath her chin to tilt her head back until she met his gaze, "I have no doubt you will succeed at your job."

Solas seemed confused, and he wouldn't elaborate. He was still working through the conundrum of his reaction to his near death experience.

TEN

"This is foolish." *I am defective*. It was the only plausible explanation for her behavior with him. Angry about her evident weakness of the flesh, she shoved to her feet with a huff and met his scrutiny head-on. "Why didn't you kill me for paralyzing you? Or for trying to kill you?"

Any other paranormal creature would have. *She* would have if placed in a similar situation. Then again, she'd never been bested... *until yesterday when he broke my wings.*

Solas swallowed, the thick lump of resentment nearly choking her.

"I don't want you dead." He combed his fingers through his love-tousled black hair. The slight change in his hair color failed to detract from his handsomeness. The bastard. It wasn't fair he could beat her without using an ounce of his godlike strength, and be this good-looking too. And seriously, why'd she give in to him? What was it about him that made her so weak-willed?

So what, she'd been practically in love with him when she fell. The man she'd watched and refused to kill was not the man standing before her. Or was it?

She'd seen him do good deeds, giving funds to children charities, and donating time to those events. He'd bandaged a child's scraped knee and even managed to tease giggles from the little girl despite her tears of pain. He'd aided pregnant women, the elderly, and even rescued an animal or two. Sure, he'd hidden the truth of who and what he was from her, but had he really tricked her with who he was at heart?

Neither could she deny he'd been right earlier. He could've left her on the street banged up after her fall from the three-story building without her wings. There'd been more than one stranger that passed her by that evening. But not Loki. He'd offered help and shown kindness, genuine concern that had made her uncomfortable. No one had ever shown her that much compassion. Not even her brother and friend, Michael, had been so charitable. Michael had been tough on her, even bullied her, offering her no measure of consideration until she reached the level of skill he demanded of her. Even then he hadn't applauded her skill, but instead had made her feel as if she'd been slow measuring up to his expectations.

She was thankful for the return of her wings, but it didn't mean she owed Loki anything. Hadn't she paid for them with her virginity?

Instead of clutching him close while he ate her out just now, she should've ripped the strands of hair out as she wrenched him away. Her willpower required fortification or better yet a complete overhaul.

Disgusted by her weakness, she glared at him and contemplated his trickster abilities. She should investigate them because maybe he possessed the ability to arouse her against her will, delivered with his kisses or a magic slithering from his fingers as he touched her. The administration could come in any form since he was the trickster and no one knew much about his powers. He shielded his magic like a magician guarded the tricks of their trade. That made him a loose cannon and difficult to kill.

"Right." Didn't want her dead… she snorted. That lie was so cringe worthy it should've felt sour on his tongue. Neither was she gullible enough to fall for it. "Like you didn't ponder ways to kill me after I overpowered you and left you paralyzed on your kitchen floor. Rendering you powerless was quite satisfying for me."

"I thought of ways to *punish* you. Might still punish you more. Especially for that last sentence."

With his confession, her gaze narrowed on him and she bristled. The demi-god's arrogance astounded her. If he tried to discipline her, Solas would show him what she was made of, and she wouldn't be playing this time.

"Denying you your *shatterings* until you promise me anything to find relief was and still *is* at the top of my list of punishments. I could do it too, and I'd enjoy it." Oddly enough, that form of castigation intrigued her. She hadn't realized a person could be kept on edge the way he described. Before she put forth any queries on the topic, he continued. "Spanking your ass bright red until you can't sit for a month. Second on my list. I really want to discover how you'll react to a heavy hand. Mostly I want you to *submit* to me."

"Never." Solas was a leader, and she'd submit to no one ever again. All her life had been spent yielding to her father's demands, and that'd bought her a free mutilation job and an eviction from family and home. Her days of submission were over.

Loki ignored her. "Shoving a butt plug up your ass too fast so you feel the burn would leave a *nice enough* reminder too, don't you think? Tied for second on my list."

That was twice he'd brought up the words 'nice enough'. Were they used because she'd told him before she left him paralyzed that the shatterings he'd given her were 'nice enough'? If so, someone had a bruised ego. She wouldn't even reflect upon his butt plug and ass comment no matter how much the concept titillated her. He'd touched her there when he fucked her on his table, and she surprisingly liked it. She craved examining the act more, but she held no plans of admitting that. Such an admission gave him power over her, and she wouldn't hand him that much sway over her body. He already enjoyed too much control over her.

"Not once did I ever contemplate your demise. You gave yourself to me, admitted you are my wife, and I won't bring you harm."

"I wanted to shatter, I would've agreed to anything in that moment. Even being your spouse."

"Doesn't matter." He gave a hard headshake. "A vow was made. You are my wife."

He could *not* be this ignorant of her kind. "You fool, a reaper lacks the capacity to wed."

"You were tossed away like common refuse. I claimed you. That makes you *mine!*" He bellowed the final word so loud she winced.

True to her lineage, she remained stubborn. "I'm no man's property."

"I'm a god. Man is my inferior."

Solas gave him a slow, sardonic grin. "If you have to repeat it this often, you're not much of a god, my dear, dear, *pretend husband.*"

A tick in his jaw evidenced his escalating temper. "What are you afraid of, Solas?"

"Nothing." *Everything.* Being an outcast and never seeing her homeland again saddened her, but what truly terrified her was the way she reacted to Loki. The way she wanted to bend to his will and give him everything he demanded. Submitting to him would be the easiest thing she'd ever done, and she feared losing herself in the process. It was bad enough she might be stuck in her deal with him. That worried her less than losing her identity to his will. In his presence she became senseless, a mindless beast bent on quenching her hunger for *his* orgasms. It should be the other way around, and while she enjoyed him getting her off—merciful Heaven did she ever enjoy those shatterings—it was her joy for *his* climaxes that perplexed her. They fed her power over him in a way she couldn't comprehend. This truth had her shrugging off her earlier suspicions that he drugged her with his magic. Loki might be capable of many things, but not that. His arrogance alone would require a sense of fair play when it came to sexual favors because it'd serve as evidence to him that he was the best at everything he did. Even making a woman shatter. And if there was one thing she'd learned about Loki, it was that he *had* to be superior to the lesser creatures because the other gods minimized him. "I already proved I could best you, so I'm assuredly not afraid of you."

Protest too much, maybe?

"Oh but you are afraid of me, just not in the way you would have me believe." Before she could argue, he stepped forward and stroked one of her wings. Solas stifled a groan and slammed her palm in the center of his chest to halt further advancement on his part. She yanked her wings into her body rejecting his caresses. In response, he cupped her chin and forced her head back to meet his gaze. "You're a worthy adversary, more powerful than I gave you credit."

"Did that hurt to admit?"

"No. It excites me that you're not a pushover. I like that my wife—"

"Repetitively reiterating the word wife doesn't make it true."

"—can protect herself." His fingers pinched her chin. "The baby in your belly proves otherwise."

"I've given that assertion some thought and formed my own conclusions."

"Which are?"

Snubbing him, she walked to the lounge chair and selected the skimpiest G-string she'd placed in the pile of clothing she'd planned to purchase. "Oh, by the way"—she said as she stepped into the bit of lace—"I lied about my intentions with your platinum card. I planned to max that bitch out and leave you with the obligation." She'd seen that on a T.V. show once when she passed the long, boring hours of watching a mark before taking her life. The pettiness of her intentions had chafed her pride only a little.

"So max it out, I don't care."

Surprised, she glanced at him as she adjusted the panties into place, the thin strips of red fabric stretching over her hips. His focus followed her movements.

"I would've magically zeroed out the balance." The purple was in his eyes, and a moment later he was fully clothed, decked out in a black suit and crisp white shirt. "Angel, all you have to do is ask and I'll worship you."

His gaze traveled her body, and she shivered at the renewed heat in his perusal. Her nipples tightened to the point they ached. No, he damn sure had not magically roofied her.

That he was attired and she remained only in panties increased her arousal, dampening her fresh new pair of undies. Were sex addict meetings a thing? She could use a few. "I don't wish to be worshipped. That's for inferior gods." She shot him a pointed glare.

Loki snorted. "Tell that to your father. He covets being worshipped more than all the other gods."

He had a point, but she gave an abstract shrug as a reply.

Loki strolled to her mound of to-be-purchased clothes. He tossed aside several garments before holding up a royal blue, skintight dress. "Wear this." The dress would complement his smart apparel. Offering her the garb, he circled her puckered nipple with his other thumb, and she sucked her bottom lip into her mouth to stifle her moan. "I love the way these evidence your arousal... for me. *Your husband.*"

She knocked his hand away and snatched the clothing out of his grasp, before proceeding to dress. The way he watched her—like he owned her, adored her, and already worshipped her—resulted in a surge of more wetness between her legs. Jesus, at this rate, her thighs would be damp soon.

With a wave of his hand, the pile of outfits vanished. A lift of his chin caused the mirrors to fix themselves. Once he cleaned up the mess they'd made, his gaze zeroed in on her breasts. "It's a pity you feel the need to hide those jewels."

Deciding she wouldn't touch that comment with a ten-foot pole, she finished adjusting the dress into place and smoothed the skirt over the tops of her thighs.

She cleared her throat to draw his gaze off her cleavage. "Loki *Agod*. Really? You couldn't come up with a more original name to put on your credit card?"

"You have to admit there's a certain sense of rightness in the irony of it."

She grunted her disagreement. "Why even bother with a credit card if you're going to wipe the balance anyway?" *Why bother when he can attire himself without purchasing a single thing?* The trickster made little sense to her practical mind. "Why not just walk into a store and mentally accost the workers like I'm sure you did in this boutique?" The workers were noticeably vacant so it was a credible assumption. "Or create your own clothing? By the way, what'd you do with *my* clothes?"

"Accosting workers leaves a magical imprint. The advantage of getting to you outweighed the disadvantaged this time."

Ahh… now she understood.

"I have your clothes, but it'll be a while before you're allowed to wear them. That's part of your punishment."

"Trickster, you're delusional if you think I'll tolerate punishment of any sort."

"We'll see," he said noncommittally.

Damn right, we'll see.

"Something else is bothering me." Her confusion over his need to appear human with the credit card reminded her to ask. "Why have a pretend job at the grocery store when you clearly don't require employment?"

Loki chuckled. "That was a hallucination spell. What do you think the boutique is wrapped up in right now? You think

I'd permit our vulnerability while distracted with my tongue in your pussy?"

Solas gaped at him, not for the crassness of his words, but because that was strong magic if he could delude her with an illusion.

"What of the good deeds I saw you do? Was that a hallucination?" She held her breath, waiting for his answer, and very much afraid she'd fallen for a lie.

"Depends on the deed." He raked his fingers through his hair. "If it involved children or women that was me." She breathed a sigh of relief as he continued confessing. "I never played basketball with that group of churchmen. They were uptight fuckers, all adulterers who didn't cherish their wives, but I still created the hallucination that I was involved. It gave the appearance of being human, but I've no tolerance for that type of hypocrisy."

She could see through most spells... unless performed by a god.

A twisted grin curled his lips. "I keep telling you I'm a god, angel. Even your parent would be fooled by the magic. I use it to hide who I really am and protect myself from those who would *attempt* to kill me."

Arrogant asshole. He had to rub it in that she'd failed to kill him when she had her first real chance. Any further opportunities to get rid of him would be limited.

Spying a sexy set of five-inch black stilettos, she slipped them onto her feet and fastened the slim clasps around her ankles.

"Fuck me," he said, swiping his hand over his mouth.

With a saucy grin, she pivoted, and strode straight for the door, putting *a lot* of sass in her hips.

Solas pushed the door open, and the bell jangled above. No more than five steps on the street, he fell into step beside her... and grasped her hand, lacing their fingers together. Startled by the non-sexual touch and the intimacy of the act, she stumbled.

He caught her with one arm, stabilizing her footing before he released her. Stepping in front of her, he blocked her path as people milled around them seemingly without a care for the way they clogged the walkway. Thanks to the high-heels they were on equal eye-level, and he held her regard with what… emotion? She couldn't decide, except it caused a contradiction of emotions to surge through her. Excitement and terror to name a few.

"I'll always catch you, Solas."

Suddenly, all the air was vacuumed from the atmosphere. The vow terrified her and promised more than she offered him. She couldn't figure out why he was so eager to accept their unexpected relationship when she struggled against the new landscape she navigated. Nothing made sense and everything was out of control. For the first time she had choices, but she had no idea where to go or how to proceed.

"It's okay to be scared, angel." His understanding alarmed her, even though the slight squeeze he gave her hand should've comforted her. The fingers of his other hand sifted through her hair at her nape. "The sooner you admit you're mine, the easier it'll be for you to accept our future."

Taking a deep breath, she averted her gaze, noting the pedestrians but not really seeing them. He offered her an alternate home. She wasn't sure she could allow herself to accept it despite her craving for him and the pampered lifestyle she knew he offered.

"Tell me what you've decided about the baby." The topic change confused her, and her expression must've said as much because he said, "You said you'd given my assertion about the baby some thought and formed your own conclusions." As he waited for her explanation, his fingers massaged the back of her neck, soothing her.

"It's impossible for me to be pregnant. Reapers can't conceive."

"The fallen can."

"There's no proof to substantiate that claim." That was the official Heavenly statement. But she knew the truth. A few of the fallen had spawned children with humans. The offspring were Nephilim and were often gifted in some remarkable way.

"I've no desire to dispute this with you when the evidence of the infant is all the argument I require to invalidate your belief."

That right there *was* her answer. In the less than twenty-four hours she'd been with him he'd argued with her over everything in an attempt to validate his beliefs. "There's no way you could've known I was pregnant after less than a day, Loki."

"Your brothers told me about the baby. They'd been sent to retrieve you to await your father's punishment."

"Don't dress up why they were here, Loki. They were sent to kill me."

He shrugged. "The one with his blade to your throat—"

"Jares."

"—he said the baby was an abomination and deserved to die. There was something in his tone though, so I doubt he truly would've killed you."

She thought about earlier in the alley. Her siblings must've told Loki this mistruth about the baby after he ordered her to return to his home, because they'd said nothing of the sort prior to her departure. "If that is true, there'd be no punishment just an execution."

He scoffed. "I doubt that. Why kill you when your father could use the baby for His benefit or against me. That was more likely His intention, but when Jares realized I'd defeated them, he lied, hoping I wouldn't guess His real purpose."

"Probably. The end result would be the same, and I would be executed." He made a face, and she quickly detailed her argument. "He kicked me out of my home for disobeying Him. You kind of saved me—"

"You ingrate. I *did* save you."

"—and He's angry. If—and I'm not admitting that I am—but *if* I am pregnant, I cannot see Him viewing that as anything but a betrayal. One worthy of nothing but death. I will also concede that I can believe Father would use any child of ours against you. Having that type of power over you would be a victory in His book, so that's definitely within His wheelhouse of tactics." Her parent would do almost anything to take Loki down, His hate for the demi-god was well known in Heaven. Before her fall, she'd never questioned His loathing. After her fall, it was as if her eyes had been opened and she saw things through a new set of lenses. Father's animosity couldn't possibility be a simple aversion to competition because He owned the most souls, so why'd he despise Loki so much? "You should know, though, reapers often lie so they can achieve an advantage over their opponent, making it easier to defeat them. My younger siblings like this morning require the distraction because they cannot rely on their abilities alone."

Loki stared at her, twin frown lines forming along his forehead, and he considered her for a long moment. "Then they picked the wrong lie because this one gave me greater motivation to triumph over them."

That made sense to her, and would've sparked her desire to survive at any cost as well. The only reason she hadn't killed him earlier was because of his baby allegation. She allowed him to live for the sole reason they might've created life. A father wasn't required for a child, but if she were pregnant, then her creator would come for them, and Loki was the baby's best chance at surviving.

"Why didn't you kill me when you had the chance?" he asked as if he'd read her mind.

Startled by his question, Solas met his stare. "I'm a fool." *So accurate it isn't even funny.* She should've obeyed her father and killed him. Life at this moment would be the same as it'd been for epochs if she'd followed through with his death. Watching humanity and waiting for a mark. If that's what she wanted, then why'd she wince at the lackluster memories of her former life? "What transpired in the boutique is *all* the evidence you need to know that I'm the biggest fool alive. I miscalculated how long you'd be incapacitated. On another it'd have put them down for twenty-four hours or longer. Had I been smarter, I would've ditched this town the moment you hit the floor."

"I would've found you either way."

"There you go pretending to exceed your limitations again."

He chuckled, and the deep sound rolled over her like a lick of his tongue between her thighs. Just that fast she wanted him to debauch her again. What a hopeless cause she'd become. In a paltry effort to hide her responsiveness to him she glanced away... and tensed.

Five of her siblings blocked the sidewalk. Walkers gave them a wide berth, even though she knew none of the humans could see them.

"Lucky me, more of your siblings. I really must set some ground rules for in-law visitations." Loki's sarcasm almost made her laugh.

If her kin represented anything but danger, she would've allowed her amusement freedom. Instead she manacled Loki's wrists in magic. The mystical handcuffs marked him as Solas' claim, eliminating her siblings' ability to steal him from her. It was a safety measure, but she elected not to divulge that information to Loki. Let him stew on the ease with which she'd fettered him.

"What the—" He wrenched his wrists apart, but the chains held, all his efforts failing at breaking the mojo. Not giving up easily, her unwanted *husband* twisted his wrists in opposite directions, but they still remained secure.

Solas gripped the smoky magic connecting his wrists and yanked. He jerked forward a little from her hard tug, and it harvested his full attention. Furious purple eyes glowered at her.

"Underestimating me again and so soon, trickster? Tsk…tsk…" She shook her head in mock disappointment, when she wasn't the least surprised he'd misjudged her.

Loki ground his molars together.

"I like you in chains, *husband*." Wearing a saucy grin, she stroked his cheek with her fingertips.

I will spank her ass for this perfidy. Not that now was a good time to call out her misconduct, but he was agitated nonetheless when she turned her focus on her siblings, giving him her lovely backside. The same backside he'd bare while bending her over his knee. The same one his palm would descend upon with heat until her buttocks flamed bright red. No mercy would be given even when she begged for clemency. Oh no, he'd—

"State your purpose, Mozeb."

Solas' demand jerked his focus back to their current situation, causing his scrutiny to drift to her family. The four reapers standing in front of one sister testified to their soldier status. He deduced Mozeb was the one behind them since she wore the air of command. A quick scan verified no evidence of magic, either that, or these goddamn shackles stifled his power.

Mozeb's white hair glittered in the sunlight like ice crystals. A shiver ran along his spine, not in fear but aversion because of the slimy feel her vibe emanated.

"You fell for *him*, Solas?" Mozeb asked, her tone haughty, as her mini-army parted in the middle for the ice-queen to step between them. "How the mighty have fallen."

"At least Loki is dependable. Unlike my family," Solas shot back.

Loki grinned, his smile growing bigger when he caught the eye of Solas' sister for a split second.

Mozeb's mouth pinched about the edges, detailing her displeasure of Solas' statement. He liked the way his woman defended him. *That's my girl.* She wasn't nearly as indifferent toward him as she pretended to be. Otherwise she wouldn't endorse his character. Even though she delighted him with her words, he would still offer no sympathy as he reddened her ass.

"Get on with your purpose." The hard edge of Solas' voice captivated his cock. Wouldn't be the first time he faced off against a foe with a hard-on.

"Hand over the trickster." A shimmering sword that gave off a crystal-like appearance descended into Mozeb's grip.

The weapon classified her as a Grim Reaper. Marking her as the best of the best. They were not only the oldest, but also the most elite of the reaper squad. Her father had upped the ante if He was sending Grims after Loki. Even so, a Grim offered him no contest, and while Solas had proven she was capable, he doubted she could hold her own against a Grim. Few could.

"I'll go with option number two, please and thank you," Solas' sarcastic quip surprised Loki with her lack of fear. Outgunned and outmanned by Grims would've resulted in cowering from even the most powerful paranormals.

"Giving me the trickster is your only option."

Loki's wife palmed a short blade, flat black and without any sheen. The weapon's texture would make it easier for her to kill without notice. He'd never seen anything like it.

"*Your* only option is to come through me to get him." Silence raged between the two sisters as they stared at one another.

"I have soldiers," Mozeb indicated the others that flanked either side, "and Father's directive."

"Father's directives no longer concern me." Solas gripped the foggy-chain between his wrists so hard her knuckles whitened. "If your soldiers are expendable, then attack. I've no qualms deploying them to eternal death."

Was his woman crazy? She acted like the superior of the two. With that sword, he might not be able to identify her rank as a reaper, but Grims were the most elite of the assassin angel squad. Then again, he'd never witnessed a reaper use their feathers as a weapon before either.

Mozeb lowered her gaze and turned her head to the side just a little. It represented a clear relinquishment of power.

What is *my woman if she intimidates a Grim*?

Their telepathic chatter was clear, but in a language even he couldn't discern. A moment later the reapers vanished.

"What'd they say?"

Solas looked over her shoulder at him. The breeze ruffled her hair, and her lips pulled up into an ironic grin. "Obey or die. What a paltry and pathetic warning really."

Her blasé attitude over her safety and their potential child's well-being unnerved him. "They could've killed you, Solas."

"*Pfft...*" The acrimonious exhalation amused him. "If Father wanted me dead, He wouldn't have sent *them* after me."

"You're discounting the abilities of a Grim." Either she wasn't as versed in her kin as she should be or she was more lethal than he even gave her credit for.

"Yeah, and I could've bested her and her buffoons with both my hands tied behind my back."

He thought of her wings and how she'd used them as a weapon. "What *are you* if you're superior to a Grim?"

"Grigori."

"A former Watcher?" That confession surprised him. Watchers came from the beginning of time, created as sentries to humans. Lore divulged most of them lusted after mankind and mated with them, resulting in Nephilim, but she'd denied rumors of their offspring just a moment ago.

"I still watch humanity, report their activities to Father, and wait for His commands." Solas grimaced. "Or I did."

"But you're a reaper."

"Yes."

"How can you be both? A reaper and a Grigori?" He was so fucking confused, but then many of God's doings were shrouded in mystery, often proving to be falsehoods or misrepresentations. The cryptic lent for different interpretations, making it easier to control mankind.

"All Grigori are reapers. We're the first reapers. I was one of the first born after Creation. I told you, I am the best at what I do. That wasn't a lie, Loki."

She basically qualified as a myth and that explained why her maker wanted her back. *But she is still no god.*

"I was one of the few unfallen, until now."

Solas sounded so sad that he stepped into her personal space. Loki lifted his chained hands and draped his arms loosely around her neck. He ran his lips along her cheek and smiled when her breath hitched.

"I don't know what to do with myself now that I'm fallen."

With her confession, he buried his hands in her hair and angled her head back so he could stare into her sparkly gaze. He loved how her passion was reflected in her eyes, going from black to iridescent silver.

"I don't know why I admitted that to you." The tiny creases at the corners of her eyes displayed her vulnerability.

He would do anything to see it erased from her psyche. She was strong, but his presence further strengthened her.

Loki claimed her mouth with his, thrusting his tongue between her lips, as he teleported them to his residence. Safe in his domain, he vowed, "I know *precisely* what to do with you, Solas."

ELEVEN

*O*r at least he thought they'd be safe. Once they appeared in his bedroom, the vibration of another power pulsed inside his domain. With his arms still wrapped around Solas, he felt her body stiffen and watched her eyes narrow with alertness. Good to know her senses were astute enough to detect another paranormal creature.

Loki moved his arms from around her neck, and cocked his head. "I think you should remove your magic cuffs now, love. You *are* powerful, I'll give you that, but whatever has broken through my magic... will likely eat you up. And, that's my job." At his wink, she rolled her eyes and then tapped the swirls of smoke circling his wrist. "Thank you. I'll be right back to deal with you—"

"To *deal* with me?" A frown stole across Solas' brow. Her annoyance with him, the way she challenged him and broke his balls, made their dance so much more fun. How odd that he enjoyed her defiance.

"Yes. I'll handle whoever has dared break into my home, then return momentarily to run my tongue over your wet pussy." He delighted in the way she tried to hide the quick intake of her breath. But there was no mistaking it when her magnificent breasts lifted so quickly and her nipples tightened in response to his lurid promise. She could pretend to be angelic all she wanted, in fact, defiling an angel made him come harder than ever before, and he could tell she loved his crudeness too.

"I'm coming with you, Loki."

"Yes, indeed, you will come with me... Now get naked, lie on the bed, and wait for me like a good wife. I'll be right back." Before he closed the door behind him, he saw her face heat up with desire, and even caught the quick swipe of her tongue along her bottom lip. Her anticipation increased his eagerness.

He wanted to refuse her orgasm as punishment, but whom did that really punish? *Me, because I love watching her come undone.* Her enjoyment was so pure and honest, without any hint of dishonesty—he didn't think she'd know how to fake an orgasm if she tried—and he couldn't remember the last time he'd fucked someone that wanted *him*. Most of his lovers joined his bed because he was a god, and screwing a god came with privileges. Not to mention epic climaxes. Others wanted something from him, and even a few attempted to trap him with fictitious offspring. Humanity would be surprised how many immortals used the same ploy to ensnare a man.

Funny that the others that'd attempted to deceive him with an heir had enraged him. But give him one fallen angel with the likelihood of carrying his offspring and he suddenly wanted the possible child.

Confused by his unusual desire, Loki shrugged her from his mind as he followed the trail of power to the kitchen. Spying his interloper, Loki rested a shoulder against the wall and sighed. "I should have known it was you." Býleistr, Loki's adviser, was the only one granted entrance into his home or personal space. Myths convinced the weak minded that Bly was his brother, which put the poor man's life in danger. Bly had been by his side for centuries, making Bly loyal and trustworthy—to a point. Loki trusted no one fully.

"You're interrupting something very important. I hope this is good." He stared at the man leaning against his counter, arms folded across his chest, and ankles crossed. A casual stance, but he could feel his first in command's anxiety. When Býleistr tilted his head, his shoulder-length dark hair fell and brushed against the tattoo on his bicep. His gold eyes were alight with a defiance Loki hadn't witnessed before.

"Is *she* your something important?"

Loki moved so fast he was before the man in a blink, encroaching on Bly's personal space and eliciting a shocked gasp from him. "Is there something on your mind... *brother?*" Taunting Bly with kinship, as the myth suggested, always pissed him off, and the slight tensing of Bly's jaw verified now was no different. Loki stepped back, giving Bly room to squirm under his scrutiny.

Býleistr scratched the stubble on his chin, cleared his throat, and lowered his gaze long enough Loki noted the subservient action. "There are concerns amongst your Naglfar."

"We're still on track with Ragnarok. What's so concerning that warrants you disturbing me—*unannounced?*"

Bly palmed the back of his neck before snapping his eyes back up to Loki's. "The fallen slut. That's the concern!" By the look on Bly's face, Loki knew his always-calm demeanor had fallen and was replaced by blazing, pissed-off purple eyes.

In two steps he had the man bent back over the counter with nothing more than his presence in Bly's space. "If you ever utter a foul word against my wife again, I will fillet you like a fish and drip venom from a serpent onto your gaping carcass until you scream your apology to her—and that still won't be enough to end my torture." A knot bobbed at Bly's throat, evidencing regret for his harsh words. Loki turned away from him and took a deep calming breath before he ended his longtime counselor.

"I'm not the enemy here," Bly said.

"Aren't you?" Maybe if he paced the floor it would prevent him from killing Bly. "You come in my home, say foul things about my wife! Next you'll want to kill her!" Loki halted and spun to face the man, leveling a penetrating glare on him. The look of sheer terror reflected in Bly's eyes was evidence he'd hit on something.

"Not me—"

"Liar, liar..." A new worrisome thought came to him. Loki conjured a blade and palmed the handle. "How did you even know of Solas?"

"You know how the grapevine works."

"I claimed her only last night. The grapevine never works *that* fast, Bly."

"I'm trying to do my job and protect you, and you're worried about how the word got out?"

"Deflecting, Bly?" Holding his man's stare, Loki waited. One wrong word and he'd reduce his counselor to rivulets of blood.

"This is a whole new level of paranoid when you're doubting my loyalty." Bly pointedly glanced at the knife in Loki's hand. "It's my job to keep my ear to the pipeline. I have angels in my pocket, some fallen, some still on Heaven's payroll. You know this." His first in command pinched the bridge of his nose. "Celeste, you know the angel with the scar across her face—"

He knew her well. "The one playing both sides."

"Yes." Bly nodded. "She told me some angel chump named Jares was bragging about how his father was sending him with a regiment to return Solas to Heaven because she'd gotten pregnant by you. At least a hundred of us were sparring when she showed, so a good majority of the Naglfar heard what she said. You should know, there are many Naglfar that want Solas dead."

"Why?"

"They feel she's delaying the Ragnarok." Bly averted his eyes. "Or that she'll kill you despite her fall."

"Go on." There was more, Loki could feel it.

"And the baby, Loki, some want the baby…"

When his advisor trailed off without finishing, rage like he'd never known swarmed inside him. "Dead? They want to kill my child?"

"Some, but others,"—Bly paused and grabbed a small paper bag off the counter—"others say the baby is the key in winning Ragnarok."

Loki eyed the bag in Bly's hand with caution, contemplating how Bly had learned of the potential baby when he'd only been informed of the possibility. Distrust burned inside him. Bly's knowledge was epic and couldn't be dismissed. Loki'd been cursed to this earth, chained to this rock, and had been working on overthrowing the power of Gods for centuries. Ragnarok, Fate of the Gods, had been foretold throughout his history since his birth, and it was Loki's hope to lead all of his people, the Naglfar, to the heavens to destroy the angelic sanctuary. Now they were turning against him? They wanted to harm his wife and child? He considered Býleistr with a glower. The man had never crossed him, and he must determine whose side held his alliance. One thing he could count on, Bly was a shitty liar.

"I'm going to ask you this one more time, Býleistr, so it's very important you get it right." Loki moved until he stood in front of Bly once more, but kept his distance this time and leaned against the kitchen table. "Did you come here to kill my wife?"

"No, Loki. I'm here to help you, like always." He settled the little brown bag in his hands on the counter behind him, and turned his back on Loki. Even though he couldn't see the sack, the crinkling sound of the paper bag implied Bly removed something from it.

Suspicious of his 'friend's' motives, he asked, "How are you going to help?"

Bly turned around with a weapon of unknown origins. Loki held a blade to Bly's throat before the other man could blink.

"This is how I'm going to help!" Bly shoved the object into Loki's chest. "Here. You know, for a god, you're very jumpy."

Loki ignored his comment and pinched two fingers around the weird stick.

"What on earth is this?" He flipped it over, examining every angle, but felt no magic coming off it. "What power does it yield?"

"It's a pregnancy stick."

"Really?" Waving his hand in the air, Loki made the blade disappear and focused on the magic stick. "How does it work?" Excitement replaced his anger. Was he close to finding out if he was a father?

"The human I'm fucking says you pee on it."

"I pee on it?"

"No! The woman pees on it."

"That's... disgusting." He wrinkled his nose at the thought. "There's only one problem."

"What's that?" Bly relaxed, confidence returning to his posture.

"Solas doesn't have to urinate."

"Angels can't have babies either, yet here we are."

If she'd conceived in human form, it raised the question could she use the bathroom? She was exuding other human traits, so maybe this would work.

"What do you want the outcome to be, Loki?" Bly's question refocused him on the world-domination clusterfuck he was in with *his* people. This new information changed the dynamics of things, or at least it should, but as he thought about his response to Bly, he could only focus on the weird feeling inside of him. A child. It would be the first person to love him unconditionally, without hesitation or doubt. As Ryan Sinclair, he'd seen a lot of shitty parents, and their children still loved them. How could he possibly fuck this up? The thought of being loved after centuries of hate cracked something deep inside of him. What would this mean to his faithful Naglfars though? "Loki?"

"Yes." His gaze snapped to Bly's, and he quickly masked the emotion he felt.

"You don't have to answer me, but if she is pregnant, do you know the value of that child? A child born of a god such as yourself, and a fallen angel—a reaper no less—would have unimaginable powers."

A nod was the only thing Loki could muster. Bly didn't know the half of it and hopefully, no one else knew Solas was a Grigori. Their child had the potential to crush the entire world with a flick of its little finger. Solas' maker had to know this, and that's why *He'd* sent His best assassins, but his angel had scoffed at her parent's sincerity in killing her since she outgunned even His Grims.

"If the child fell into the hands of her god, He'd use it to destroy you and all the Naglfars. If one of the Naglfars gets the child, it would be a chance to overthrow you. If you care about the child, your own people *will* use it against you."

"I can destroy all of them, they wouldn't dare."

"They *would* dare, *there is no honor amongst thieves.* You know that, my friend."

Loki eyed the magic pee stick in his hand. The weight of the underworld made him weary. "Where is your alliance in all this, Bly?"

"Haven't I made myself clear?" Býleistr looked offended, and a touch of hurt flashed across his features. "As always, my loyalty is with you, Loki."

"What do you propose we do?" Loki placed the magic stick on top of the brown bag and tapped his finger against the counter.

"I don't know how you feel about any of this, so don't shove another blade against my throat for trying to help when I'm in the dark. Being your advisor is a daunting task at times."

"Fair enough." Bly was a smart man though, and Loki assumed Bly already concluded where his mind was concerning the child.

"The child will be your demise, either way. The reaper has already gotten under your skin—kill them both—they're making you weak."

"Do you think I'm weak?"

"No. I have faith that you have a plan, and know what you're doing. But there are others that don't know you as well as I do. They think you're weak. I've already heard whispers of them leading an uprising, and they will come for the child, Loki."

"They'll have to wait, if she is with child, it's only been twenty-four hours."

"Unless they come and take her from you and hold her until she gives birth."

Fuck. He'd never considered that option. They would do unthinkable things to her that went way beyond torture. They would *touch* her in ways that made his blood boil with pre-planned vengeance. The vile things his people could put her through sickened him. And once they had the child, they'd leave her for dead. He knew this with every fiber of his being, because it was exactly what he would do if placed in their position.

"It's not an option," Loki said with affirmation. "I can't—"

"What's not?"

"Killing her."

"Who are we killing?" Solas' voice had both men whirling around and poised in a battle stance. Loki's weapon of choice was the magic pee stick. He would have laughed at himself if he weren't confused and for the first time, worried.

"I thought I asked you to stay in the bedroom?" Loki clenched his jaw at her defiance. How much had she heard?

"No. You *told* me to stay in the bedroom." She glided her fingers across the table as she walked toward him. "Besides, wasn't your tongue supposed to be licking something by now?" She tilted her head and tapped a finger against her jaw.

"Remind me, where is your tongue supposed to be *right this moment*?"

Bly choked on a laugh.

Loki didn't find anything funny about her defiance. "Býleistr, meet my wife, Solas."

"Your brother?" Solas stared at him with wide eyes as Bly made a noise of disgust. Now, that was amusing, Loki thought.

Bly nodded and moved to extend his hand. Loki's attention was drawn back to the magic stick in his hand, a plan simmering in his mind as he palmed it. One that could make Solas run from him again, but it would save her life and his child's. "Bly has come at my request to help us with something."

Bly angled his head, regarding Loki, but then nodded.

"Is it with the licking?" Solas teased, and he didn't like it one bit. The thought of another man touching her had his fist curling around the pee stick in his hand.

"For an angel, you sure like to seal a man's fate. Be assured that I will kill anyone who touches you." Loki grabbed her arm and held her limb out to her side.

"What are you doing?" She asked, smacking at his grasp.

"Be still, wife!" He tightened his grip on her wrist until she lowered her arm assaulting his hand. "This is a magic stick." Loki held the item in front of her, watching as she studied it.

"What does it do?"

"It tells us if you're with child." *But by my manipulation.* "See,"—Loki flipped the stick so the wording faced Solas— "Two lines pregnant, one line means you're not."

"And how does this magic work?" Her distrustful gaze snapped to his, a dubious smile upturning the corners of her mouth so slightly he would've missed it had he not been watching her closely.

Earning her trust after this deceit would be difficult, and he had no doubt she'd make him work hard for it. If she ever trusted him again. He tried hard to maintain eye contact, not wanting to see the light in those hopeful dark eyes fade if she caught on to his trick. "You wave it over your belly, and it can sense the energy from the child inside you."

"Really? Like the crystals from the magic lake? The ones the Seers use?"

"Yes. Just like that, angel." When he held the stick over her belly, her body stiffened. Anxiety replaced excitement, or maybe it was apprehension he saw in her black pools. Loki pushed everything aside as he glided the stick over her stomach. Twisting it to make sure only one line showed before he revealed it to her. This time when he showed her the stick, he didn't have to try so hard to mask his emotion and let his disappoint show. "One line. Not pregnant."

Solas stared at the stick briefly before her glare turned deadly. "What kind of trickery is this?"

"What do you mean?"

"There are two lines on that stick." Solas crossed her arms over her chest and stared at him.

When Loki flipped the stick to see for himself, two lines taunted him. It couldn't be? Did he will the two lines while trying to make one? Was the thought of a child unconsciously tainting his magic? "Angel, there was one line when I looked at it." Loki turned to Bly who stood behind him in silence. "Can I do it twice, Bly?"

"Yes, of course. In fact it's suggested, especially since the child would've been conceived a mere twenty-four hours ago. It's called a false positive."

"Oh, thank you, Bly. I had a charge once that had a false positive, but I didn't know what she was crying about," Solas said with a funny tone in her voice, but then she waved her hand at the pregnancy test. "Proceed, *trickster*."

Was there a hidden meaning in the way she called him trickster? Or was he seeing ghosts that weren't there?

Loki held her gaze for a long moment, neither of them blinking. Deciding there was no subterfuge coming from her,

Loki waved the stick over her belly once more. He focused all his energy into the test to make sure it didn't change this time. This was harder to do, because he also had to mask the evidence of his power from Solas. Once the two lines turned to one, he showed it to Solas. Her lips tightened, and she nodded. "Very well. Now we know."

Why do I feel as if there is a double meaning to her words?

Many things crossed over her features, too many for Loki to sift through. He'd thought a negative reading would have made her happy, because she'd made it obvious she didn't want his child. And, he knew she would run from him again soon. With the child out of the picture, she had no reason to stay with him. As he watched Solas turn and leave the room, he was more confused about everything. Whose side was she on? After he gave the stick to Bly, and asked him to spread the lie about the child, Loki followed Solas.

TWELVE

Solas crouched on the ledge of Loki's rooftop and contemplated the foot-traffic of humanity below her on the streets. Stalking them with her gaze lent a strange sense of tranquility and quieted her mind, allowing her thoughts to drift as she tracked the souls with her observation. Uncertain if they could see her, she remained frozen in her position as she focused her power on cloaking her presence.

Before her fall, she'd been invisible to mankind unless she wanted to be seen. Falling had brought about her humanity, but then Loki had fixed her. People could still see her as if she remained mortal, but her abilities had returned with her wings. None of it made sense.

Flashes of the dream that'd woken her and roused her out of Loki's warm embrace flitted through her mind. Solas zoned in on the foot-traffic below until she found herself in the comfortable mental-ambience of meditation.

Not a dream but a memory.

Memories she'd forgotten right before her fall. She grimaced as the recollection skirted through her mind.

"Kill him or have your wings taken." Father's command boomed around the stark, white chamber.

"I cannot. I tried, but I cannot." Ashamed of her defiance, she'd turned her gaze aside. She'd obeyed without question all her life, never defying Him. She'd killed children for Him, but she'd sensed the evil they could craft once they reached

adulthood, so her mission had been just. But to follow His demands on this felt wrong. To kill an innocent was wrong. He'd taught her that. "He's pure. I cannot turn my blade upon an unsullied."

"He's tricked you. He's the biggest sinner of all. A trickster. Worse than Lucifer." Father's lip curled in disgust. He smoothed His palm over her head. "You were my favorite, my most dependable. Until now."

It stung to lose His favor, but in her heart, she knew she'd made the right choice.

"Such a disappointment." Jesus stood behind their father shaking his head. "Twelve before you failed. You were lucky number thirteen, the one that we knew could get the job done."

Just because she'd always been reliable and executed without hesitation before, didn't mean she couldn't fail. That they expected a perfect track record perplexed her. None but Father was perfect.

I will find solace in standing up for the righteous. There is honor in that.

Happiness and contentment had been her constant companion before she refused to execute her mission. That she could feel His displeasure created an ache in her breastbone. Was this what it felt like when God shunned Adam and Eve and ejected them from the Garden?

"Forgive me, Father." The words were hollow, spoken only to appease her parent because she felt no guilt for her inability to follow His will.

"Punish her." He strode from the room, leaving her to the Lamb of God's judgment. Jesus held his flaming sword in his grip. Father would have her mutilated. She accepted the outcome since she'd made the right choice.

"Bow before me, child."

Solas went to her knees because in Heaven she had no choice but to obey. Only on earth could she refuse to do His bidding, and she'd failed to follow through three times before she returned home and confessed her insolence. That she possessed freewill surprised even her. She hadn't known she could defy Him as the fallen angels had.

Head bent, she could see only the edge of Jesus' white pants and his glossy white shoes as he circled her. He stopped at her side, and she held her breath waiting for punishment to commence.

Searing pain went through her as his sword hacked one of her wings from her body.

Screaming, she attempted to flee by crawling away, but Jesus halted any escape with a foot pressed to her back. In the sensitive spot between where her wings connected. She wept and begged for forgiveness. The angels in attendance sang hymns to Father as they watched her sibling saw off her remaining wing. Slowly. In a back and forth manner as if he used a hacksaw to chop down a tree. Solas screeched for mercy until her cries turned to hoarse whimpers. Thanks to the sensitivity of her wings, the sawing motion slowed her punishment and caused her to suffer more than a straight-through cut would have.

With the mutilation complete, Solas remained on the floor, weeping as blood pooled around her. Living in a bubble of protection, she'd never before endured pain, and this... well, this was crippling. Her sibling kneeled beside her. Their gazes locked for a second, his impassive and cold, before he ran the tip of his sword along her wounds, cauterizing them from the heat the weapon possessed.

"Solas, since you love the humans more than our father, He grants you humanity. Live among the filth they've created and be one of them."

Her brother's foot connected with her hip, and he pushed her to the opening that'd been created.

Fear and adrenaline gave her strength to fight against the fall being forced upon her. "Forgive me, Father, as you forgive your mortals." Even though He'd left the room, she knew He could hear her prayer.

Jesus booted her through the hole. Without wings, she experienced a moment of dead-drop, but Father appeared from nowhere and caught her hand, halting her descent. Relief swelled inside her as she peered into His eyes. He'd forgiven her, like she knew He would, like He did all of His offspring.

"Redeem yourself, and I'll allow you to return to your homeland. You have one week to kill him or I'll cast you out of Heaven for eternity."

Surprising her with His lack of forgiveness, He released her, and she fell, her arms rotating as she attempted to break her fall to Earth.

Solas shook her head, dissolving the memory. Shivering from the chill in the air and what she'd seen in Father's eyes as He released her, she pondered her dilemma. One week to kill Loki. Was that a mortal week or a godly week? She had no idea. Either way, time grew scarce.

She sighed, her breath fogging in front of her from the cool night air. Loki was an ass, but he had shown compassion and come to her aid during her time of need. He'd also taken her virginity as payment, claimed she married him, and gave *shatterings* that provided the most profound sense of peace she'd ever experienced.

Her and her self-proclaimed *husband* had done nothing but go in circles since her fall. Killing him presented her with a chance to return home, but... the same problem remained. Knowing Loki's true identity, knowing he wasn't a mere mortal man like she'd believed, she couldn't bring herself to kill him even though he made her angry enough to follow through at times.

Father had accused her of choosing a mortal over Him, had punished her by turning her into a human. He'd lied about

Loki's identity and pretended Loki an ordinary mortal, but she'd sensed his uniqueness despite her parent's duplicity.

There's more going on here.

She could've returned home if she'd followed through with her intentions to kill Loki. Could've had what she thought she wanted without remembering this one memory and all the ramifications that went with it. She'd be lounging in the comfort of Heaven right now if Loki hadn't discombobulated her by professing her pregnancy and she'd stayed her killing play.

A test proved I'm not pregnant.

Palming her belly, she considered the test he'd done. The first one had been positive, the second one negative. But his eyes had shimmered just a moment the second time around, long enough she suspected he tampered with the results, long enough she recognized the visible sign he channeled his power.

The trickster thought to trick her. Not much of a surprise really—she'd known from the get-go he thought to deceive her—but what chaffed was that he played her for a fool thinking he could speak and she'd believe anything he said. He wasn't *that* charming.

Solas had been watching humanity since the dawn of time. No doubt she was ignorant of nuances because she studied their actions and movements, not their words that were oftentimes lies more than truths, but she wasn't as gullible as Loki believed her to be either. The test he'd used to disprove her pregnancy was for mortals and had been operated incorrectly. And while she'd been reduced to mortality for a few horrible hours, the trickster had put her back together again. Given her a new lease on life, immortality returned, and all powers at her disposal. Because of her fresh start she doubted anything intended for human means would work on her.

He also believed she was unable to kill him. Sure, his arrogance was warranted. Many had tried to execute him, and all had failed. That testified to his skill and his strength. But she'd proven earlier if she wanted him dead he'd be the hottest fucking corpse in all gods-dom right now.

If she carried his offspring—and she'd begun to believe she might because she couldn't think of one good reason for Loki to fudge the results unless she *was* pregnant—he'd make a formidable ally.

Why did Father want him dead?

The answer didn't matter. Father wanted Loki dead. *That* was what mattered.

She rose from her perch, and a human below stopped mid-stride to gape. That settled that, they could see her regardless if she attempted to cloak. A breeze ruffled her feathers, and she stretched her wings over her head to drive out the ache from her forced immobilization. The individual made a cross-like motion with his hand from head to sternum, and from shoulder to shoulder, as if he attempted to dispel the presence of evil. That was amusing.

Making her way downstairs, she found Loki sprawled on the bed, his forearm thrown over his eyes, and his other hand rested on his belly. Shirtless with just the waistband of his lounge pants peeking from the sheet, she would've admired his display of maleness if not for the black streaks of his veins.

My poison lingers. Much longer than she would've anticipated.

This explained why he'd been fatigued after they returned from the boutique, and after following through on the licking he'd promised, he'd collapsed on the bed and fallen asleep. He'd been expending his magic to hide the effect of her toxin on him. Impressed he managed to conceal the extent of his weakness from her, she smiled because she saw his action as a maneuver to trick her. Proof he didn't trust her. Further evidence of his trickster ways, and that he likely lived a lonely existence much like she had, or maybe she was delusional because it saddened her that Loki could trust no one.

What's it like to live eons hiding from those who would murder you for... she had no idea why any of the gods would want him dead? She knew the lore, but obviously little of it was accurate if he was walking and talking and not chained in a cave with venom being dripped on him.

Was he so powerful all the gods feared him? Could it be as simple as that?

Always being on guard would be exhausting. *But it was little ol' me that brought him low.*

Solas crawled onto the bed, plucked two feathers, and straddled his waist as she expanded her wings.

"Not now, angel." He didn't budge, not even his muscles tensed, proof he dismissed her as a danger. "I require a brief siesta before I can service you again."

Conceited moron. She didn't seek his sexual help. He'd taught her how to do that all on her own, although it was more fun with him.

She leaned over and bit his bottom lip hard enough to draw blood. His cock twitched, and a groan rumbled from his chest. "Keep that up and I'll give it to you hard up your virgin ass for interrupting my rest."

Solas sat up and rolled her eyes. He wasn't just resting, but attempted to heal himself and was doing a poor job from what she could tell. Every erotic act he'd done to her had been divine, so she didn't expect anything different with sodomy even though it was believed to be the most abhorrent of all deviant acts. "My fearsome demi-god threatens a mere reaper with sexual sadism."

A grin curled his lips. *Sexy fucker.* "Not a *mere* reaper, but *mine* to do with as I please."

It was way past time he took her seriously, as more than his sexual play toy. Despite his demi-god status, they were equals.

She jabbed the feather stems into his heart, a quick motion that buried them deep into the organ, only an inch of each stalk left showing. He jerked, going into immediate action, arms lifting to grab her, but his adrenaline worked against him. She caught his wrists and wrestled them to the bed on either side of his head. That she was capable of overpowering him so easily proved the liquid in her feathers pumped through his system. "I'll remove them in a moment. You need all the serum."

"What've you done?" He panted, a shimmer of purple in his eyes lending suspicion he resisted the antigen polluting his system. She could expound on the futility of his efforts, but his stubbornness wouldn't allow him to listen anyway, so she held her tongue.

"Father wants you dead. Just before I fell, He gave me a clause out of my sentence. A week to kill you and I'd be granted permission to return home." At her confession, his eyes widened, and panic threaded into his green orbs, the purple eradicated in a single burst as if he conceded defeat. Solas knew better. Loki would never give up until his last breath, and she admired his tenacity. He winced as she yanked one, then the other feather from his chest. "I just remembered His promise as you lay here all vulnerable, asleep in your toxin-ridden state, dismissing me as a viable threat." She lifted his arm and traced one of her fingers along his black veins. "You wasted your magic hiding this from me."

"Not wasted."

"Liar." She released his limb, and his hand moved to her throat. A grin twisted her lips, taunting his labors when his squeeze lacked any force. "Your magic is depleted or you'd be able to fight what I just put into you, and you'd be capable of choking me with conviction."

He didn't back down, didn't remove his hand, but his voice emerged thick and hoarse, evidence her serum weakened even his vocal chords. "You'll be bored as fuck in two minutes once you return to Heaven. Only *I* can give you the life you want."

"No, Loki, only *I* can select the life I want." Solas drew her short sword, and he eyed the weapon of death with caution, his fingertips digging into her neck for all the good it did him. "I can plunge this into your heart or slit your throat." She shrugged. "Either move will kill the infamous Loki."

Using the tip of the blade, she brushed his hair off his forehead. His hand trembled against her skin, and his breath caught, their gazes connecting. Genuine apprehension reflected back to her. With her first objective successful, she tossed the weapon aside on the bed.

She pulled her wings into her body and jerked off her shirt and bra. Loki's gaze zoomed in on her breasts as she wiggled a bit lower until she straddled his cock.

His thumb caressed her skin, and she bet he didn't realize he'd gone from threatening her with his fingers on her neck to stroking her?

She rubbed against his dick, and his pupils dilated just a hair. "Or I can chose you and snub Father's offer. So I repeat, only I can select the life I want."

"You planning to fuck me to death?"

"Ballsy to the very end. I like that. What I want you to remember is that everyone is a threat, Loki. *Everyone.* You of all people shouldn't forget that."

Confusion drew his eyebrows together and furrowed along his brow. "Ironic that a reaper seeks to educate me on threats."

"Ironic that I could've killed you multiple times, but yet I have spared your life. Father demanded honesty from me in all things, but He mislead me about your origins. What else did He lie about? What did you do that makes all the gods want you dead?"

"I won't conform to their ideology."

"Hmm... I bet there's more to it than that." Solas anchored her hands on either side of his head and drew almost nose-to-nose with him. "To answer your question, if I planned to fuck you to death." She cupped his jaw, digging her fingers into his flesh and forced him to meet her gaze. In response, his hold on her neck tightened, stronger this time. "If I wanted you dead, Loki, you'd already be dead. I've proven my skill to you twice now. I had multiple opportunities to kill you before I was revealed to you. If I wanted you dead, I wouldn't have given you any final last words before I offed you. That's not my style. Instead you'd be choking on your blood right now."

Something unnamed flashed in his eyes. "Then why the venom?"

She rubbed her breasts against his chest. Like always, he felt decadent against her nipples. "You've dismissed me as a threat more than once. That's disrespectful. A reaper has some pride too. If I don't have my husband's respect, then…" She sighed at the slip, but the renewed spark of purple in his eyes testified to his pleasure and the return of his power. "I gave you a paralytic to articulate how easily I *can* bring you low. My lethality is legendary, and I'm not bragging, but that's a truth. It just *is*. That I'm not a demi-god doesn't mean I'm not as dangerous as you."

"I'm aware of your ability. Made all the more obvious with this life lesson." Yeah, and he sounded as happy about her stealth as a lamb having its throat ripped out by a lion.

Solas draped herself over him, resting her ear over his heart, the steady thump of the organ soothing her, and confirming she made the right choice. She slid her fingers down his neck to circle his nipple and in response the little bud coiled tight. His cock flexed against her core, and his abdomen jerked against her belly, a warning that her serum would run its course soon. "I reaped what Father wanted until you. Never forget, I've chosen you over my homeland not once, but twice. Father wants you dead, and I don't understand why. But for now, I've chosen you."

The hand that clutched her neck shifted to clamp on her nape with more force than a moment before.

"The second drug was an anti-toxin to counteract my earlier venom. Given how fast your metabolism is, you'll be back to your old self in a few minutes." *Probably back to his arrogant self too.* "You're fucking welcome."

"You healed me?"

"You don't have to sound so shocked."

The moment his erection batted against her core at full staff, she knew he was back to himself. A second later, she found herself beneath him and her arms pinned over her head, a hand caging and anchoring her wrists.

"I should spank you for your subterfuge." He'd used that threat one too many times without follow-through for her to take him seriously.

"Get over yourself, Loki. Father sent not one or two after you before He put me on you. I was reaper number thirteen. He'll send more."

"And all of you have failed."

"Did I? If you believe that, you've not learned a thing thanks to your overinflated arrogance."

Scowling, he released her hands. Loki lifted her sword. Surprise spread across his features. "It's cold."

Death is a cold occupation. "The spill of blood heats it up."

"Should I spill yours to verify that?"

"It won't cut me." Catching disbelief in his eyes, she dragged her wrist across the edge, but the most damage it did was catch on her skin and vibrate in his clasp. "See." She turned her arm so her wrist faced him.

"Convenient that it can't be turned on you."

"Just about as convenient as a reaper not turning it on you when ordered."

A slow grin, much like she imagined the one the cat wore right before it ate the canary. "You admit you're my wife?"

"For now." He scowled at her again, and she said, "Don't be greedy. Take your victories however you can."

"I won't let you go."

"Why do you want to keep me?"

He looked away, rammed a hand through his chocolate hair, his conflict evident. Ignoring her inquiry, he asked, "Where do we go from here?"

"Intel." At his confused scowl, she explained. "I want to know why Father wants you dead all of a sudden."

"He's wanted me dead longer than you've been alive." He handed her the sword, handle first, and she grasped it, sheathing the blade back into her body.

"I've been too busy fighting my unnatural response to you to realize there's more at play here. Your friend, what'd he want?" Silence lingered between them, and she took his lack of response as his intention not to confess. "You've got to trust someone."

"As you so eloquently showed me just now with feathers jammed into my heart—that hurt like a sonofabitch by the way—no one is trustworthy."

"Don't be a whiny baby. It doesn't suit you." She sat up and shoved her hand into his hair, cupping the back of his head. "If anything, I just proved you *could* trust me. I saw your vulnerability, I could've ended you and gone home, and instead I chose you... and the baby."

He was off her like a lightning strike, putting distance between them. "There is no baby."

"You attempted to trick me on the test, and now you would lie to me about the baby." Solas gave him her back as she pulled her shirt back on, the pain of his deception cutting deep. "I'm a fool for trusting a goddamn liar." She'd never used that particular curse before and found liberty in uttering it. "I'm not a fool. I know how pregnancy tests work, and since I don't have bodily waste, it was impossible to operate it in the manner in which it was intended."

"I am protecting you."

"Have I not just proven I'm a formidable enemy?" She rubbed her temples with her fingertips. "I could be your ally. Together we're almost indomitable."

"Bly warns my people—"

"The Naglfar?"

"Yes." She refrained from looking at him, but she could hear the hesitancy in his voice. Trusting her wasn't easy for him. "Some want you and the baby dead. Others believe it's the key to winning Ragnarok."

"Ragnarok?" Stunned by this admission that her child might play a role in destroying her homeland, she twisted to look at him. He leaned against the wall, ankles crossed, arms folded, and eyeing her cautiously. "Go on, Loki."

"If God has possession of *our* child, it's believed he'll use *our* child to destroy me and all Naglfars."

She nodded, realizing he used the word 'our' to bind them, while it dawned on her that she'd been an instrument of battle for her parent. It explained everything. "He's omniscient, so He would've seen this, would've known I'd conceive."

"Omniscient is arguable, but I won't quarrel since it's not the issue."

"You not quarreling?" she teased. "Has Hell frozen over? The underworld suddenly been crippled with peace?"

"Hush your mockery, wife, or I'll make good on my punishment."

Solas rose and strolled to him. When she neared, she trailed her fingertip down his chest to hook into the waistband of his lounge pants. "Which one? Spank me or fuck my ass?"

"Jesus fuck." His arm shot out, and he clasped her nape with his hand, fingers digging into her skin as he dragged her against him. "Both. I'm going to do fucking both at the same time just for taunting me."

Grinning, she rubbed her pelvis against his erection prodding her stomach. "Tell me what else Bly said, I'm guessing there's more."

"Bly worries if one of the Naglfars gets ahold of our child, it would be a chance to overthrow me."

"Anything else?"

He shook his head. "That's it, the truth of it all. My Naglfar may be a bigger threat to us than your father. How do you feel about carrying my child?"

She took her time responding because she wasn't completely sure. The concept was still too new, but on the one hand she'd loved the smell of mortal babies and since they could see her when others couldn't, she'd loved engaging with them. Their innocence was refreshing. But a child from her own loins? That engineered a little fear, and she wanted to think of something other than a wee one ripping from her womb.

"Mixed." Her admission elicited a grimace from Loki. "How do you feel?"

"Same."

"Another lie."

He scowled. "Fine, Ms. Honest Angel, a child threatens my kinghood, threatens all I've worked for. I could kill it—you in other words—and be on solid ground once again."

"But you won't." She witnessed the truth in his eyes, the softening at the corners, and even the way his lips slackened. He would *never* raise a hand against their child.

"The allure of having someone love me unconditionally... that's an addictive idea, one I cannot kill without profound contemplation. I wouldn't sleep too deeply if I were you." He added the last in a begrudging tone.

Solas' heart took a direct hit. Had she ever heard anything so tragic? Everyone deserved love and acceptance... but even she had been denied the treasured affection. She'd moved through life doing her job, watching mortals, and reporting to and obeying Father. She'd cherished many things over the centuries but never felt the same devotion from anyone else. Loneliness had been her constant companion. Until Loki saved her from the streets and introduced her to excitement and *shatterings*, she hadn't realized how apathetic she'd been.

"I stand by you unconditionally. I hope that's enough." Until this moment, she'd been blind to her longing for love. She wanted Loki's, and that terrified her so much that if not for her vow to him and her decision to see this through to the end, she'd flee.

Heartbreak is the only thing that'll come from remaining with him. Despite that likelihood, she resigned herself to the ultimate fall. Looked like the joke was on her.

THIRTEEN

$\mathcal{L}$oki hooked the heel of his boot under the motorcycle's kickstand and leaned the bike to the side. He watched the hardened dirt crumble under the bike's weight, much like he felt his world was crumbling. The feeling was unsettling. Why couldn't he gain control of the cracks in his foundation? The cracks weakened him and allowed Solas to wheedle into his heart. Her tenacity was compelling, and he liked it. But to give her a piece of him jeopardized his safety. Sighing, he let his gaze slide over the compound. Neither could he hold her at arm's length. At this point, he figured he was screwed either way.

"Daydreaming?" Solas pushed on his shoulders as she swung her leg over the backrest of the bike.

She stood before him, removing her helmet and looking like a supermodel. When those gorgeous raven locks fell against the black, leather cat suit, Loki drank her in. One swoop from the tips of her thigh high boots to the depths of her onyx pools, and he knew exactly why he couldn't control the cracks in his foundation. He was thinking with his dick. And those cracks would continue to spider like a motherfucker because no power in the world would ever take her from him. Something else unfamiliar shifted inside him, and he desperately wished he could decipher the feelings. Being able to name them might offer some consolation. It went beyond mere lust. When he looked at her or thought about her a softening occurred in his chest. Tender emotions women endured, but never the infamous Loki. Was his affection for Solas or his child? Both maybe?

"Loki?" This time when she spoke, there was an edge to her voice. Concern if he wasn't mistaken.

"Are you sure this is the place?" Loki observed the large fence surrounding the piece of property. "This looks more like a compound than a biker bar."

"They're understandably distrustful." Solas gave him a pointed stare, as if to accuse him of being the king of distrust. His cynicism had kept him alive for millennia, would keep her breathing too, apparently, since she trusted when she shouldn't. He would never apologize for his misgivings of anyone, not his Naglfar, strangers, angels, or kin for that matter. Everyone could be turned. It was simply a matter of the incentive used. "Easy to comprehend why they don't like company." She hung the helmet on the backrest and surveyed the area. "Someone was to meet us at the gate."

"Could be a trap." Loki observed her eyes as they narrowed. "What?"

"There may be no honor among thieves but—"

"But you think fallen angels are more dignified—more decent." His angel lifted her chin and squared her shoulders. Loki hadn't thought it possible to want her more than he had earlier, but her confidence made her more desirable. "You're forgetting the whole, cast the fallen into Hell and commit them to chains of gloomy darkness."

"I don't find that an accurate description of what happens."

"No? Where would you be if I hadn't kept you?" Loki realized his mistake when fury lit her eyes.

"Kept me?" Solas inched closer to him. "You mean raped me then impregnated me with your dammed seed!"

Is that what she thought? Loki reached for her arm, but she pulled away. Over her shoulder, he noted the guard at the top of the fence, a large-power rifle in his grasp. "Come here." Using his godlike speed, he grasped her and held her against his chest. "You're making a scene and causing suspicion." Locked onto her gaze, he loosened his grip but kept her close. "Raped?" He seethed at the thought. "I seduce, angel, never rape. It's much more fun to corrupt the soul. Forcing my way in is too easy, and not very sportsmanlike."

"Let's just do this…"

"Not until you admit you wanted me and gave yourself to me *willingly*."

"Why do you care what I think of you?"

"Because of *your* guilt you like to demonize me, and I will *not* tolerate that any longer, wife."

Solas looked away from him, and the biker on the platform at the top of the gate drew Loki's attention.

"You're right. I was scared but excited." She conceded, but sounded guarded, like maybe she admitted her sins with reluctance. "I gave myself to you willingly, even though I was manipulated."

"You said before we came here that you chose me."

"I did. I do."

"Solas, I need to know before we walk through those gates that you are with me because I sure the hell am with you." Solas met his gaze with a mixture of emotion. A jumble of feelings he understood well.

"Is there a problem down there?" The man at the top of the gate yelled. His accent was all Alabama, but his skin had the Florida sun etched all over it. It was the perfect combination for the BamaFlora Beach, which rested on the line of the two states.

"I'm with you, husband," Solas said, as she turned to face the man above them. "There will be a problem if your representative doesn't hold their end of the deal."

The deal was to have Loki present. It's the only way her fallen would agree to meet with Solas. Of course, Loki wouldn't have allowed her to meet them alone. No way in hell would he let her walk into the line of fire without his protection. That they demanded Loki's presence resulted in his increased suspicion. His wife could have all the faith in Heaven toward her brothers and sisters, but this was a trap indeed, he felt it in his gut. And he'd survived too long on gut feelings to ignore them now.

The gates slid open, pulled by two men on each side, and Loki took in the scenery. Not what he expected. The dilapidated, wooden gates made him think an abandoned junkyard waited beyond the security. Instead, beach cabanas surrounded a large tiki-hut style bar. Motorcycles lined the back gate, and the smell of barbeque drifted on the wind. Loki's gaze followed the smoke to the grill, and he mentally started a headcount of enemies.

The man on the ledge motioned them forward with his gun. Loki would've smirked at the human weaponry and its ineffectiveness to harm him if he wasn't so worried about protecting his angel.

Frustrated by her eagerness to trust, he fell into step next to Solas whose fearless stride had her nearing the gate much too quickly for his peace of mind. "This should be a good indication of how your fallen relatives are living."

"What's that supposed to mean?"

"If you feel there is no honor among thieves, you better watch your ass." Loki pointed toward a garage, the ground in front covered in grease and oil. "Chop shop. They're parting out stolen motorcycles."

"Now you're an expert on motorbikes?"

"It doesn't take an expert to know you don't rip apart a brand-new Harley into that many pieces unless you're parting it out and hiding evidence."

Solas stopped to face him. "Why is it so hard for you to think that the fallen are good?"

"Sweetheart, there're different kinds of good—different kinds of bad. I'm not saying that they're murderers, although I'm not ruling it out, but you have no idea what they've had to do to survive." Stunned at her hypocrisy after schooling him on threats just hours ago, Loki shook his head.

"This again." She huffed and looked adorable doing it.

"Please remember how you felt when you fell from that three-story building at my feet. You had no one, and neither did they."

Tilting her head, she stared at him, and an array of emotion moved through her eyes. Solas nodded, and they continued walking to the bar. Loki hoped she remembered the desperate need for forgiveness after her fall—the need to make her parent happy—the isolation that seeps into your soul. She forgot he was cast out and shunned by his family long before her. Loki had cataloged each painful memory, every struggle, the feelings of desperation and abandonment, because holding on to such memories kept him grounded and always on guard.

Loki wrapped his hand around the bar door, pausing briefly to say, "I hope they are just the way you want them to be, angel. I wish that for you." His honest angel sucked in a breath and met his gaze. "It's the truth." *Because I want to give you your heart's desires.*

He tightened his grip on the door handle before he reached for her. Keeping alert had become difficult with Solas around. These *feelings* for her grew stronger, harder to control. If both sides were against them, he needed to deaden himself to her. Solas was his weakness, but his child was his strength—the perfect balance he required to get through this meeting.

Without further thought, Loki opened the door. Solas was two strides ahead of him when the room went silent, and she stopped in the middle of the bar. The bikers stared at them in silence for several minutes before eleven people, ten female and one male, came forward and kneeled before Solas.

The fallen.

One woman swayed her hips as she walked around the bar where she served drinks. Her eyes stayed on Loki, moving up and down his frame. She looked familiar, but he couldn't place her face.

"Kneel, Sephora!" The woman closest to Solas commanded.

"Is she really a Grigori?" Sephora moved closer. "Why should we kneel? Even if she is a Grigori, she's fallen—just like us. Without our wings, *if* she has any magic, it's no more powerful than ours."

Loki cursed under his breath. His angel shifted beside him, her ego taking a hit Loki knew she'd have to defend. Before he could protest, black wings spread wide pushing him back behind her. Solas stepped forward and pointed to the floor, glaring at the woman. "You were saying?"

Movement from behind the bar caught Loki's attention. A large man who looked familiar rounded the bar. Something silver in his hands reflected the light as he moved toward them.

"No!" One of the fallen leaped to her feet and ran toward the man. She jumped, flying through the air toward him, only to be swatted away like a fly. The action allowed Loki to see the man's tattoo, a mark all Naglfar bore. Recognition hit the pit of his stomach just as *his* Naglfar assassin used his magic and vanished.

The fallen drew their swords, Solas included, just as the Naglfar reappeared in front of her. The demon looped strands of thick silver around Solas' wings before she could close them. The sound of her whimper twisted in his gut.

Loki spotted two more Naglfar coming from both sides toward them. With the fallen in front, swords drawn in battle position, and three Naglfar closing in on them, Loki acted fast. He could feel the depths of his destruction in his very soul at the thought of losing her. Because of his emotion, his power surged inside him, and he knew if his Naglfar disappeared with Solas, he'd create an earthquake with such force Florida would break off and be swallowed by the ocean. That meant he'd have to leave another atmospheric footprint, one that'd bring more enemies—ones much more powerful than the fallen and his Naglfar.

Cursing under his breath, he held out his arms. "Now, now..."

At his command the room stood still, as if they were frozen in time. As much as he hated leaving a trail of his magic, he also missed the look on his enemies' faces when he used this particular power. He'd be lying if he pretended the ease with which he overpowered them all didn't make his cock hard. Defeating his foe always had this effect on him.

He walked around Solas until he faced her and the Naglfar. Seeing the indention of the knife in his wife's belly wielded by *his trusted* Naglfar, where his child rested, caused rage to simmer just beneath the surface. "How dare you."

The Naglfar tried to move his head but couldn't. Loki kept the room suspend in motion, but allowed them to talk. "My lord, it has to be done. I swore to protect you, and the baby will ruin everything. It is prophesied to be your downfall."

Loki briefly met Solas' gaze. Trepidation, with a touch of disbelief stared back at him. Of course, she would now question everything between them. He saw it there in her eyes. Did she really have the upper hand? Could her poison really have killed him? Those were the questions she'd most likely ask. The inch of trust he'd gained from her vanished with this show of his power. As much as he wanted to discuss her fear and doubts with her, there was a threat holding a blade against his child.

"Like *this* has to be done?" He held the man's gaze as he walked to the Naglfar on the right side of the room. Ignoring the fear in the Naglfar's eyes, Loki lifted his index finger and touched it to the demon's forehead. From head to toe, the Naglfar turned to ashes, leaving a pile of residue on the floor. All about him the fallen gasped, and he thought he saw a new measure of respect enter a few of their eyes. Tending to his recalcitrant children in a harsh manner would deter other

Naglfar from rebelling against him. His wife seemed unimpressed, though, and continued to glare at him, fury and wariness bleeding from her black eyes.

When Loki finished ashing the other Naglfar on the left side of the room, he turned back to the bastard holding the blade against his child.

"My Lord, please… don't kill me. My devotion is to you."

Did his minion take him for a fool? Words were useless when his devotion was evident in his insurrection.

Taking Solas' sword from her stiff hand, Loki held it out to inspect as he responded to the Naglfar. "Kill you?"

"I was only doing what's best. Please," the man begged, but Loki saw no real regret in his eyes.

"I'm not going to kill you." Loki turned the blade in his hand. He had other plans for his wayward Naglfar.

"Thank you, my lord."

"Don't thank me yet."

"Loki, you can't use my sword—" Solas tried to interject.

"Silence!" A man threatened his child, and she worried about the weapon in which he chose to employ to mete out justice? Loki shoved the sword through the Naglfar's stomach. Instead of turning to ash, he screamed in agony before disappearing on a thread of Loki's magic.

Once the threat was gone, Loki bent to pick up the dagger dropped by the Naglfar. As he rose, he paused to press a kiss against Solas' belly. An act he did without thought. He'd probably regret his public show of affection later. For now, he buried his feelings to deal with the current clusterfuck. Later, he'd start picking through the many emotions stirring inside of him. A choice needed to be made, one he feared he couldn't make, and it would lead to his death.

"You," Loki said, pointing to Sephora. He wagged his finger in the air and released her from his hold. "Come here."

When Sephora's lips tilted in a sultry smirk, he thought he heard his angel growl. Loki pushed the silver ropes dropped by the Naglfar aside with his boot and walked a couple steps forward. Once Sephora reached him, she lowered her lashes and purred, "You, I will kneel for." When she looked up from her kneeling position, Loki remembered her with clarity. For it was in this position he'd had his cock rammed down her throat.

"It wasn't Sephora when we met."

"No. It was Scarlet." Sephora's excitement at his memory of her was evident in her thickened tone.

Scarlet.

He chuckled at the name.

"Did you fuck her?" Solas' voice held a touch of darkness, a raspy tone that he recognized from when she went for blood in his kitchen. Loki angled his head enough to brush his gaze against hers. The only thing he had fucked was Sephora's mouth, but his wife would have to wait for an answer.

Loki lifted his head and stared at each of the Fallen. *Scarlet. Scarlet....* Except for the one male, a room full of *Scarlets* stared back at him. Why hadn't he put this together sooner? Were the attacks on his life spread out enough not to see the connection, or was he so blinded in his lustful ways he didn't care what their names were? A brilliant plan by their maker, but he'd admit that only to himself.

"How did you do that?"

Loki followed the voice to a face that was startlingly familiar compared to the rest. Waving his hand through the air, he released the raven-haired woman. "Come closer." She moved toward him on his command. Loki glanced between Solas and the woman, noting slight differences. If it weren't for her short hair, they could pass as twins. When she stood in front of him, he lifted her chin and tilted her head side-to-side. Amazing resemblance.

"Don't touch her!" Solas warned, and he could feel her magically struggling against his restraint. "Release me from your hold."

"Who is she to you?" Loki asked his angel who had fury creeping into her gaze.

"My sister, Suriel. Let me go, Loki."

"Your sister?" He looked back at the fallen replica of Solas. "Your sister as in, *We're all God's children?*"

"No. She's of my blood."

Excellent. This could work to his benefit.

"I'd like to know how you did that as well?" The male angel asked, but Loki didn't release him.

Loki had many questions too. "You want me to reveal how I suspend the room or turned the demons to dust?"

"No," Suriel answered. "We'd like to know how you used a reaper's weapon to kill, especially one like Solas'."

The questions were stacking up. Solas had said her sword wouldn't cut her, not that no one other than a reaper could kill with it. Was it a lie? Or had something shifted, allowing him to use her sword. It would have to be a powerful magic to release a spell on a sword forged by *Him*.

Loki bent and scooped the silver chains into his hand, noting the gasp from Solas. The chains were something she feared. More questions, but Loki thought it best to hold them for now.

"How do you still have your wings, sister?" Suriel asked Solas. There was a longing in Solas' gaze, one he wished he could soothe by setting her free to embrace her sister. Letting her out of his hold wasn't an option at the moment because he knew if he released her, she'd move among her siblings, and he couldn't protect her as easily then.

"Father is sending someone for you both." Suriel looked panicked.

"I think *He's* already failed at that. Thirteen of you stand before me, all of you failed." That Solas elected not to challenge his statement verified her doubt. "Can he afford to lose more angels?" Loki paced the room contemplating his next move.

"Solas, Father is sending a powerful source. I dare not speak his name." Suriel whispered the last sentence as if mentioning this 'powerful source' would draw him out.

"Speak his name Suriel, or lose your tongue." Loki stood before her, hands clasped behind his back at ease with his power.

If you hurt her, I will gut you. The threat echoed about in his head. None of the other fallen reacted to the vow, so he glanced sharply at his woman, her stare sent the same message as the words. He knew Solas spoke telepathically to her siblings on the street, but could she have telepathed to him without intending to? Was it even possible?

Suriel swallowed, and he took the reaction as a genuine sign of fear. "Michael."

Solas struggled harder against his hold, hard enough it pulled on his power. Impressive.

"Loki, please." The desperation in her tone matched the fear in her eyes.

He walked to her, placed a hand on her belly and leaned forward to speak against her ear. "Nothing will harm you, wife." He felt her shiver. Concern still marred her expression.

With a snap of his fingers, Bly appeared by his side. "You called—"

"I will discuss everything with you in depth once we are safe. For now"—grabbing Suriel by the arm he shoved her toward Bly—"take her." With a nod, Bly disappeared.

Loki turned back to the room. "How would all of you like your wings back?"

"Blasphemy!"

"It's against God!"

"Imagine the power." Sephora purred. Loki had one chomping at the bit to receive new wings but judging by the look in Solas' eyes, Sephora may not live long after getting them. He'd have to smooth this over if his plan was to work. Was his woman jealous of the other angel? Surely Solas knew

Sephora didn't appeal to him. He was interested in only one angel.

"No one leaves this compound. I've sealed it, so don't waste your energy trying. I'll be back for you." Waving his hand, he released them all from his hold.

"Except for her." Jaw set, Solas went straight toward Sephora.

Loki halted her with an arm around her waist. "Let's think of the big picture, angel."

"I am, you narcissistic ass. But does your *big picture* involve a sick threesome with *my* sister and this harlot?"

He hadn't thought of that, but his naughty angel's mind resulted in his cock going hard. "Sisters? Why, angel, what a nice suggestion."

"You son of a bitch!" She elbowed him, and he laughed at her attempt to break his hold. When she reached for a feather, he froze her again. He'd deal with her fury later. "How's that for not underestimating you? Thanks for the warning earlier."

Loki turned toward the room as he hefted her over his shoulder. "We're having a little domestic argument. I will return."

Moments later, Loki walked through the gates they'd entered when they'd arrived, with many things on his mind and too much to deal with. Michael was coming. First priority was getting his wife and child to safety.

FOURTEEN

*I*mmobilized like a fucking powerless pet. In that moment if Solas had possessed her blade, she would've gutted Loki like the pig he was without an ounce of regret.

If I could.

The joke was on her again. He could've neutralized her at any point he wanted, but instead he'd played with her.

Toyed with me like a cat does a mouse.

How many times had he laughed at her when she thought she held the advantage? His good buddy Bly was probably in on it.

Just last night he'd had her believing her immobilization serum worked on him as she'd healed him. If he'd even required healing in the first place. She couldn't trust anything between them because she wouldn't put it past him to manipulate her by any means necessary. Creating the black veins to determine how she'd react would be an easy trick.

Not that she would've been shocked if he required none of her healing serum. He was a demigod. His power should eclipse hers, but she'd needed this lesson in inequality because she'd fallen for the belief she was—or could be—his equal. Blinded by her first experience with romance, she could live with her stupidity.

What'd I ever see in him to make me fall? Besides an easy hand with children, his affection toward animals, and his kindness toward others, not sensing evil in him shouldn't have been enough. Proof the monotonous eons of watching and killing had influenced her ability to rationalize.

Now he's trivialized me before my siblings. That, she couldn't live with.

"Angel, I need to know before we walk through those gates that you are with me because I sure the hell am with you." He'd said it with such earnestness before entering the compound, she'd done the unthinkable and put her faith in him. Again. The trickster. The king of fucking lies. With his actions, he'd proven he sure as shit hadn't been with her, but thought her just another one of his puppets, easily controlled and manipulated. Wasn't she?

He used his power on me in front of everyone and undermined my authority.

She could've aided him, had practically begged him to release her—it added to her humiliation, weakening her further, when her husband ignored her pleas. Instead, he'd shunned her need to appear as his equal. They had *not* been the united front he'd pretended they were.

I was never his equal, only fooled myself into believing I could be. And she wasn't talking about power, but rather their relationship.

Solas couldn't decide if she wanted to scream or cry. The fury and sadness that blended inside her might result in her doing both.

Loki settled her on her feet next to the motorcycle they'd arrived on. Cars zoomed past them on Highway 292, the rush of air from their movement blowing her hair away from her face.

Solas could feel Loki's stare like an accusation from a teenage drama queen for some trumped-up offense. Unable to meet his eyes, she focused on his chest and attempted to swallow the thick knot in her throat. Witnessing his smug satisfaction would be more than she could tolerate in this moment.

He still held her flat-black blade in his grasp. None but her should've been able to operate the short sword. She didn't know what to make of that unexpected outcome and mostly didn't care. Tomorrow she'd drum up the energy to care. Right now, she wallowed in her misery and anger. Misery over the proof he only 'kept' her because of the baby. Anger because he'd duped her, and like a naïve reaper she'd fallen for him.

Fallen...

Yeah, she'd fallen again. Fallen for his lies, his glorious shatterings, and his declaration that he was with her. She'd even fallen for the belief that he *wanted her*. She'd put her faith in him, and the disappointment was crushing.

This fall hurt worse than the first.

She lifted a hand and rubbed at the odd ache in her chest threatening to strangle the oxygen from her lungs. That's when she realized he'd released his magic and she could move.

Solas said nothing, didn't even look at him or attempt to retrieve her sword, just turned on her heels, and walked away from him and all she'd *fallen* for.

"Solas..."

Ignoring him, she kept walking, putting as much distance between them as she could before she did the unthinkable and attacked. Of course, that'd end in her own death, but at least she wouldn't be suffering from heartache any longer.

To think I defended him against Sephora's plans. The newbie reaper's thoughts had been amplified like she spoke into a megaphone, and Solas had been unable to turn them off or lower their volume.

"Solas!"

Solas kept walking.

Sephora plotted with the Naglfar to take them down. Plotted still to catch him unawares and put her sword through his heart. She'd take everything Loki offered her, but she wouldn't give him her full loyalty in return. Oh, no, Sephora wanted back inside their homeland, and she'd stop at nothing to return. Killing them would buy her a one-way ticket back into Heaven, along with a higher perch in the ranks... or so

Sephora believed. Solas was realizing the truth now. Before her fall, she'd been aware of the promises her ranks vomited to the fallen, all the while intending to renege on those deals in the end. Yet her loyalty and love for her home made her turn a blind eye to the truth, accepting the explanation given for the revoked promises.

He'll kill you before you breathe on him, Sephora. Good riddance, you double-crossing bitch.

Maybe she should be cheering her sibling, but she couldn't bring herself to wish for or want Loki's death. Even after his betrayal, she still felt the wrongness of ending his life. Had she felt differently, she would attempt to do the job herself.

Loyal to the end, and I'm the one spurned instead of the real traitor.

Solas was pretty sure Loki thought her reaction to the other fallen was borne out of jealousy. She couldn't deny the jealous bug had bitten her when she realized he'd fucked her sibling, but she hadn't been all that surprised either. But as usual Loki thought everything revolved around him. He probably thought *he* was the source of creation. The egotistical bastard hadn't given any consideration to the possibility that Sephora's excitement to join his ranks had nothing to do with him or getting back at their father, but everything to do with betraying Loki. And even though he'd had Solas trussed up like a bondage master, she'd still foolishly sought to protect him against her sibling.

I don't know what you are, but you're worse than a fool. Worse than a moron or a—

The sudden pinch on her arm jerked her to a halt, and a moment later Loki yanked her about. "Go ahead, let me hear it so we can move on."

Solas still refused to meet his eyes and instead gazed at the white sand, almost blinding against the sun. "If you value your hand, you'll remove it from my arm."

Without her sword, she couldn't make good on that threat, but she'd bluffed her way out of worse situations. Well, no, she hadn't. Loki *was* the worst situation she'd ever encountered.

Loki chuckled. She didn't know what to make of that. He shocked her still when he offered her sword, hilt first.

An ironic smirk teased her lips, but she fought it back. "You trust me not to ram it through your deceitful heart?"

"Everything I did back there was to protect our family."

As she curled her fingers around the blade's hilt, she met his eyes. *Fucking liar.*

"I'm not." Had she projected her thought? He kept talking before she could ask. "You were outgunned back there."

"No question."

"My Naglfar would've killed our child... and you."

I'm the afterthought in that sentence.

"You're not." He sighed, as if weary, while she processed their conversation, certain he heard at least some of her thoughts since he kept responding to them. "I had to do something."

"Sure. No question."

"Goddamn it! Scream and rail at me. Do something, but don't pretend indifference."

"Fuck. You." Proud she'd managed to keep the cursing to a neutral tone, she elevated her eyebrows, and asked, "Does that please you, Loki?"

Purple prisms hit his eyes a moment before his hand tangled in her hair and his other one went to her waist, wrenching her against him. On instinct, she reacted to his manhandling and pressed the blade against his throat, a two-inch line sliced into his skin before she halted. Blood pooled over her blade, darkening his shirt and heating up her weapon, but the wounds healed almost instantaneously.

"Finish it," he challenged, angling his head to the side as if he truly dared her to complete her job.

Bold words for the master of duplicity. No doubt he'd freeze her—or demonstrate some other colossal power that belittled hers—before she went much further. "Like you couldn't stop me. You've been in total control, toying with me, since the day I fell at your feet."

"That's technically untrue, angel." She stared at him trying to decide which part was untrue, and he must've realized her unspoken question or heard her thoughts because he explained. "Yeah, I could've halted your attack in the kitchen. Sparring with you showed your cards, I couldn't let that opportunity pass by, but never doubt your venom—"

Solas kneed him in the dick. A burst of Loki's magic struck her, causing her hair to fly back from her face. He dropped like a meteor, the pavement beneath him caving and creating a crater-like indention from his mojo. His fingers remained in her hair, tightening, and nearly taking her down with him.

A passing vehicle honked at them. They ignored it.

"You bastard!" She worked his fingers loose as he gagged through his pain, cupping his family jewels.

A glimmer of thought surfaced. In this moment, she'd weakened him like any mortal man. He was unprepared for an attack, which meant now was the perfect time to slice his throat or thrust her blade through his insincere heart. And after everything she still stayed her hand.

No bigger fool than me.

"I put my faith in you, trusted you like I did Father, and you both betrayed me. Twice I've fallen for you. First when I refused to kill you and second by trusting your *lies*." Struggling to withhold tears, she breathed through the burning in her sinuses. The weakness pissed her off, but she was mostly mad at herself for putting her faith in the trickster. She knew all the lore, so she had only herself to blame for her current predicament.

Fool me once, shame on you. There wouldn't be a twice.

Admitting her ultimate defeat at the hands of the trickster, she sheathed her weapon and pressed her empty palm to her chest once more. Why'd she hurt so much right here?

She was only halfway in control of her emotions when he tilted his head back and peered at her. His dark hair glistened in the sunlight, and she hated him for his magnificence.

"Your venom did weaken me and last night, I was down for a few moments before your elixir healed me. Had you wanted to kill me, you could've, and there was nothing I could've done to stop you. Thank you for caring enough to fix me and for *not* killing me."

Solas snorted. "I won't fall for your lies a third time, Loki."

"I didn't betray you."

"You did." He shook his head, and before he could speak she said, "The show of power didn't surprise me all that much, just reminded me I'm out of my league with you. That I ever thought I was your equal is on me, not you. That was my pride and wishful thinking, wanting to be more than a mere reaper."

"You are more. You're the mother of my child."

There's the ache in my chest again. The baby was the only reason she was 'more' to him. No one had ever wanted her just because of who she was. Father valued her skillset, but He'd only ever used her, never demonstrating any affection toward her. After eons of obedience, the one time she wanted an explanation, He'd punished her. Loki was no different. He wanted the child, not her.

She swallowed through the lump in her throat, and reminded him, "Says the demigod—"

"I'm a god."

"—who reminded me just last night to sleep lightly because the child threatens your kingdom."

"You're twisting everything I say."

"Maybe, Loki, but I'm not twisting your actions." She held up her hand when he would've argued. "Before walking in there we established we were in this *together*. You said, and I quote, 'I sure the hell am with you,' and I agreed with you. I believed we were equals, portraying a united front. You wanted it, demanded it, and misled me into believing you. The joke was on me when you so eloquently reminded me of your nature, tricking me, and rendering me insignificant in front of the fallen when you refused to release me from your power. Initially, sure, I understand, but once you had the situation under control you still held me captive."

Silence lingered between them, their gazes locked. She might've thought she hit a nerve, but she couldn't trust her assessment where he was concerned. Not any longer. Not after his recent actions.

"Tell me about this." He indicated his hand. The thin silver rope his Naglfar had used on her was coiled about his palm. A memory surfaced, flashing through her mind, something she'd forgotten about the events that led to her fall. A lesser reaper had used a silver lasso on her, towing her before their father to account for her failure. The pain had been unbearable. Her wings had sizzled and smoked like acid dripped on them. It had *felt* like acid dripped on them. In those moments, she'd known true fear for the first time in her life. The same agony had touched her for a brief moment when the Naglfar used it on her.

Trembling at the jumble of emotions and trying to remind herself that was then, and they no longer burned her wings, Solas attempted to pull herself together as she took a step away from the instrument of torture. His eyes wrinkled at the corners, narrowing, as his lips pressed together in a tight line.

A second later, the lasso vanished, and he pushed to his feet, drawing her against him. "I vow to kill the reaper who hurt you and brought you fear."

He just verified my assumption that he can at least read some of my thoughts.

She almost believed his promise. If not for today's duplicity, she no doubt would have. Shrugging out of his grasp, she said, "Your betrayal hurt me more."

He flinched and put his fingers through his hair as he stepped away from her. "Please understand I was protecting you, angel."

"You were protecting your ego." They didn't even really know if there *was* a baby. A rumor based upon her sibling's attestation was not confirmation. "Tell me this, demigod—*ahem*. Excuse me. Tell me this, *god*, could you read Sephora's thoughts?"

Loki shook his head. "No. I'm only getting some of yours."

That's what I thought. Solas grimaced. She'd have to work on correcting that. "You would've known her thoughts had you given me even a fraction of the benefit of the doubt. Instead you were too busy throwing your weight around in there to even consider a peon like me could help. But that's all right—"

"Clearly it's not," he gave a half-hearted chuckle, adding insult to injury by making light of his actions and her offense.

"Clearly it's not my problem anymore. My unsolicited advice, watch your back with that one."

"What do you mean by it's not your problem anymore?"

Of course, he'd focus on *that* rather than her warning. Typical. Arrogance never looked so good on anyone, and she loathed him for it.

"I'm done with this charade of a relationship."

FIFTEEN

From nowhere, Michael appeared behind Loki. Startled by Michael's abrupt arrival, Solas froze for a moment as she noted minute details. Michael's crystal sword caught the sunlight and shimmered like diamonds, the sharp edge translucent where faint-white flames licked along the blade. Recognizing the blade as the god-killer, her breath hitched in her chest. Forged from Father's special blacksmith, it was a legend among swords. Lore told God blessed the alloy, imbued it with His magical imprint, and the weapon hummed when it neared one of His foes. Rumor had it that it'd been crafted specifically for Michael and that he'd slain more than a dozen gods with the blade.

The archangel elevated his weapon to strike a deadly blow to her trickster... from behind like a coward. *"Behind you!"*

Loki reacted. Spinning, he parried Michael's blow with... *my sword*? How in the hell did he do that? That he could call forth *her* weapon would *not* do.

Michael frowned at the short blade Loki palmed, most likely recognizing it as hers since they'd practiced often by dueling one another. "What is this trickery? How does he call forth your sword, sister?"

"I'm a god, that's how." Insert Loki's ego, once more. Solas shook her head as a convertible full of teenage boys whooped and hollered at them as they passed.

They drew apart, and faced off. Loki put her behind him. She allowed his protectiveness for a moment while she confirmed he indeed possessed *her* weapon. The fucker. Not only was he a liar, and a trickster, but a fucking thief too. She couldn't have him stealing her sword whenever he desired. Chances were, at the most crucial moment she required *her* blade to defend herself he'd pilfer it from her very grasp. Given the recent turn of events, that'd be her type of luck.

"Solas," Michael said as he gauged Loki. "The rumors of the baby are untrue."

"Trickster, I told you reapers lie so they can achieve an advantage over their opponent. The same goes for angels of all rank." Staring at her mentor, the angel who'd taught her everything, she couldn't even bring herself to trust him, having been burned one too many times lately. One set of siblings claimed she was pregnant and wanted to return her to Father for punishment, while her oldest and dearest friend declared the opposite. Or Loki lied about what her brothers had said the other morning.

"I didn't fucking lie." Loki shot her an aggravated glare over his shoulder.

She offered him a saccharin smile. Didn't matter because either way... *I'm surrounded by goddamn liars.*

"It is the truth." Her brother flicked his gaze in her direction for a heartbeat before returning it to the greater threat—Loki, of course. She was nothing but a nuisance, like a bug either of them could easily swat aside.

"You also told me that your younger siblings, like those the other morning, require the distraction because they cannot rely on their abilities alone." Loki nodded toward Michael. "He's an apex predator. What's his excuse?"

"You're still stronger than him."

"If we join forces, with all we know about him between us, together we can defeat him." For the first time, Michael leveled his focus on her. A steady stare, which told her he believed what he said, and that he put his faith in her and believed she remained on Heaven's side.

"I have her sword." Loki showed off by spinning her blade. "How's she going to aid you without it, pansy motherfucker?"

Michael elevated an eyebrow. "How indeed?"

She should save herself the headache and feather Loki right now and get it over with. Not in the mood for sibling drama or Loki's ego, she elected to wrap up this little altercation. She placed a finger to her lips. "*Shh…*"

Only her brother could see her, and he didn't even acknowledge her motion. After plucking two feathers, she flung herself onto Loki's back.

Upon impact, "*oomph,*" was the only noise he had a chance to make before she sliced both feathers across his throat in opposite directions.

She yanked a third feather, dragged the tip across her tongue, coating it in her blood, and jabbed it at an angle so that it'd enter his brain stem at the back of his neck. Loki growled, and the quill quivered.

Against the back of Loki's ear, she whispered, "Only the blood of your maker can heal you."

Her bloody and violent attack lasted less than fifteen seconds, but it was all the time she needed. His miscalculation gave her the opportunity she required to execute a deadly blow.

As he stumbled, she jumped off his back, mentally counting out the seconds before he collapsed. Loki held his throat with one hand, blood covering his fingers, and slapped at the feather lodged at the back of his head with his other hand. A futile effort because he never had a chance of dislodging it.

"His maker will not come to his aid." Her brother sneered at Loki. Michael had taught her to never glory in those moments before death. *And yet here he stands doing the thing he claimed to abhor, claimed was unethical.* Was anyone who they pretended to be?

"What've you done, angel?" Loki's gargled words were almost unintelligible, proof she'd cut through his vocal chords.

"The only thing I could." She yanked the quill from his neck, pressed her thumb to the blood and venom seeping from his spine, leaving behind her thumbprint on his neck directly over the wound. Snapping the feather in half, she released it for the wind to carry it away.

"The mighty has finally fallen," Michael gloated, his eyes alight with profane merriment. "All of Heaven will rejoice, and many other gods as well."

What'd Loki ever do to Michael to warrant so much hatred? "You will report our success to Him?"

Loki twisted toward her, lurching in his sudden movement, and teetering into her. She caught him, and stabilized his footing, as she called her weapon back to her.

"Yes, sister. I proudly return to Father, who doubted, when *I* alone knew you were the right choice."

"Why?" The single word from Loki was so mangled she barely understood him.

"Your ego will be your ruin." She glanced at Michael over Loki's shoulder. Why wasn't he leaving to crow about their achievement? "Forget about my feathers so soon, husband? Or did you just expect me to fall in line?"

Loki's eyes rounded, the purple prisms of his godly magic burst forth. His mojo punched her and stung, but petered out without any effect. Weakened from expending his power, he drooped against her, chest-to-chest, his arms anchored over her shoulders. His breath grew ragged, coming in quick pants. Lifting an arm, he dragged a bloody finger along her cheek, the wetness sticky against her skin. In that moment, she saw the recognition of his death reflected in his eyes.

"Would've given you the world, wife."

"Didn't want the world. I only desired an equal partnership."

His eyes slid closed and opened much too slowly, as if all his energy went into forcing the lids up. Pulling her thoughts in tight, so neither man could read them, she said, "You underestimated me for the final time, Loki."

Her trickster slumped to his knees, his face pressed to her stomach and his weight heavy against her. With her fingers digging into his shoulder, she held him in position.

"Little one," she thought he murmured. "My surprising joy. You are... loved," and then he said nothing more, his muscles going flaccid. But a small blip of magic, like a light kiss, tickled her belly. Eyes wide, she stared down at her broken husband. Had that been Loki's last surge of power or... could it have been the baby responding to its father?

A car whipped past them, shocking her with the sudden burst of air. *Homicide on Highway 292...* and not a single human had stopped to aid Loki. That was humanity for you.

She tightened her grip on Loki's shoulder. If she released her handhold on his shoulder, he would crumple to the pavement. She wouldn't give Michael the satisfaction of seeing Loki in such a defeated manner.

"Tell Father I would never betray my maker."

Her brother gave her a huge smile. "Give me the body, and I will find you when the hit has been lifted from you so you may return home."

Solas knew better. She'd rebelled, an unforgiveable act. There'd be no amnesty for her, not for any of them regardless of promises. "No. I'll secure him in a safe place, but I'll have my pardon first."

They stared at one another. "Father will not like your distrust."

"I don't care."

"Very well. I will contact you without delay."

Solas nodded. The moment Michael departed, she stepped behind Loki, wrapped an arm around his neck in a swimmer's hold, and took flight. Thankfully she managed to catch Bly's trail of magic somehow and surf it, which helped with Loki's weight, but not as much as she would've liked. The two-timing bastard was heavier than he looked, and she expended too much power carrying him to safety. By the time she arrived in a cavern unfamiliar to her, exhaustion pulled at her consciousness.

Her arrival in the room could be described as nothing more than a crash landing. They both hit the floor, Loki face-first with her draped over his back. Not a graceful entrance, but when she lifted her head from Loki's shoulder she could make out the runes and wards splashed across the walls. Powerful magic she didn't understand and shouldn't have been able to penetrate without Loki's magic.

A moment later, Bly ripped her off Loki and shoved her hard against the wall, knocking the breath from her lungs. "You killed him."

"If you want him to live, you'll release me."

Suriel mercifully came to her aid, settling her blade against Bly's throat. "If she was your enemy, he'd already be dead."

"I'm about to drop from flying his heavy ass here. Let me heal him before the last of my magic is depleted."

"Do anything but heal him, and you're dead."

Fair enough. But she wouldn't go down without a fight.

Solas nodded, and walked straight to Loki, dropping to her knees beside him. Fatigue threatened to send her into a heavy sleep to recoup her overtaxed magic, but she managed to blink several times and force herself to remain conscious and upright. She would've said by the grace of God, but she knew He had nothing to do with her determination to stay awake.

Thankfully, Bly rolled him to his back, and she pushed Loki's arms to the floor at his sides.

She snagged a new feather, her wings drooping against the floor, causing a cringe to surface because she usually protected them from filth. Too weak, there was nothing she could do. Once more, she cut her tongue.

Leaning over Loki, she settled against his chest, not because she wanted to be near him—she didn't, they were *done*—but out of weariness. Solas pulled his chin down and pressed her open mouth against his. Flicking her tongue across his and spreading her blood and serum from the feather, she continued the movement until his fingers curled in her hair and he snatched her head back.

The accusation in his eyes intensified her weariness. "You murdered me."

Dizziness slammed into her as the last of her magic winked out. "Not that I'm expecting a thanks, but I bought you some time. Michael wasn't playing fair. He wielded the god-killer." The room spun, and she blinked and rubbed her eyes. "For now, Michael and Father believe you're dead."

"What happens to you when they realize you duped them?"

Solas would think of that later. She shook her head and attempted to rise, to get away from him, but she was too gone, and collapsed across his chest. The last thing she heard before she went into a magic-depleted coma was Loki barking orders.

SIXTEEN

$\mathcal{L}$oki paced as he barked a laundry list of orders to Bly. Every new demand inspired another. If he kept moving and continued to direct his man, maybe, *just maybe*, he wouldn't have time to think about his wife's lifeless body laid out on his bed.

He rammed his fingers through his hair, and his heart amped up. At first, when she'd collapsed across his chest with her face turned toward him, he'd thought it some sort of trickery. A new tactic on her part, and he'd been amused by the ineffectiveness of the plot. But when she wouldn't respond to his nudges, and he couldn't detect any signs of life, he'd panicked. Not his proudest moment, and he still struggled with the absolute fear holding him hostage. Terror for another was a new experience for him. That's when he'd begun to spew orders, and truthfully he couldn't remember most of what he'd requested.

His blood from where he'd dragged his fingers down her cheek had been stark against her too pale features. She'd had no breath. No heartbeat he could detect either.

Drawing her into his arms, he'd clutched her to his chest. The earth rumbled with his emotions, and he'd been so caught up in his grief he'd been useless to control his power. "Breathe, goddamn you, *breathe!*"

"She's alive, Loki." At his hostile glare, Suriel had shown bravery when most would've backed off. Instead she'd placed her hand on his shoulder. "She expended all her magic and hibernates to rejuvenate."

The sight of Solas' weakness sickened him, even with the knowledge she was in an angel's deep sleep. Brought low by her inferior creator—if Loki had crafted her he would've given her strength so her mojo never waned—and all because she'd drained her magic for him. But why aid him when she'd been the one to kill him? Why, when she'd known depleting her power would incapacitate her? Leave her vulnerable to his revenge?

Terror gripped him again as the image of her lifeless form limp in his bed slammed through his mind, reminding him despite Solas' perceived strength she was very fragile. He hadn't realized how breakable she was until now.

Many questions swirled in his head. He pulled at his lip, lost in thought, until a wave of healing magic vibrated against his skin. With a jerk of his head, he locked eyes with Bly.

"Were you injured?" Loki asked his man.

Why did Bly fidget, as if nervous to answer? Even cleared his throat before he spoke and wouldn't meet Loki's gaze. "No. Suriel was injured." Bly reached beside him where Suriel stood and lifted the hem of her shirt to reveal a slice from a blade just below her naval. "I'm healing her."

Did Loki detect a defensive tone from his first in command?

Loki walked toward them. Bly made the slightest move, but it couldn't be mistaken for anything but a protective stand. *Interesting.*

"Did you attack my men?" Loki asked Suriel.

"No. When your men arrived, I refused to help them with their plans to trap you and my sister. They retaliated."

Fury burned through him. By the hard set to Bly's jaw, he felt the same. Unless in defense, no angel was to ever be harmed without Loki's consent. Killing angels was about balance and control. That his once-trusted Naglfar hurt Suriel on top of trying to harm his wife and child would not stand. This was anarchy, and the uprising against him would end today. Loki nodded to Bly. "Send a message to those who'd betray me. Go now."

Bly stepped to Suriel and caressed her bare arm. "Can you describe the man who cut you? Show me the image in your mind."

"So much was happening at the time. I'll try."

A fizzle of blue and white magic snapped and popped between them, visible only to Loki. A moment later, Bly's lips curled before he vanished.

Before Loki could open his mouth to question Suriel, Bly returned, surprising Loki with a head in his right hand.

"Is this the one who harmed you?" Gripping the hair, Bly lifted the head until it was eye level with Suriel.

She clutched at the edge of the table, her strong demeanor slipping before she straightened her stance. With a tight jerk of her head, she said, "Yes."

Bly must have sensed her discomfort because the head vanished from his grasp. Drops of blood remained on the floor, and Suriel focused on the glossy liquid, her horror evident in her wide-eyed gape.

"You weren't sent to kill me, were you?" Loki asked. Without her confirmation, he knew Suriel was no reaper. The evidence was in her reaction toward Bly's brutal vengeance in her honor. Later, he'd address his man's need for retribution for a woman he just met. Bly's loyalty was to Loki, but Suriel's loyalty remained in question. At least Bly's message to his men was clearly sent. Decapitation had a way of getting the attention of even the most stone-hearted warrior. And Bly had executed his mission at a speed that shocked and impressed Loki. No doubt, Suriel was the cause of Bly's unusual speed to carry out an order. Bly always got the job done with efficiency, but never this fast. Even though he saw the possibility for trouble with Bly's obvious infatuation with Suriel, he'd have to reward her for trusting Bly enough to share her vision of the traitor in Loki's midst.

Suriel lifted her chin. "No."

The similarity between the two sisters was startling. One would have to look closely to isolate the differences. Suriel had dark grey eyes, not the onyx pools of her sister. And her vibe came across as younger than Solas.

"Why were you cast out, then?"

She held her tongue, her lips thinning into a tight line.

Loki walked around, circling her, an intimidation tactic he'd used on the most hardened of adversaries. With each rotation, he'd release a speck of magic, letting it trickle down his enemy's spine. Minutes ticked off the clock until he gained a response, and she shivered.

Impressive that she managed to hold out so long.

Then and only then did he face her once more, with his feet braced and his arms crossed over his chest. "You are my wife's sister. I will not harm you." Suriel visibly relaxed, and if he wasn't mistaken, so did Bly. "You're going to swear your loyalty to me, Suriel. In exchange, I will grant you your wings and my protection. A place by your sister's side for eternity."

The look in her eyes was the same he'd seen in Solas' the night she fell. Desperation. Uncertainty. Resolution finally entered her gaze, and she stuck out her hand. *Cute.* Did she expect him to shake on it? Yes, Suriel was much younger and more naïve than Solas. Her presence was softer and less commanding.

Loki stared at her hand until she dropped her arm to her side, her fingers twitched, a clear demonstration of her uncertainty. Better she learned how he operates from the get-go. "You are of Solas' blood?"

"Yes."

"This agreement is binding. Everything I ask of you, you'll do without question." Normally, Loki wouldn't take the time to explain the extent of his power over someone. Solas' sister was a different story. He didn't want to manipulate her.

"I understand, Loki. There is much more going on than you know about. I stand with my sister. She's made it obvious her position is beside you."

When had she made that obvious? She'd sliced his throat and stabbed him in the neck. As he died in her arms, befuddled by her duplicity, she'd turned a blank face on him, and he'd experienced betrayal and the cold kiss of death like... those he'd victimized. He was very uncertain of Solas' alliance with him, but if she was against him why had she saved him?

Tired of going round and round with his confusion, he shook the thoughts aside to ponder at a later time.

"Your wings." With a snap of his fingers, Suriel fell to the floor, and her agonizing screams ripped through the room. Loki clasped his hands behind his back and watched Suriel squirm on the ground as her wings regenerated. Bly looked away, grimacing as she suffered her rebirth. Memories of the night he'd gifted Solas' wings flitted through his mind. The way she'd proudly bore the pain of their regeneration, and taken his cock, gifting him with one climax after another. The memory centered him and reminded him of his purpose. "Tell me more, Suriel."

She grasped at her neck as if something obstructed her throat, but he recognized the attempt to fight him and ignore his request to divulge secrets about her sister. But they'd made a pact. Her lips started moving at his command whether she liked it or not. "Michael has been sent to kill other gods and demigods." She winced in pain, struggling as her wings cut through the flesh on her back, and a seizure gripped her for a long moment before she could speak again. Gasping through the agony, she picked up the conversation without him having to issue a request. "The balance to humanity has shifted; too many are worshiping false idols. Evil is growing." She choked as feathers budded between her shoulder blades. "The halls of Heaven are filling more rapidly than ever before."

Her maker was concerned about population? Since when? God had wrestled for control of humanity's souls for centuries, so why did He suddenly fret about receiving too many?

A quote from the Book of Revelations wormed through his mind. *Man will pray for death, and death will not come.* This was worse than he thought. Had he been so preoccupied with his own life that he hadn't realized the evil spreading throughout humanity? This explained why He sent an army for Loki. By taking out the bigger gods, *He* would have a better chance of making the less powerful gods fall in line. If the balance had shifted to the point of overpopulating Heaven, evil would soon rule humanity. No more sliding by the pearly gates on a technicality. God would have to be pickier about who He allowed into His precious kingdom. This would leave more souls open to Hell. And God did not want to gift a single soul to Hell.

Being the evil, selfish prick that he was, even Loki didn't want Hell gaining more souls. Where would the fun be in manipulating the evil? He'd be challenged more for his position as well. It's a headache he didn't need.

Suriel sat on the floor. Her shirt ripped, shredded off her body by the force of her wings. Sweat beading on her skin. With her arms guarding her breasts, she continued like a sinner confessing to a priest. "I was cast out because I tried to save my sister."

"I will reward you for your rebellion."

"I don't need a reward for loving my sister, asshole," Suriel grated. Loki chuckled. If he'd doubted her relationship to Solas before, with her attitude he gained all the verification he required. Although he detected a slight cringe at her swear word.

"If you didn't fall from trying to kill me, then there is one more reaper not accounted for." One more to make the thirteen that fell trying to assassinate him.

"Yes, your men have him."

"Him?"

"Elyon. He was the strongest of us present, the oldest too. When he swore allegiance to Solas and refused to agree to harm her, your men took him so that we'd all fall in line."

Why did that knowledge heat his spine more intensely than his men betraying him earlier had? He must meet this *man-angel*, who had put his life on the line for his wife. "Bly, I want him here. Chained next to the other fallen, Sephora." Loki pinched the bridge of his nose, the pull to join his wife strong. He needed to be with her when she woke so they could settle a couple of things. "Where is the seer I requested earlier?"

"The seer will be here in five moons." Bly's shoulders slouched as if weary from Loki's growing list of commands.

"I asked that she be here today." Loki snapped his fingers, a robe appearing in his hands. Spinning it around, he covered Suriel and then lifted her to sit in a chair at the table. "I can't move forward with my plans until I speak to the seer."

"I'm not sure how cooperative she'll be if we force her."

"Tell her I'll make it worth her trip!" His impatience escalated. When Michael and his god realized Solas' deception, Loki feared the worst. Maybe they'd come for her again and he could defend her. But if what Suriel said was true, Solas' deception was proof of a darker uprising, since they believed she'd been swayed by Loki's evil. Solas told Michael she stood with her maker. Loki was her maker, a false idol in God's eyes. *He will not take her from me.* But to which *maker* did she make her vow? He couldn't be certain it was him.

Loki lifted Suriel's chin, forcing her to meet his gaze. "One more thing, love." Pain gave her eyes a glassy appearance, as a single tear rolled down her cheek and over Loki's thumb. Such an opposite to Solas, or maybe he had her in a fragile state as he did Solas when he remade her.

"What do you want, Loki?"

"Tell me about your sister." She didn't pull away from him, but her lips curled in the slightest smile. The corners of her eyes softened, her love for Solas evident, and Loki envied their bond. Would Solas ever have that look in her eyes when someone mentioned his name? "She and I seem to be having trouble communicating."

"No shit." She cringed again at the curse word, but he liked her initiative to continue trying.

"What's that supposed to mean?"

"The way you stripped her power in front of everyone back there... wow. Could you be a bigger douche? What were you thinking?" Suriel laughed, but there was no humor in the action.

"I was trying to protect her."

"But you took away her choice to be protected."

Perplexed, his brows drew together. "Explain."

"You made her weak in their eyes, and even angels won't follow a weak leader. They'd planned to put their faith in her earlier, before you minimized her strength. Now..." She shrugged. "I can't say what they'll do now. Put yourself in her situation."

"I tried. I was protecting her. She should have known that."

Sighing, Suriel stood. Angling her head at him, she said, "Solas is like a female Loki—minus the evil and trickery. Now, put yourself in her situation. How betrayed would you feel if she did the same to you?" At his glower, she elevated her eyebrows and challenged him with her unflinching stare.

Uncomfortable with that request, he pondered her a tense moment. "You're a Guardian."

Her confirmation wasn't required. He knew. Suriel's guidance came with ease and without fear of speaking her mind. This is why she'd cried earlier. Was there a human she'd been looking out for before her fall? One she failed because she didn't complete her task? With her wings back, she may have felt the pain of her failure.

But her words haunted him. '*Solas is like a female Loki. How betrayed would you feel?*' What kind of logic or help was this information? Loki scratched at his nape, deciding he'd meditate on her guidance later. Much later, when his head wasn't spinning with his near-death experience at the hands of his wife. A woman he'd protected without a stitch of thanks, and whom he'd foolishly put his trust in.

She saved you, can't you trust her, the devil on his shoulder mocked.

"Bly," he growled his man's name, but with his emotions running high, he didn't attempt to soften his tone, "I'll be in my chambers. Come for me when the seer arrives."

SEVENTEEN

$\mathcal{L}$oki sat at the foot of his bed in a Victorian high back chair, with his legs crossed while waiting for his wife to wake. It was the night of the third day, and Solas had barely stirred during all that time. A twitch of a finger or a toe, and once or twice her breathing escalated to the point he thought she'd hyperventilate. Otherwise, she hadn't so much as budged from where he'd placed her three days ago.

He'd left her side only long enough to shower. Many things traveled through his thoughts. How easy it would be to kill her while she slept. She was fragile after all, made all the more obvious by her angel-coma. After she brutally murdered him without a thought, his like-minded revenge would be justified. But then he'd remember her lifelessness, and his anger would wash away as he grew protective of her once more.

Without the seer, he couldn't be certain if she was with child. After witnessing the love in Suriel's eyes for her sister, Loki had come to the conclusion killing his child was not an option. Just because Solas didn't love him, didn't mean his child wouldn't. He chuckled at the irony. An evil prick in search of love. Love without a price—without conditions. He probably didn't deserve love, but he craved it like a lifeline.

A moan sounded from the bed. Loki unfolded his long legs and stood. Fuck, she was breathtaking. But it wasn't like she was the only beautiful woman he'd fucked. So, why'd no one else had this effect on him? From the moment she'd fallen at his feet, she'd been his, and he'd been protective.

He placed his palms on the footboard and waited for her to wake.

"Where am I?" Solas jolted into a sitting position, hand poised above a feather.

"Where you belong, angel. Do *not* pluck that feather." No desire to fight her—not when he had other more delightful desires in mind—he executed a waving motion with his hand and stilled her just as he'd done at the biker compound. "You're with your *husband*. You know, the one you tried to kill?"

"You fucking bastard!" Solas struggled against his power, but only managed little movement. Still, it was more movement than any before her had managed, and the evidence of her ability hardened his cock. "I should have left you for dead and watched the vultures pick your carcass."

"Now, now, angel." His gaze slid up her frame. "I'll release you after we get a few things straight." He tugged his shirt over his head, and slicked back dark locks still damp from his recent shower. As his base hunger grew, he could have sworn Solas felt his desire—a connection they shared maybe?

Solas worked on swallowing. Her eyes intense with specks of silver shimmering through them. "You'll release me now, trickster."

"Why? So you can brutally slit my throat again?" Loki tossed his lounge pants to the side but remained locked onto Solas' gaze.

"Gah! You thickheaded demi-god, you didn't learn your lesson at all." If he freed her, Loki expected she'd storm away from him like she had on the side of the road.

Loki crawled up the end of the bed until he knelt by her feet. He would have smiled at her struggle to not look at his growing erection, but determined to see his plan through to the end, he hoped he managed to keep his expression unreadable. "Ah, but I did learn a valuable lesson, angel. One I will never forget." Especially after speaking to Suriel. "Now it's time you learn *your* lesson." Holding his palm toward her, he nudged her with his power, gently, until she lay back against the pillows.

"What lesson will this teach me? That not only can you cripple me in front of my peers, you can own me in the bedroom too? Thanks, but I already learned that lesson."

"It'll teach you to know the difference." When she'd collapsed in his arms he'd almost lost it, until Suriel revealed her deep sleep. Even though he'd been relieved by what caused her sleep, his emotions had been high. He had bathed Solas, washed the filth from her wings, and then wrapped her in the purple silk he pulled toward him now, unveiling her lush body. "Do you remember how you felt when I froze you at the compound?"

"I will never forget that feeling. Never trust you again either."

"You will learn the difference."

"Difference of what?"

Inching closer, Loki spread her thighs until they draped over his, and he sat back on his heels. Needing more contact, he rubbed his palms over her knees. "When I am finished with you, tell me how it felt to be... how did you say it—*Immobilized like a fucking powerless pet.*"

Inhaling sharply, Solas gaped at him. Wide black eyes sliced through him. "You read my thoughts."

Ignoring her, Loki lifted her leg and pressed his lips against her ankle. "I've sat here for days thinking about killing you."

"Loki." There was a slight plea to her voice, for what he wasn't sure. His angel cowed to no one, especially not him. Could she sense the change he felt within himself? "Do it then." The defeat in her voice unnerved him. "As you proved it only takes one finger."

"Yes. Just one." He held up the one finger he'd used to kill his men. When he stroked it down her thigh, she shivered. "And at any moment... I. Can. Take. You. Out." Her breath hitched, and he wondered if his power excited or frightened her. Using the same finger, he walked it across her stomach to punctuate each word. "But would it change anything, wife?" He slithered his deadly digit from her navel, glided it over her pubic bone, and straight through her wet folds, making sure he hit her clit.

"Loki!" Excitement mixed with apprehension settled in her eyes.

"Do you want me dead, wife? If I closed my eyes forever, would your world change for the better?" He rubbed her clit in small circles with a feathery touch. "You could run back to your father." Sliding his finger through her wetness, he circled her entrance, stroking lightly, entering her with just the tip of his finger. "Would He take you back, risk His life for you?"

"Would you?" Solas asked in a low breathy tone.

"I already have, angel."

Her eyes clouded over, and a quizzical expression scored her forehead. *When has he risked his life for me*, her thought hit him.

Instead of responding, he continued with his confession. After the bar, she'd been closed off, not allowing him to explain his actions, so he used her body against her to weaken her, giving her no choice but to listen to him now.

He shoved two fingers inside her, watching as her hips tried to fight against his magical restraints. "This relationship has been many things, but *never* a charade." While hurt over his actions, she'd told him their relationship was over, hurting him with those words as surely as if she'd sliced his throat again. "We are *not* over. You don't walk away from me, wife."

Loki gave her no time to argue, but lowered himself between her legs and covered her clit with his mouth, sucking hard.

"*Loki!*"

With the knowledge that God was pulling out His master soldiers, Loki's uncertainty with Solas and the way she'd killed him without a thought, made his need for her grow out of control. If he was going to die, he'd do so with the taste of an angel on his tongue.

Loki hovered his fingers over Solas, swiping across her skin from hip to hip, before he buried his face between her thighs. Freeing her hips was selfish on his part because he loved when she ground her pussy against his face, lost to her own need, and desperation. He'd force her to fuck his face again, even when she fought her desire. "I'll release you when you lov—" Loki stopped before his internal thoughts were out. He wouldn't manipulate her into loving him. No. He wanted to give her so much more—the world, an army to fight for her, his devotion, and to share his power with her. It would bind her to him, and entwine their souls the way he craved. But Solas had to want him and accept his power, or the union wouldn't take.

With the world on their shoulders, maybe he didn't want to know the truth of her love. Lost in his thoughts, in Solas' scent as he licked her, and in her soft, desperate whimpers, Loki hadn't realized she was so close to the edge until she swirled her hips, rubbing herself against his eager tongue. "Yes, angel, shatter for me."

Little sounds of pleasure turned into pleas. Pushing his fingers back inside her, he pumped them at a steady pace as he lapped at her, licking circles around her clit but not touching her nub.

"Please…"

"Please what, angel?"

"*Please*, Loki—"

"That's not quite what I want to hear." He released her from his hold, but she was lost in her need, so hungry for her climax, she didn't realize he'd freed her. With a frustrated sigh, she moved her hips, her desperation to command where his tongue touched her made his cock harder. "Come on, wife, you can say it."

Fisting the sheets, she lifted her hips and cried out, "Please, my husband, make me shatter."

Simple words to some, but hearing them from Solas' lips caused him to release a burst of magic and resulted in the earth shaking beneath them. Just a little tremor showing how deeply this woman affected him. Loki shoved the tip of his tongue inside her over the two fingers he still pumped furiously, then dragged his tongue up slowly to flick against her clit. Once, twice, she shattered...

His angel's cries shot straight down his spine and slickened the head of his cock. After kissing her clit, Loki crawled up her body until he was poised above her. If Suriel's observation was correct and Solas was his kindred spirt, Loki had an idea of what she may need. It's the same thing he desired. Love. To be cherished the way she deserved.

Cupping her face, Loki stared into black eyes infused with silver, detailing her angel magic was once again operational. "I did not lie to you about your venom, angel." She looked so vulnerable, as she always did after she took sexual release. He ignored his cock throbbing against her entrance and her wet heat that tempted him to thrust deep and hard. But the next words he spoke were much more important than his desire to be inside her. "Yes, I could have released you at the compound when I had things under control, but I'm still unsure about you, Solas."

"Loki, I—"

"Shh... let me finish or I'll never say this. I've never fought beside someone who I value, except for Bly. It's-it's a weakness I can't afford when there is so much at stake."

"I don't understand, what's a weakness?"

"You are, angel."

Her eyes closed, and her bottom lip trembled as she turned her head aside.

"You weaken me more than your venom ever could."

"I've no power over you. That's been proven."

His fingers curled in her hair, and he turned her head so he could look her directly in the face. Without request, she opened her eyes and returned his intense stare. She *felt* something strong in this moment. He could feel her emotions, but he'd blocked her thoughts, because to take them now without her permission... well, even a trickster respected her too much to do that to her.

"Never doubt your power over me." He pushed his cock inside her, slowly entering her and losing his soul with each inch she took. She gasped when he was seated deep inside her. Her eyes held many things he couldn't pick through, but he did see her confusion. He'd always gone fast and taken her with a roughness to avoid this depth of intimacy. Just this once, he was going to show her love by his actions. Even if it left him vulnerable. He'd fight for his soul later.

Moving in and out of his angel, fucking her gently was indescribable. Maybe he didn't want to know the truth, if she loved him, if she could, because if she couldn't she would break him.

With his forehead against hers, he closed his eyes and continued the tortuous pace for love. He felt her soft palm against his cheek, the tips of her fingers brushing against his hairline. Loki would shatter this time, and into far many more pieces than ever before.

"Loki." His angel breathed against his ear and arched her back to meet his slow, deliberate movements. Black wings expanded beneath her, rounding in the middle like they were trying to embrace him. She lifted his head and locked onto his heated gaze. Solas moved her hips faster beneath him. Maybe she was the one hiding this time, but he wouldn't allow it.

Loki kept his pace steady. Balancing on his forearm, he palmed her ass with his hand and lifted, making his plunge deeper. His angel moaned against his ear, and his sac tightened. Everything felt heightened. He could feel her nipples scraping against his chest, her gaze locked onto his with such intensity his seed rushed to the head of his cock. Faster he pumped, with more aggression. His angel—his wife. She tightened around his shaft, a purposeful move, as if she knew it's what he needed. Their breaths mingled, faster, heavier.

"Yes, my husband!"

Loki came with Solas wrapped around him, encased in her wings, her thighs looped over his, and her ankles locked against his lower back. Something shifted between them. He could feel the change as they both shattered into a million pieces. She closed her eyes in what he thought was an attempt to hide from him.

With a palm by her ribs, Loki pushed against the bed to give her space. Feathers brushed against his fingers. Had she pulled them in an attempt to kill him again? Two more feathers fell from the bottom row of her right wing, and he grasped them with the other three. "Angel?"

Her eyes fluttered open. "I'm tired, Loki, so tired."

"Your feathers are falling out."

Solas bolted upright. She turned pale and yanked the feathers from his hand. The last thing he saw before she fell back against the pillow was raw fear.

Hours had passed since he'd sent Bly for the seer again. His gut soured, and the sense of doom hung over him like a dark cloud. While waiting for Bly to return, he sat on the edge of the bed holding Solas' hand, watching her sleep, and rehashing the final moments of their conversation.

She'd turned away from him, curled into a fetal position. With her feathers clutched to her breastbone, she'd wrapped her wings around her body, cocooning herself and refusing to talk. After sharing such a sweet moment with her, her dismissal stung.

Loki had slid his fingers through her hair. "Talk to me. What does the feather loss mean?"

"I... nothing." She shivered, and goose bumps broke out along her exposed skin. "Doesn't matter."

Does fucking matter. He dropped his block and attempted to snag her thoughts, but she'd erected hefty blocks of her own.

He pulled the covers over her. "I know you're not telling me something."

"I just need sleep."

"You've slept for three days already." Guilt slammed into him. Had he pushed her too fast? She'd been comatose for three days, barely breathing—fuck he'd thought her dead because of her lethargic inhalations. And what'd he do the moment she woke? He'd jumped her like a pervert, and she'd expended more magic, he'd seen the silver evidence against the black backdrop of her eyes. Maybe he was the rat bastard she called him.

Bly returned well after midnight. Loki felt him before he presented himself and entered Loki's bedchambers. He released Solas' hand and stood by the side of the bed. "The seer is here?"

"Yes. Are you sure about this?"

"I must protect my wife and child." Walking to the door, Loki paused to look over his shoulder at Solas. His angel slept in his bed, peacefully. *Protected. A man isn't a man if he can't protect his family.* So, why'd he feel like his world was about to upend even though she was safe?

Loki entered the living room with Bly on his heels. With the cave carved in what the humans would call an open floor plan, it was easy to watch everyone regardless which area they inhabited. The open structure also provided him with enough space to defend himself if someone attacked. Suriel sat at the table where he'd left her earlier, and the seer stood in the center of the room. Such beautiful creatures for being so bitchy, but seers were known for their crankiness. Her hair was covered in silk, overlaid with a beaded chain. At the center of the chain was a bright-blue crystal that lay against her forehead. The crystal changed colors with her eyes until her vision manifested.

"Thank you for coming." Loki kept his tone neutral. Upsetting the seer wouldn't benefit him. He shouldn't have to thank her either since he was paying her a goddamn fortune. And he'd had to send Bly three times to finally secure her, and still she protested coming immediately as he commanded. For now, the seer had him by the balls. He needed answers only she could provide, and she knew she had him at a disadvantage. Loki couldn't even threaten her, and she knew he wouldn't kill her. He *loathed* being at someone else's mercy, but he'd make any sacrifice for his woman and child.

"I was under the impression I had no choice." Her tone was raspy, like the sound of a human's voice that smoked too much. Loki knew the cause of the roughness to the beautiful creature's voice. Some of the seer's visions were so terrifying, the creature screamed until her voice was no more. He'd never heard a seer with a normal voice.

"No, you didn't"—Loki held his hand up when she would protest—"I said thank you, and I'll make it worth your time, and your loyalty."

A nod.

"Is my wife pregnant?" Loki held his breath as the seer turned toward him and closed her eyes. The stone in the middle of her forehead flashed different shades of red, blue, green, then went sold white. When the seer opened her eyes, they were bright-white, almost blinding orbs.

"Yeeesss." Her gravelly voice drew out the word.

Excitement had Loki's heart pounding in his chest. He had a child. *I will be a father.* Something he'd never thought to be. *Now to secure their safety.* Loki turned in Bly and Suriel's direction when he asked the seer his next question. "Do Suriel and Solas share the same blood?"

"Yes." The answer sounded more slithery than the first.

Loki placed his hand on Suriel's shoulder. "You've become very valuable to me, *sister*."

"What are you going to do, Loki?" Suriel studied him, concern resulting in grooves spreading across her forehead.

"Seer, can Suriel carry my child."

"What—" His sister's face paled, and she shook her head. "Silence!"

"The short answer is yes, my lord." Something strange crossed over the seer's face. "It comes with a price."

"Will my child be safe with what I plan?"

"Yes."

"Seer, what of Solas? What does her future show?"

"She's marked."

Worry punched him in the gut, and he struggled to breathe, but his reaction made little sense when the seer's proclamation could mean anything. Could even mean marked for greatness. "Marked for what?"

"A hell of her own making."

His blood ran cold. Suriel sniffled, but he maintained his focus on the seer.

"Only you have the power to save her, trickster."

He pinned Bly with a stare. "Locate me a human with a child in the same development stage as mine. This is your first priority. All other commands come last." He leveled his gaze on Suriel. "You and I will meet with the fallen while Bly is busy."

"My God, what are you going to do?" Suriel's fingers curled around her neck as horror bled across her features. No doubt she thought the worst.

"I'm going to protect my wife and my child—at all costs."

EIGHTEEN

$\mathcal{T}$he pounding in Solas' head woke her from a dreamless slumber. She rubbed her forehead with her fingertips, but her skull still threatened to crack open any moment. Cottonmouth, throat scratchy, she swallowed several times without any success at alleviating her dry mouth.

How long had she slept this time? She ached everywhere, like when Michael had pushed her hard in prep for battle.

Sitting slowly, nausea rolled in her belly. She swung her legs over the side of the bed and spied two more feathers free of her wings. Clutching them with the others, she forced herself to rise from the bed. If she were pregnant like Loki believed, she'd gift them to the little one. Her legacy to her offspring, they'd hold their power until used, and hopefully any child of hers would be able to discern their usage like she could since they shared the same genes.

She took her time showering and washing away Loki's seed from between her legs. *I wasn't out long enough that he bathed me after fucking me.*

Something had changed between her and Loki during their lovemaking, but she couldn't decide what. He always fucked her in a rough manner, with little tenderness, as if he forced her to accept her desire for him. As if he knew she attempted to resist him, so he navigated her quickly through the stages of lust to discombobulate her and annihilate any resistance.

This time, he'd been tender, almost as if he cared, totally opposite of what was normal. She liked his domination, craved it, but his gentleness brought out a different need in her and created an ache in her breastbone.

She'd tried to block him from her thoughts, but her magic had sagged, and there at the end she'd felt... loved. Cherished even. She knew she was wrong. Loki loved no one but himself, his kingdom, and governing the weaker populace. He'd even admitted he wasn't sure he wanted the potential child she might carry because the baby held the ability to overthrow his authority.

He'd called her his weakness too, crushing her with the confession. It wouldn't have hurt as much if he'd just carved her heart from her chest. Respecting his feelings, she preferred the coldness of his honesty to a lie.

She knew how this story ended.

Death. Death's how we end, either way.

Sighing, she turned off the shower, dried off, and went in search of something to wear. All she found were Loki's clothes, so she tugged on one of his silk shirts. Black to fit her mood, to fit her fate.

Barefoot, she shuffled down the hall in search of the kitchen to drench her parched throat. She'd swig magic if she thought it'd help, but knew no amount of enchantment would resolve what came for her.

She stopped in the doorway, the girl with dark, short hair sitting at the table reminded her of... "Suriel?"

Her sister swiveled and then launched from her seat, crushing Solas in a hug. They staggered backward from the impact but somehow managed to find a steady footing. Suriel's gentle nature engulfed her. She'd missed her sibling so very much.

"I need your help, sister, and I don't want Loki to know about it." Against her, Suriel stiffened, before pulling away.

"You look exhausted. I'd thought you'd be one-hundred percent by now."

"I should be." Solas located the fridge, retrieved a bottle of water, and guzzled the contents. It didn't ease her dehydration, which meant it was a symptom of her doom. "I'm sorry to ask for help when we're finally reunited after so long. I should just be happy to see you." After Suriel's fall a couple of centuries ago, Solas had searched the planet for her, but she'd been hidden. A punishment for both of them, thanks to their merciless parent.

"Talk to me."

"Where's Loki?" The last thing she needed was for him to walk in unannounced and hear a part of their conversation.

"Making allies or enemies, I don't know which. What's wrong, Sol?"

A grin tugged at the corner of her mouth. Her sister couldn't help but attempt to aid her. Guardianship was as much a part of her makeup as killing was a part of Solas'. "Promise not to tell Loki?"

Suriel looked away.

"He's gotten to you." Solas wasn't surprised, he'd charmed her out of her panties in less than an hour. He captivated everyone with little to no effort. But right now, she needed an ally, one that wouldn't gainsay her every step of the way.

"He offered me protection for the return of my wings. I thought you'd approve since you stood behind him."

Yes, *behind* not *beside*. He'd made that clear in the bar, despite his allegations as he fucked her—to a mind-blowing orgasm that still made her core quiver at the mere thought—that he immobilized her because she weakened him. She believed him, maybe she shouldn't, but she did even though they weren't words any wife wished to hear. Solas wanted to strengthen Loki, not be his weakness. That wasn't a marriage. She could forgive him the slight, even understood his motivations. If his enemies got ahold of his wife, it wouldn't matter that he didn't love her when his pride would dictate he put his life in danger to save her. She wanted no part of that.

In death, I can empower him without weakening him. It would have to be enough.

"I do approve." She patted Suriel's hand that rested on the table. "He keeps his promises. He'll take care of you." For her wings, he'd only promised to make her come. With little working sexual knowledge, she hadn't understood the impact of that promise until he made her shatter. She'd been addicted to him since.

All his promises to keep her safe from her father came later, after their pact for her wings, so honoring them wasn't required. Her throat thickened. He'd demanded she agree she was his, and she was, she didn't argue that. He owned her body and soul. She'd willingly handed herself over to him and damned herself in the process. If she could redo their relationship from her fall up to now, she'd make the same choices, but maybe not the same mistakes. She'd never regretted a single person she reaped for the Kingdom of Heaven, and she didn't regret falling for Loki.

"What do you need, Sol?"

"Reishi mushrooms." At her sister's frown, she struggled with the need to tell her everything. She required a confidant, and maybe she could use Loki's power over Suriel against him. What'd she have to lose? Even if he forced her sister to confess everything, he'd discover the truth anyway. "The reishi will help with my longevity and strength. If Loki asks what I told you, you tell him I said I'm fine."

Suriel nodded. "Promise, but I can't guarantee it'll work."

"I'm dying." Tears shone in Suriel's eyes, but emotions would bog down Solas' plan, so she hardened her heart and made no attempt to soothe her sister's pain. Also, as a guardian, Suriel felt more than the average angel, so there wasn't much solace she could offer Suriel anyway. "If I'm carrying Loki's child, I need help to secure its survival before I pass."

"You should talk to Loki."

"Why? So he can bitch about how every idea I have is stupid? He's smarter than all of us and thinks only about himself."

"That's unfair." Solas knew it was, but she gave her sister a *look* anyway, prompting Suriel to admonish her with, "You don't give him enough credit. No wonder you two can't get along. You're both stubborn and prideful. Two peas in a pod."

Solas rolled her eyes at Suriel's drama until a sharp stabbing pain struck her temple. Wincing she rubbed at the ache and said, "I give him plenty credit. He thinks he's the only one with the right answers."

"All gods are arrogant, but he cares for you."

Solas' knee-jerk reaction was to argue her sister's claim, but in some respect her sister was right, Loki cared for all his progeny, but expending her energy arguing over something so minor wasn't worth her time. Loki had returned Suriel's wings, and that made her sister naïve and starry-eyed toward Loki. Solas knew the feeling.

"Does your head hurt?" She nodded, and Suriel rose from her seat to trail her fingertips along Solas' brow. "Let me try to soothe it with my magic, and then I'll get you some reishi. But I want you to promise to *think* about talking to Loki."

Solas gave her an offhand shrug. Let her sibling take that however she chose.

"I understand he's your husband."

Heat from Suriel's magic settling against Solas' temple bloomed along her skin. She wished she could say it felt good, but it prickled like needles against her skin and she grit her teeth. This reaction was her body's way of verifying she rejected another's healing magic.

"Yeah," her voice sounded a tad scratchy, and Suriel glanced at her sharply. Solas cleared her throat and continued, "He gave me my wings with nothing more than a promise to make me come, and to show my appreciation I sold myself to him and became his wife."

"I'm disappointed in you, Sol." *Here comes the lecture.* At her silence, Suriel went on. "You stalked him for two years."

"How'd you know that?"

"I might've fallen, but I still have angelic sources. That any better?" She lifted her hands from Solas' temples.

"Yes. Thanks." A tad better, but not a lot, which was odd when angelic magic could've healed wounds in the past. *Maybe her magic isn't the magic I need.* The soft look on Loki's face as he moved inside her flashed through her head. She would *not* ask him for his mojo.

"I know you love him, Sol. Stop shaking your head at me. I knew the moment you walked into the bar you were in love. It's the way you look at him, the fire in your eyes. Admit that to yourself, if not to me, or I'll go straight to him and tell him *everything* you said."

Solas rose from her seat. "You're his, bound to him in ways I'm not, so I've no guarantee you won't tell him everything anyway."

***

Returning to Loki's bedroom, she settled in the middle of the bed to meditate, knowing the contemplation would allow her to communicate with Michael. It was just a matter of if he'd open the door to the mental knock she sent him. The two of them rarely spoke verbally. That he'd verbalized everything during his attack on Loki indicated he'd wanted her husband to hear everything he said.

It wasn't long before her sibling answered. *Solas, I'm disappointed. I expected more from you.*

She sent him a mental shrug. *I didn't contact you to discuss your disappointment in me, or my disillusionment with you. Father called in my marker.*

I know. I have requested to be the one who punishes you in your afterlife.

Betrayal slammed through her. She'd battled by his side. He'd been her mentor, taught her everything she knew. She'd saved his life more than once, and aside from being her brother, he'd been her friend. That should've bought her some mercy from him if no one else. It was further evidence everyone she'd ever trusted wasn't as honorable as they pretended.

With no point in drawing out their conversation, Solas got to the point. *I have the Holy Chalice and Seeds of Creation. I'll return them to Father if, and* only if, *He agrees to release His hit on Loki.*

No deal, you traitor. You will return them now to their rightful owner! Michael's voice boomed in her head.

That she'd hit a nerve resulted in her sending him a grin. She could feel his fury through their mental link. Father had given the holy pieces to her for safekeeping after their last battle. The heavenly raid by Odin had surprised all. Somehow they'd defeated the attack, but just barely. No other soul knew the location of the items, and she'd use the advantage to secure the safety of Loki and their maybe-baby. *My terms are non-negotiable. If He agrees, I'll expect a soul oath to my terms.* That way if Father reneged on His deal, He'd join her in her hellish afterlife as a victim instead of a torturer. Motivation for Him to do the right thing for a change. *He has twenty-four hours to make a decision. If I hear nothing, I'll assume my offer's been rejected. Also, Loki will receive all my powers when I pass.*

Blasphemy! Those angelic powers belong to another angel who deserves them. They were not meant for an evil trickster demi-god.

He's a god. Repeating Loki's declaration gave her a sense of satisfaction. And he wasn't evil, but nothing she said would convince her sibling differently. As for the bequeathment of angelic powers, she'd received many over her lifetime, and

Loki was the best candidate to inherit them. *Just leveling the playing field, brother.*

I will enjoy being part of your hellish afterlife.

Anger bled from him so strong it managed to sting. Once he realized she'd deceived them and had no intention of handing over the Holy Chalice or Seeds of Creation, her afterlife would become worse. For Loki and the maybe-child, her suffering would be worth any agony Michael could dole out. Knowing her husband and child were stronger for her deception and the gifting of her legacy would make her hell bearable.

Twenty-four human hours, brother, and not one second longer, or—

You will die with the abomination in your womb.

I thought the baby rumor was a lie? She volleyed back. *Or did you show me your true colors with another lie to bend me to Father's will? It's hard to have* freewill *when everyone you once trusted is a goddamn liar.*

A minute pause from him, but long enough that she realized she'd hit another nerve. Michael ignored her taunt. *I will enjoy ripping the brat from you and making you watch me kill it over and over again. I will show you no mercy, sister. You deserve none.*

Somehow, some way, she'd save the infant first. Despite Loki's uncertainty over the child and the threats the infant could pose to him and his reign, she knew once the baby was born he'd love his son or daughter. In his final moments before the death-stasis took him, he'd been thinking of the little one. Called it his 'joy'. Loki craved love and acceptance more than she did. Any doubt she'd once carried about his devotion to the child evaporated in the moment the death-stasis took him under. Loki was many things, misunderstood, a pain in her ass, frustrating, even tender when he wanted to be, but he wasn't the monster her father made him out to be.

Even though she didn't want to go to Loki for help in this moment, with the sound of her brother's anger lingering in her ears, she realized her husband might be her best option at success.

Solas disconnected the call and slumped on the bed, exhausted from the expenditure of this bit of magic. She took only a moment to relax before calling forth her blade and plucking a feather. Using the tip of the quill, she etched her last will and testament into the metal, giving Loki all her magic, the Holy Chalice, and the Seeds of Creation. If her unborn child existed, then her offspring would receive her feathers. If the rumors of her pregnancy were unfounded, then they'd go directly to Loki. *And he'll become the benefactor of everything I am.*

Once finished etching the angelic lettering into the metal, she pricked her finger and dragged her blood along the words, sealing her final testament.

It is done. There was no way her action could be undone except by her own hand.

NINETEEN

*L*ater she sat in the wingback chair in Loki's bedroom. Knees folded beneath her, she added three more feathers to her pile. Ten precious commodities gone in too little time, the loss made her want to cry, but emotions weakened her, and she had no time for them. She tossed another reishi into her mouth and munched, hating the taste and texture, but then she didn't require sustenance so the act of eating was foreign to her. Thankfully the mushroom gave her a kick of energy, and she felt a little more like herself.

If not for the pile of feathers stacked on the table, she could almost pretend she was back to normal.

When the door opened without any forewarning, Loki joined her. Expression pensive, he caught her eye and strode across the room toward her.

"Suriel said you were awake." What else had Suriel told him? "Feeling better, Solas?"

Talk to him, Suriel's words skipped through her mind. "Better. How long was I out?"

"Day and a half."

Almost five days.

"Yes."

"Can you pick and choose when you hear my thoughts?"

He sat on the edge of the bed, his gaze almost hyper-focused on her. "I blocked you yesterday." A crooked grin briefly curled his lips. "Wasn't sure I could make love to you properly if I could hear your thoughts."

There was her cocky god. It was the one time she adored his arrogance, because he excelled at making her shatter. And of course, at the mention of yesterday's lovemaking, her core clenched. Seriously, her pussy was a junkie for sex, and Loki was her fix.

"Want to tell me what's wrong with you?"

She peered over his shoulder. "What gave you the impression anything is wrong with me?"

"Ten fallen reapers." That snagged her attention, and when their gazes locked he said, "They had *a lot* to say about your slowness to rejuvenate."

"What were you doing with the fallen?"

"Changing the topic. All right, I'll play along. *For now.* But we *will* revisit this conversation." He kicked off his shoes and dragged off his socks, such a human chore for a god when he could make them disappear with a flick of his finger. "I recruited them to our side and returned their wings."

He'd stolen her sister from her first, and now he claimed the fallen. Typical Loki, but she didn't blame him since he increased his numbers and attempted to secure his future with the alliance. "*Your* side, not *ours*. Don't pretend you did that for anyone but yourself." At least the extra firepower would keep him and the potential baby safe.

"Solas—"

"I don't need to hear your defenses, Loki. I don't care that you claimed them as yours."

"You're angry with me and not slitting my throat. Now I know something's wrong."

"My first inclination isn't violence. And I'm not angry with you."

"Trust me, love, violence is your go-to reaction." He stood and came toward her. Leaning over, he braced his hands on the arms of her chair, getting in her personal space. "My balls still ache from your well-placed knee."

"I was pissed off."

"I got that loud and clear."

He eyed her mouth as she said, "Your balls seemed to be working just fine yesterday when you fucked me."

His gaze snatched to hers as if surprised by her comment. Heat poured from him. "I didn't fuck you. I made love to you. Big difference, angel. I hope you received my message?" She elevated her eyebrows, pondering what message she should've received. He explained. "You were *my pet*, gifted to me for my pleasure, so I could gift you with your shatterings. When you're taking my cock, that is the only time you are my pet. In everything else, we're equals."

Solas' heart took a direct hit. "None of that matters any longer, Loki." Facing imminent death and an eternity in angelic-hell, made everything so much clearer, and the little things didn't matter. "As a Grigori, my expertise and abilities were never in question. My rank and legend inspired respect and fear. That made me prideful. I believed I was more than I am. I couldn't see my error in thinking until you showed me my ineptness. I learned a valuable lesson."

He sighed, a weary sound that caused her to lift her hand and trail the pads of her fingertips along his jaw. Selfish on her part, but she didn't want to spend her last days fighting with him. "Don't despair, husband, I've always been a fast learner."

"You've not learned a fucking thing, wife, but I don't want to fight with you either." Solas jerked at the last part, but he went on as if he failed to notice her reaction when she knew he caught the effect his words had on her. "All ten fallen swore fealty to *you*, angel. Yeah, I gave them their wings, but they're yours to command, not mine."

She couldn't think of one thing he could've said that would've shocked her more. "Why?"

"Every goddess requires a regimen to command."

"I'm not a goddess."

"You're my wife. I'm a god. That makes you a goddess."

She rolled her eyes at his preposterous logic.

"I should spank you for that disrespectful eye-roll." Without warning he lifted her from the chair, turned and sat in the furniture, drawing her across his lap.

"You make that threat much too often and never follow through."

"I find I'm unable to punish you the way you deserve." He nuzzled her neck, and she felt a soft, unnamable emotion coming off him. Whatever it was, it calmed her. "After your reaction to my immobilization power, I'm a little afraid if I did spank you you'd cut my dick off. I'm rather fond of it."

He didn't worry, that she knew, so she realized he teased. "I am fond of your dick too." And she wasn't teasing.

Purple blazed over the green of his irises. "Tell me what's wrong, Solas."

"What'd the fallen tell you?"

"Everything or nothing. Either way I want to hear it from your sinful lips." He caught her chin, turned her head, and forced her to meet his penetrating gaze, the purple of his godhood reflected in his eyes. "I could steal your thoughts, but I won't. I trust you to be forthright with me so we can determine a favorable resolution *together* as husband and wife."

"There's no possible 'favorable resolution' this time, Loki."

"Solas..." he warned, then shook his head. "You still don't trust me to pick you first?"

"I'm trying to protect you."

"The same way I protected you in the bar by immobilizing you?"

Solas looked away and swallowed hard.

"Tell me everything right now or I swear to you, I'll strip you, put you in our bed, and fuck you with my tongue and fingers, withholding your orgasms until you confess all. I can hold you on edge for hours, Solas, until you're so desperate to shatter it's a physical pain, and *then* you'll give me what I want just to find relief."

"As always, you're not playing fair."

"Not when your life is at stake."

Her eyes widened. "How much did they tell you?"

Loki remained silent, his eyes going all-god as he drew her to her feet. The fabric of his shirt she wore gave free when he gave it a hard tug, ripping the silk off her.

"No—" Before her next breath she found herself on the bed, legs spread, and his grip firm as he held her open. Loki settled between her thighs, his features determined, but he halted when she said, "Wait! Let me talk, Loki."

He paused, his mouth so close to her core his breath puffed against her sex. "You've got five seconds or I continue with my promise."

"Ages ago, I made a soul oath with Father. If I ever betrayed Him…" She closed her eyes trying to find the right way to deliver the news.

"Just say it."

Opening her eyes, she met the fury in his. "I'm dying." Pushing him away, she sat up and leaned against the headboard. She drew her knees to her chest, crossed her ankles, and wrapped her arms around her legs. "Since no one but Father can rescind the marker on my life, I have to determine if I'm really pregnant, and if I am, save the baby somehow. I won't live long enough to give the infant life."

The purple sparks in Loki's eyes diminished, and he pushed to his knees.

Solas called forth her blade and tossed the weapon on the bed between them. "See the words on the blade?"

"Yes, but I don't know what it says."

"It's angelic lettering bequeathing all my magic to you, along with the Holy Chalice and Seeds of Creation."

"How'd you acquire those holy relics of immense power?" He seemed impressed, or maybe she read his expression all-wrong.

"Long story, doesn't matter, they'll be yours. You and the maybe-baby are my legacy. The child will get my feathers, even though they're falling, the power inside them remains intact. If there is no baby, then they're yours by default. Through you, I'll survive, and giving you all of me and giving all of my play toys to you is my only way of protecting you after I'm gone."

Loki moved so fast she couldn't track him for a second. One moment he was on his knees at the foot of the bed, the next dragging her across his lap, and against his solid chest, tightening his hold on her. She'd mistake his grasp for a hug if that gesture weren't out of character for him.

"I called a seer while you slept to confirm your pregnancy once and for all." His palm settled over her belly. "Our miracle child is inside you."

Love hijacked her system. She hadn't known she could feel such immediate and profound sentiment for a single creature.

Solas rested her hand over his. "Give me a bead of your magic, and I might be able to connect us with it since it's part angel."

He shifted the positions of their hands, hers resting against her naked belly, and his settling over the back of hers, lacing their fingers together. A slight bubble warmed her palm, and she gasped at the pleasurable effect of his mojo. Focusing beyond the hedonism of sampling his divine magic, she fixated on the infant, locating their unborn child almost immediately.

"The heartbeat of our miracle is strong," he said, awe tingeing his voice. "A *son*."

Maybe because of their connection in that moment, Solas could *taste* Loki's emotions. They were strong, feral, and so protective moisture stung her eyes. She was thankful their child would know the love of his father when she hadn't.

The connection dropped thanks to her weakened state. But the moment they lost the connection, he lowered his lips to hers and forced her to take his tongue, fucking her mouth the way he always did, with domination. In seconds his hunger became evident in the way his hard-on prodded her hip through his jeans.

"I can't let Him have our son to torture too," she said against his mouth. "Loki junior—"

"His name will *not* be Loki junior."

"—is innocent." She smiled at his immediate and vehement dissent to the name. "You'll be a better father than mine."

Loki's palm cupped her neck, and he dragged his thumb along her jaw. She couldn't decide if anger or *what* particular emotion burned from his eyes, but it was savage. "You knew this would happen when you told Michael you would never betray your maker?"

"You heard that?" He nodded, and she explained. "I thought you were out then. For the record, I never killed you, just wanted my brother and father to think I had. If I hadn't been brutal with you, Michael wouldn't have believed I killed you. For that, I'm sorry. The feather I jabbed in the back of your neck was a death-stasis spell activated by my blood. Only my blood could release you from the death-sleep."

"I could've beaten Michael."

"Yeah, you could've taken Michael. That was never in question. I told you that, but one nick of the god-killer and you'd have sickened and died. That he wielded that particular weapon told me how desperate my father is to have you dead. It's cheating and a dishonorable death. No one as prideful as you should be murdered like that. Even if I told you one nick would be your demise, you're so fucking arrogant, I couldn't take the chance you wouldn't engage him just to prove you're superior. So, I protected you the only way I knew how. I guess just like you protected us by immobilizing me in the bar."

"Did that hurt to admit?"

"A little." She punished him for the jab by biting his bottom lip. His eyes flamed, and his cock jerked. "When I told Michael I'd never betray my maker, he heard exactly what he wanted to hear. Only once it was too late for him to collect your *dead body* did he realize I'd betrayed my creator, not my maker, and by then you were safe. I bought you time."

"And damned yourself." Oh, there was explicit anger in the grit of his words.

She palmed his cheek. "I fell for you, Loki. I regretted that more than once, but now I see the truth. You remade me, and I *experienced* life rather than surveyed the world through the eyes of a watcher. I underwent a change. For the first time, I felt something more than the wet work of death on my hands. I embraced the pain when you returned my wings because it was a novelty. I'd only ever experienced pain a time or two, and after my fall the sensation was different, more pronounced, but it affirmed no one controlled me any longer. Knowing no one governed me any longer was a heady feeling, Loki. I craved your kisses, desired your lovemaking, the exquisite feel of your dick pushing into me." She shivered, and her channel pulsed for him. "I felt passion for the first time, and I longed for more of it. I would've felt none of that without falling for you. You freed me even before I ever met you." What doomed her was when... *I fell in love with him.* She choked on a breath with the revelation, her eyes widened as she peered at him. *Yes, my god, yes, I'm in love with Loki.* Clearing her throat even as her heart swelled with her admission, she forced herself to continue. "I was—*I am* good at killing, and I enjoy it even though I shouldn't. If I could do everything all over again, I would still make the decision to die for you." In her head, she finished that sentence with, *because I'm in love with you, and there is no sacrifice too big to keep you safe.*

TWENTY

*T*en minutes had passed since Loki abruptly left Solas in his bedchamber. He'd heard the words as clear as if she'd spoken them aloud… *Yes, my god,* yes, *I'm in love with Loki.* There was no spark in her eyes, no light of love that lit up her face and made it glow like he'd witnessed with Suriel when she spoke of Solas. No, his angel looked shocked, even as if she gagged on the thought. His stomach gave a lurch. Were the words a trick she'd orchestrated in her thoughts to best him at the end of her life?

Loki chuckled. Irony swirled inside him like pollution in a clear lake as he descended the stone steps into the dungeon. He hadn't meant to hear her thoughts. His block was in place to respect her privacy. *I'm dying,* spoken from his angel's lips collapsed everything inside him like an avalanche. He'd known the truth, the ten angels had disclosed her condition, but it hadn't felt real until she spoke the words. Just like the last words she'd thought, were they real? Did she love him? Hope burned so strongly inside him, it was almost emotionally crippling.

The words he'd waited so long to hear he couldn't trust. And if they were true feelings, Solas was dying. His *son* was in jeopardy. *Talk about a kick in the balls.*

Pushing open the door to the dungeon, Loki turned right to enter the main room. His mood reflected in his fast, long strides eating up the path to the angel named Elyon. When Loki rounded the corner, he stopped and stared at the fallen. The angel's appearance wasn't what he'd imagined. But his imagination also had this man doing things with his angel that made him twitchy to kill the other man right where he was shackled. At six-two, Elyon looked like a god with blond hair and eyes as blue as the heavens. His torn shirt, streaked in blood, showed his muscular features. Loki mentally shook the lurid thoughts of Solas and Elyon from his mind. His angel had been innocent when they met. But this *Elyon*, with his Thor good looks, risked his life for Solas, even proved to be a worthy prisoner to Loki's men. Did the fallen have information Loki's Naglfar tried to obtain? Or did they perceive Loki as Solas' weakness, and because of that they plotted to use that vulnerability against her?

Not in a forgiving state of mind, he'd ask Elyon one question. The answer would determine if his captive lived past the next couple of minutes. "Why did you swear allegiance to *my* wife?"

"So it's true." The muscles in Elyon's arms visibly flexed, and the fallen glared at Loki. "You've tainted her with your…" He curled his upper lip as if a rank stench permeated the chamber. "With all that is you."

"Are you angry because I took her before you had the chance?" Loki cupped his hands behind his back to prevent himself from caving to his desire and killing the other man.

Elyon's face contorted in disgust. "No, I'm angry because you took her before I could kill you."

"You tried, and failed, to kill me before she was sent. Did you not?"

"Yes."

"Do you still want to kill me?" Loki's gaze snapped to Elyon's.

"Yes." The angel grated, pulling on his chains as he stepped toward Loki.

"Why deny you the attempt." Loki waved his hand through the air. With a flick of his wrist, the chains unlocked and fell to the floor with a loud clank. Elyon blinked at the blade suddenly in his grasp before directing his startled gaze at Loki.

"What trickery is this, Loki?"

"No tricks. You want me dead. I've given you the opportunity to try."

"When you know I can't. I have no wings and little magic." Elyon gripped the blade until his knuckles turned white.

"After you kill me, Elyon, will you kill my child nestled in my wife's womb for your father as well?"

"I wouldn't kill you for *Him*, I'd kill you for Solas." Ah, yes, because if Loki was dead Solas might receive a pardon from her death sentence. Loki doubted it since her God wasn't nearly as forgiving as He'd have His followers believe, but the possibility remained. A reply obviously wasn't expected from him since Elyon continued to confess. "I'd protect her child from those who wish to harm it. The child is innocent."

"Yes, the child is, but it's *my* child." Loki widened his stance and held his hands out to the sides in a silent taunt to 'come and get me'. "I could kill Solas now and still manage to keep the child safe." The man struck faster than Loki had expected, pushing him back against the wall with impressive speed. Loki allowed Elyon to pin his hands against the stone because it suited his purpose to give the other man hope. "You still attack me when you know you don't have a chance."

Elyon's courage impressed him. Loki opened his hands with his palms facing toward the man and lightly pushed air magic, sending the fallen flying back into the stony wall of the cavern.

"I welcome death if it saves Solas!" Elyon growled before he lunged toward Loki once more.

Catching him by the arm, Loki swung the angel toward the wall and secured Elyon's arm behind him to immobilize him. "Why?"

"She saved my life." Elyon reared his head backward, smacking Loki in his forehead.

Twisting Elyon's arm, Loki raised his wrist upward between his shoulder blades until the fallen gave a painful grunt. Loki didn't stop, but pinned the man against the stone wall with his weight. "You will save her life no matter the consequences?"

"Yes."

"You swear your loyalty to Solas and will do as she commands."

"Yes, as always!" Elyon struggled against Loki's hold. If magic weren't on Loki's side, the angel stood a chance of beating him in strength. And his feelings for Solas were much different than Loki imagined. Something in his tone, in his eyes, showed respect, admiration, and friendship, but nothing more. Definitely, nothing in the romantic sense.

"This agreement is binding. Everything she asks of you you'll do without question." Loki released him with a shove.

Elyon spun around and locked his gaze with Loki's. A frown threaded across the angel's forehead. "What?"

"I didn't stutter."

"What if she asks me to kill you?"

"Then you do as she asks."

"You're even more psychotic than the scriptures say you are." Elyon squared his shoulders, and uncertainty shifted through his expression. "This has to be a trick."

"My agreements are never to be taken lightly, Elyon." Loki stepped back and snapped his fingers. "Your wings."

Elyon fell to the floor with a howl as his rebirth began. Knowing deep down Solas and Elyon shared a meaningful connection, Loki wanted to stay and watch him feel pain, for no other reason than the other man had something with his wife that he didn't. Intimacy wasn't in question, but there was a sense of camaraderie. The man had attacked him with no chance of survival because he was loyal to Solas and wanted to see her protected. If Loki met his fate, Elyon was the kind of man he needed to watch over his angel—even if he wanted Loki dead.

"I'd love to stay and watch your wings come in, but I'm afraid I have other things to attend to."

"Fucking asshole." Elyon gritted through closed teeth.

Loki kneeled until he reached Elyon's ear and whispered, "You live for one purpose, help keep my wife safe."

"I don't have to be asked to protect Solas, I've had her back for-for centuries." Elyon winced and yelled as light-blue tipped feathers ripped through his skin. "Asshole... Like I'd trust you to protect her."

"I don't trust you either, Elyon. You watch over my wife"—Loki snapped his fingers, summoning his second in command—"and she'll watch over you." Elyon's head tilted, and Loki knew when the angel spotted Vylyra standing behind him. His second in command was a beautiful creature. Brown hair flowed past her shoulders, changing to the colors of fire nearing the tips, to match her eyes. Vy was sexy, voluptuous, and a temptation to men and women alike. If she weren't under his command, he'd have bedded her often. *Before an angel fell at my feet.* "Ah, before you get excited, Elyon, a word of caution. Vylyra will shadow your every move. If you take flight, she will catch you." From the sound behind him, and Elyon's eyes going wide, Loki knew Vy had spread her leathery wings that were more bat like than angel. "One kiss, Elyon, and her fire demon half can incinerate you from the inside out if she chooses—*if* her succubus half doesn't fuck you to death first." Loki chuckled, patted Elyon on the shoulder, and rose to tower over the man at his feet.

When he spun to face Vy, a knowing grin pulled at his lips. No wonder Elyon's eyes were especially wide, his second in command appeared in her undergarments. At least she carried her sword. "Did I interrupt something?"

"Nothing I can't start again," Vy said in a husky tone. A wicked gleam lit her gaze as she eyed Elyon with interest.

Loki sent her mental instructions adding, "*Don't hurt him, Vy. I sense he still has his innocence. Hands off for now.*" He almost laughed at the slight pout to her lips before he walked through the hallway into the next chamber. Vy would eat Elyon alive if given sexual liberty to treat the fallen like any of her other conquests.

Trusting Vy to micromanage Elyon, he strolled out of the room and down the hall before entering another chamber. Hanging in chains from the wall was Sephora and his Naglfar that had attempted to kill Solas in the bar. Just looking at the Naglfar caused anger to leech through him, and by the flinch of his man, he'd bet his eyes tinted purple. Solas' blade appeared in his hand, summoned by an unconscious thought.

Loki wrapped his hand around the man's shackled wrist and grated out, "I will kill you a thousand times for your attempt on my wife and child's life." Using Solas' blade, he sliced the man from wrist to shoulder. Relishing the traitor's screams, Loki repeated the action to the other arm. Loki positioned his palms against the cold stone, one on each side of the Naglfar's head, getting in his face. Loki glared at the man for a long moment. The wall vibrated from his barely controlled power, saying everything about his emotions without him having to speak. Instead he savored the fear entering the Naglfar's eyes and the visible trembling that overtook his body.

Slithering, hissing sounds resonated from above, making the Naglfar look up.

"No. No!" The man shook his head in violent movements.

"When you die from the serpent's venom dripping into your gaping carcass, I'm bringing you back to start all over again."

"Please, my lord."

"You held a blade to my wife's stomach—*at my son!*" The wall shook again with his anger, and the first drop of venom sizzled inside the Naglfar's opened flesh. His man drove his head back against the wall and yelled.

Sephora screamed from behind them, but Loki was so close to the Naglfar's face that his cries of pain dimmed her sounds. Hearing Sephora reminded him he had one more thing to take care of before he returned to his wife. He resettled his fist around the blade and stalked toward her. The angel backed up until she came up dead against the wall, shaking her head, with her hands held out as he approached, the chains rattling from her visible shaking. A plea he didn't give a fuck about.

"You're a treacherous whore."

"They forced me. They—"

"*Lies.*"

Sephora kneeled, her hands held high from the chains. "Let me serve you."

Loki stood over her and fisted her hair, ripping her head back to stare into her deceitful eyes. He should save his wife the trouble and end her now. The angel's pathetic weakness would get someone killed down the road. Maybe his men tricked Sephora, that's what they're supposed to do, but she'd bought into their plan. A reaper should be more skilled at ferreting out lies than she showed a talent for. He couldn't imagine his woman falling for his men's trickery.

At the bar, Sephora had walked through the angels that kneeled for Solas like *she* ruled them instead of Solas. She'd refused to kneel for his angel. He tightened his fist around Solas' blade only to feel the bite of his nails against his palm.

"So this is where you rushed off to." Solas stood at the room's entrance. Her blade vanished from his grip and entered her tightly fisted hand. She lifted her eyebrows and gave him a challenging smirk, but then the smile fell as she took in Sephora's placement.

From the side angle she had of him and Sephora, he knew the position seemed more intimate than it was. Loki gave a mental cringe as his angel strolled toward them, while her confidence lit a different fire inside him.

She stopped next to him and Sephora, and all but ignored the angel at his feet. "You called my blade again, trying to claim your inheritance so soon, *husband*?"

With a jerk of her head, Solas snatched a look above the dying Naglfar's head. The slightest smile twitched at her lips. *A venom drip... the myth is half true.*

"Not as potent as your venom. He still lives," Loki responded to Solas' thoughts. Did she flinch from the memory?

"Did I interrupt something, my *husband*?"

Mesmerized by the sway of her hips as she walked to the Naglfar, Loki realized he hadn't moved. Sephora remained on her knees with his hand still buried in her hair. By the glint in Solas' gaze, Loki knew her question was too dangerous to answer. No, he'd learned from his mistakes and wanted to build something with her. He'd stay quiet and watch her a bit longer to determine how he should proceed.

Solas plucked a feather as she neared the Naglfar and asked, "Is this the man who threatened my child?"

"Yes." She'd reduced him to single words. The woman was fucking stunning. In a torture chamber, wearing his shirt, and she walked around as if she ruled the kingdom. She *did* rule it in half. Not one ounce of fear or anxiety from the scene before her. Fatigue was the only thing he noted in the way her wings drooped, as if they were too heavy to lift as high as she normally carried them. He wanted to stop her from whatever she planned. Using her magic would weaken her more, that much he knew.

"What happens when he dies?" she asked, twirling her feather between her fingers as she studied Loki's handiwork.

"He'll revive where he hangs, and I'll fucking kill him again."

She nodded before her focus shifted to the man half dead against the wall. The man's head hung until she was a breath away. He met her gaze. "You threatened my child." In a blink, her black feather protruded out from his chest. "Send a warning to whomever you have a mental connection with. Threatening my child *or* my husband will seal their fate." Solas grabbed the feather and sliced downward, cutting the man open from sternum to navel. She stood there watching the life depart his man's eyes without an ounce of sympathy on her features.

Jesus fuck. When Solas turned, the silver shimmered in her eyes a scant second before vanishing. Along with it vanished the arousal she'd stirred in him when she'd arrived, because she should be able to hold her magic longer. At least by all outward appearances she gave off the persona of strength.

His angel faltered midstride. Fuck, he'd jinxed her.

Loki loosened his hand on Sephora, and then thought better of running to Solas' aid. Solas couldn't be viewed as weak in front of her people—that would kill her more than death itself. He'd feel the same if in a similar situation before his men. And he wouldn't make her feel like she had at the biker compound. When a feather fell from Solas' wings, Loki wrenched Sephora's head back until her neck bent, and her gaze pointed to the ceiling. Sweeping his free hand through the air, he collected the feather, palming it behind his back. With a quick push of his power, Loki shielded Solas' thoughts from entering his mind. And by avoiding her gaze he wouldn't... *weaken her.*

The thought struck in his mind and rolled through his body. He suspected she was on the edge, on the verge of breaking down. She was on the cusp of losing her precious feathers and dying. In Solas' mind there was little hope of finding a way to survive, so he knew she had to be one breath away from crying at any moment. Isn't that what women did? And somehow he knew if their gazes brushed, she'd set her emotions free and give in to her tears.

I weaken her.

He was sure of it. So, if they didn't engage in direct eye contact, maybe she wouldn't collapse.

Numbness rolled across his skin, followed by bumps, and then the feeling evaporated. Loki mentally shook himself. The last thing he wanted was to be her weakness. And she'd said much the same thing to him, yet she planned to lift him up and give him power with her death.

Loki's breath quickened, and his chest felt tight. What was wrong with him?

As a diversion to these unnamed and worrisome emotions, he jerked Sephora to her feet.

Solas' voice sounded beside him. "You've had my husband's cock in your mouth?"

Loki flinched. This wasn't going to end well. He knew that tone well enough to know someone would soon be sporting a new injury. He hoped he survived unscathed this round.

"Yes," Sephora answered, and was stupid enough to smile.

"And he took your innocence?"

"Yes." With a tongue like a serpent, Sephora lied. Loki's gaze snapped to Sephora's, but he tightened his lips to keep from speaking, reminding himself this was Solas' angel to command—not his. He found the action difficult.

"How?" His angel asked.

"Um… with that." She pointed to Loki's crotch.

"Don't be foolish, Sephora, *that,* has a name. Tell me one thing he said to you while he was taking you. Just one." Solas' tone was impatient and her tight expression even more intolerant.

"He said it was sweet intercourse. And—"

"Stop!" Solas commanded and pointed her blade at Sephora. She cantered her head toward Loki. "Unchain her."

With a snap of his fingers, the magic restraints unlocked and fell from her wrists and ankles. Loki backed away as Solas approached Sephora, remaining close enough to counter an attack if needed. Everything inside him wanted to end this for her, and then take her to bed to rest. Instead he let his brave, fatigued, violent, dying wife have her way because... *I love her*.

He jammed his fingers through his hair. Is this how Solas felt when she realized she loved him? Like she'd been sucker punched? The air seemed to dissipate, making the room feel smaller. He stared at a spot on the back wall to help ground him in his revelation. A ring started in his ears slowly muting into deafness. The rapid beat of his heart strummed so loud the sound broke the silence in his head and then with clarity, he heard Solas' voice again.

"That was your one chance, Sephora. I wanted to see if you could be saved, to join us... to fight with us. You choose to lie."

"I-I didn't! He took me."

"He may have taken your mouth, Sephora, but he most certainly did not have... *sweet intercourse* with you. Those words are straight from the books about watching over the humans. My husband fucks hard, and rattles the earth with orgasms. He doesn't do sweet." Solas faltered again, but this time it didn't look to be from fatigue. Her gaze held something unnamed, and then she shook it off to continue. Flipping her blade in her hand, Solas grasped the sharp steel. Good thing it wouldn't cut her or her palm would be in ribbons right now. The blade had cut through his Naglfar like he pushed a butter knife through melted butter.

Sephora's gaze snapped to her actions, and tears streamed down her cheeks. "No. Please... just kill me." She attempted a half-ass run.

Seriously? Loki pitied her pathetic attempt, but not enough to let her go. He grabbed her arms, and jerked her to him, holding her against his chest for Solas to mete out her punishment.

"Let him kill me. Anything but *that*."

His angel shook her head in a slow movement that came across as a cruel taunt. It made his dick hard all over again. He saw the truth in her words now, the unholy gleam in her eyes testified to how much she enjoyed taking lives.

"Dying is too good for you, and you know that." Solas sliced the blade across her palm, then swirled the pommel in the pool of blood in her hand.

"Why did it cut you, angel, when it shouldn't?"

She gave him a sidelong peek. "It's about intent, trickster. Since it's crafted from my soul, it understands what I need."

Loki nodded, wondering if since he now held some sway over the object if that mean the blade could no longer harm him.

"You're condemned to live eternity on earth. Alone and unloved." Solas pressed the bloody pommel against Sephora's skin above her left breast. Her flesh sizzled, and she wept like a little girl with skinned knees instead of a seasoned warrior. Soon the aroma of burnt flesh filled the room. When Solas removed the blade, an insignia was permanently branded on Sephora. A piece of it would always show, peeking out above her shirt. Branded like a Scarlet Letter, to live eternity as an outcast among her kind. Fuck, but his woman was brutal.

Solas lifted her gaze to Loki. "Can you make her disappear?"

He thought she wobbled just a tad on her feet. More power she couldn't afford to use wasted on punishment when he could've eliminated Sephora without tiring. He could give her this simple request however.

"As you wish." Loki snapped his fingers and Sephora vanished. "Are you okay?" Something he had to ask, even if she may not approve of his concern.

"Call my blade again without my consent, and I'll kill you in your sleep, husband." Solas leaned into him from a weakness she refused to admit. As she settled her wings into her body, he wrapped his arms around her, cherishing the moment not because he was stronger than her but because she came to him for comfort.

An edge of humor tinged her voice when she spoke. "Take me to bed and have sweet intercourse with me."

Adorable. Loki grinned and pressed a kiss to her forehead. Her teasing was cute, a side of her he'd love to explore, but his angel was dying, and he couldn't bring himself to weaken her further no matter how much he wanted to bury himself inside her. A moment of pleasure wasn't worth the drain on her magical stores. Many things needed to be set in motion before it was too late to save his wife and child.

"No, angel. You need to rest."

TWENTY-ONE

"*I*'ll rest when I'm dead." Solas tilted her head back and gave him her best pouty face. His stone-faced features remained steadfast, but his disagreement was loud and clear through the tension in his body. Somehow he miraculously held his tongue. *Impressive.*

Mr. Sourpuss wanted her to sit back and relax while he went about saving the day. *Not going to happen.* She'd been born to fight, to kill. The savagery of her genes made her legendary in Heaven. Sitting on the sidelines cheering on the hero would never be her style. The inactive notion made her want to gag… or stab the useless cheerleader in her damn throat.

She knew Loki well enough to know he wouldn't want a shrinking violet on his arm; he'd lose interest in playing the hero. But neither did she believe there was a chance in hell of them finding a way for her to survive. That meant the baby came first, and her tall, dark, and deadly trickster needed to get on board.

"What? No 'I am a god, and you'll do as you're told' comeback?"

"*Angel…*" his tone warned, as one of his hands shifted to grip her nape, his fingers tightening. "I'm trying to be amenable, to see things through your eyes, but don't tempt me to get you under control."

"When have you ever controlled me?"

"I decline to answer on the likelihood you might relocate my balls to my throat."

She laughed and dropped her forehead to his chest. His scent cloaked her, and his strength surrounded her. He felt so good against her, like a wall of coziness, if a wall could be cozy. Anyone who wanted her would have to go through him to get her.

My father won't have to go through him.

At that sobering thought, she inhaled and focused on Loki instead of what would come soon enough. The strength in him called to her. Everything about Loki called to her. But standing here in his embrace with him freely offering his vigor and comfort without complaint... *it just feels good.*

If her parent waited until she died to come for her, she'd be surprised. Waiting wasn't his specialty. That meant their time grew shorter with every hour.

"You should use the Holy Chalice and Seeds of Creation to build a female capable of nourishing and protecting Loki junior to term."

"*Stop* calling him that name."

"What do you want me to call him?"

His palm slid upward, his fingers threaded through the strands of her hair, and he tilted her head back with his grip. The slight sting brought her body instantly alive.

"We'll decide after we solve our dilemma."

This was much bigger than a mere dilemma. "Say it, Loki." At his confused frown, she said, "Say the words out loud. Say I'm dying."

"No."

"*Say it.*"

"*No.*"

At an impasse, they glared at one another, so she attempted a different tactic. "We have to focus on saving the baby. The sooner you acknowledge I'm dying the better."

"I've acknowledged our slight problem, angel, but I've also acknowledged that *He's not getting you.*"

Frustrated, she pushed away from him. Realizing she still clutched her sword, she called it into her body. It didn't budge. She tried again, and the steel remained in her grasp. Something must've alerted him of her intention because he cast a glance at the weapon, and a tick took off along his jaw. Thankfully, the sword vanished on the third try. Light-headed from her exertion, she inhaled slowly while she focused on stabilizing her balance... and hiding her waning power from Loki. She *hated* being seen as weak. Despised even more that *he* saw her this way.

"You're worse than you're letting on." His insightfulness surprised her.

She ignored his comment. "You refusing to admit the baby is our *only* priority will get us *both* killed." Channeling a large bubble of power, she managed to call the Chalice and Seeds forth on her first effort. Fury hit his gaze, and his godhood sparkled in his eyes when she offered him the instruments. "Use them to save our son." When he refused the items, she jostled them against his chest and held them there. "Make something powerful and loyal *only* to you. Something that'll protect h-him."

Her voice broke, and she looked away before she completely fell apart. With a desperation that astounded her, she wanted to see the birth of her son, to hold him, and to raise him with Loki. She'd settle for saving him even if it was her last action. One moment she hadn't believed she could conceive, hadn't known he existed, had scoffed at the rumors, and in the next she'd loved with an instantaneous passion, and the strength of the emotion frightened her. *Similar to how much I love Loki frightens me.* That was an altogether different beast though. Either way, she was willing to do *anything* to save them both.

At least he doesn't return my love. He won't have to endure the loss of a loved one. She took comfort from that truth.

"You do it. You make the creature," his voice emerged cool and collected, but the fire in his eyes told a much different story. He was furious with her, and she had no idea why.

Why was he being so obstinate? Their end game wasn't all that different, and yet he blocked her moves. His stubbornness made no sense.

"I can't." She nudged his chest with the items once more as a reminder she wanted him to take them. The tarnished chalice looked like a piece of junk, but the vessel grew luminous when in use. The seeds sparkled like multi-colored gemstones, but with the right mixture of powers, a creature made from the seeds could conquer even Michael's ancient abilities. She met Loki's gaze. "Only a god can use them. Take them, Loki, or I'll use my power again to return them."

With a growl, he snatched them from her grasp, and they vanished a moment later. "Don't undermine me on this, Solas."

"Ensure the baby's safety first, and I *swear* I'll do anything you want. I'll be so submissive you'll doubt—"

Agony struck her temple, and she cried out as she reeled at the unexpected supernatural blow.

"Solas?"

She heard the concern in Loki's voice, but a glimmer of white light hit the back of her eyelids, sharp and glaring. Her pupils hurt like the time a ray of sunlight had burst unexpectedly between fissures in an iceberg. She'd been momentarily blinded for mere seconds then, but this lasted, remained, rendered her helpless and at risk. Another sharp strike, acute like a scalpel sliding through skin opening a seam. Grasping her head between her palms, she plummeted to her knees as a presence inserted itself into her mind. Someone wanted to talk like she had with Michael, only she'd knocked, and he'd granted permission. This someone raped her mentally and forced inside.

I felt you move the Holy Chalice and Seeds of Creation.

Father. Terror gripped her. He'd never come at her like this. She focused on breathing through the pain, but even that failed at alleviating the searing violence He created in her mind.

"Fuck," she heard Loki whisper from what sounded like a distance. More voices settled around her, but she couldn't decipher them as Loki faded.

I want them now or… His quiet demand didn't terrify her as much as the 'or' at the end did.

I gave them to Loki. The pain intensified, and her breathing altered. She panted, the noise loud in her ears, reminding her of a dog she'd witnessed who'd been run on a hot day until it collapsed. The animal had died shortly afterward.

Retrieve them, and return them to me.

It's too late. I've—

Intense pain circled her belly, ripping a scream from her. She clutched her abdomen and rode out the violence with shrieks that grew in octave as his punishment increased.

"Fuck." She thought that was Loki again, but everything felt off, out of sync like Father had managed to pull her into another dimension.

Retrieve them. Return them to me. You've two hours to comply or…

The hurt intensified in her stomach. He would kill the baby before they had a chance to save him. She knew it as surely as she recognized her parent.

Solas did the only thing she could. She fought back with her magic. Desperate to protect the innocent life she cherished more than her own, she funneled all her power toward her womb. Her father laughed, and tears wet her cheeks as she weakened, losing the battle they fought.

From a long way off, she thought she detected Elyon's voice, but that made no sense because he wasn't in Loki's domain. "She's bleeding power like Father cut her carotid artery. She's not going to last."

Was he with Father?

Amid the agony, heat slid along her arm, a pleasurable sensation. More came, like a shower deluging her, washing away the pain. Solas turned toward the effervescence enveloping her, greedy for more of it, while recognizing whatever it was and whoever provided it, somehow the warmth chased her father away and protected her child.

When the heat trailed off much too soon, she opened her eyes. Loki sat on the floor, cradling her in his lap.

"Angel?"

She lifted her gaze to his and fell apart, bursting into tears. The sobs wracked her body so hard she trembled in his arms, and he crushed her against his chest.

She clung to him, wrapping her fingers in his shirt, and let herself go. For only a brief moment did she experience the relief of winning this round before a new panic emerged. She channeled a faint cord of magic to verify He hadn't destroyed the infant.

"Loki junior's fine." They must've won by the skin of their teeth if Loki used that name. "I can feel him. Stop depleting your power."

Someone else pulled her hand away from her belly, and she turned her head to identify the intruder. "Elyon? Why are you here?"

"I'll help you." He offered his mojo, and while it was a common way to heal other angels, his tasted like bile hitting the back of her throat.

A distinct mental recoil to the angelic magic came from the baby. Solas snatched her hand out of Elyon's grasp before she had a chance to give her reaction any thought.

At Elyon's hurt expression, she said, "It won't be enough."

She could take everything he had, killing him, and it still wouldn't be enough. Over his shoulder she spied a strange woman, the most beautiful creature she'd ever seen. Awed by the woman's beauty, Solas gaped at her. The other woman's sensual charisma was so strong it seemed to drip from her. Her red-eyed stare returned Solas' gaze unflinching. Solas could sense the creature was a warrior, probably fierce and effective, without mercy.

Will she be my replacement when I'm gone? I wouldn't blame Loki. She's so stunning I can't take my eyes off her. And she's strong. She'll be a good protector for the baby. But... will she be the new mother to our son? A thick knot formed in her throat at the final thought. She would miss all of his life while this stranger—

"No, goddamn it." Loki cut off her thoughts with a low, vicious whisper, as he nuzzled his face against her neck, and squeezed her a little too tight to his chest. Surprise widened the eyes of the other woman, but Solas didn't waste her energy on figuring out what shocked her.

"If it'll buy you an extra day or two, I'll die for you, Solas. It'll be an honor." The woman behind Elyon rolled her eyes at his pledge.

"No." Forcing her gaze off the woman, she snuggled into Loki's chest, her head spinning with the slight movement. "My father—"

"I heard everything you both said. I felt a little of what he put you through. I know He tried to kill you and our child." Loki stood and settled her more securely in his arms. "The bastard declared motherfucking *war*."

Solas hadn't seen him like this, all fire, fierceness, and deadly intent. She trailed her fingers along his jaw.

So sexy.

"No time for that, angel," he said, proving he wasn't even trying to block her thoughts. A grin toyed at the edges of his mouth. "Vy, Elyon, join us."

"We have little time to save Soki," she said as he carried her out of the dungeon.

He scowled at her. "Who the fuck is Soki?"

"Our son. You didn't like Loki junior, so I mixed our names." Simple enough. It wasn't her final choice, but she suspected she wouldn't be involved in the naming, and she had to call him something for now.

"Your savagery might be legendary"—*what else did he hear of my thoughts?*—"but you're terrible at names." She bit back a laugh at his sour grimace. "I veto Soki, and probably everything else you suggest. Let me handle his name."

Like you handle everything else.

"Yes." He settled her on their bed and slid the backs of his knuckles along her cheek. "Rest."

"Not until the baby's safe."

"Give Father what He wants, and the baby'll be fine," Elyon said as he entered the room.

"He wants her too." The unrestrained violence coming off Loki was severe. "Do you suggest we roll over and just hand her over to Him too?"

Eylon didn't back down from Loki's stare. "Of course not."

"I gave Loki those items to protect him and the baby. I won't return them to Father." Solas glared at Elyon as she pushed up into a sitting position. "He gave us a timeframe, Loki, and that's *if* he doesn't renege on the time. He's not a fair player."

"Neither am I."

Well, yeah, the obvious there. Loki, the infamous trickster. If he didn't have something up his sleeve, she'd be disappointed.

"Your father has access to our progeny only because he's inside you." She nodded and palmed her belly, hating that it was her womb that made him vulnerable. "The seer verified Suriel could serve as surrogate. Inside her he'll be safe, under my protection, and inaccessible to your bastard parent."

Surprised, she widened her eyes. "She agreed to this?"

He shrugged. "She didn't disagree."

Solas could depend on Suriel. As a guardian, she was a protector by nature, and she'd been loyal to Solas since her birth. She would never betray their child. Any creature crafted from the Seeds and Chalice would be a wild card. "Okay."

His eyebrows flashed upward as if her acquiescence surprised him. "Once he's safe inside your sister, you swore you would do whatever I wanted."

"Don't give him that power." Elyon crossed his arms over his chest and glowered at Loki. "Let me kill him for you and end this now."

"Killing him won't end our fate, Elyon. You know this." She peered at Loki, knowing he plotted something. But she'd sworn to submit to him. She'd only ever broken one vow, the one that left her dying now, but she wouldn't break this one to her husband. "I vow on my tainted soul, Loki, *I swear* I will do *anything* you want so long as Soki lives."

Vy laughed. "He'll get picked on if you name him that." At Loki's sharp, annoyed glance she shrugged unapologetically. "He'll deserve the teasing."

Without a thought behind her actions, Solas flung a feather, nailing the other woman in the shoulder, with only the tip peeking out. Vy stumbled backward from the blow, coming up short and steady on her feet only because Elyon grabbed her arm. The woman clasped the feather and screeched when she couldn't tug it free.

Vy sent her an accusing glare, and Solas mocked the woman's offhand shrug with one of her own. "Hormones," she explained away her violence.

Unholy fury smoldered in Vy's eyes, making them glow. Solas held her gaze, daring the other woman to challenge her position.

Loki sighed. "When this is over I'm putting you in anger management classes."

"I'm not angry, just reminding the help what speaking freely can get her when her jest is directed toward my offspring."

"Crazy bitch!" Vy continued to pull on the feather, and it remained lodged.

"If you thought that was crazy, you really don't want to see me when I am. I'd suggest you quit struggling or the barbs will dig in. Let it alone, and it'll eventually work itself out like a thorn in a *bitch's* paw."

"*Focus*. Our son requires our attention." Loki jammed his fingers through his hair.

Scolded, Solas nodded. Yeah, she had to get her temper under control until the baby was safe. For a moment, she experienced pity for Loki because she wasn't making things easy for him. She slid her hand into his and squeezed, drawing his gaze.

"Was there any toxin in the feather?"

She shook her head. "She'll live."

His thumb swirled in her palm. "Bly."

Summoned, Loki's man appeared. Bly executed a fist bump with Vy and then grimaced at the feather.

"Bly, bring me Suriel."

Bly departed and returned in a matter of seconds, Suriel at his side.

Her sibling came straight to Solas and crawled into bed beside her. "What happened?"

"No time for explanations," Loki said, his tone unforgiving. "It's time to move the baby to you, Suriel."

Suriel sat a Solas' side and rested her head on Solas' shoulder.

Tilting her head to lean on the top of Suriel's, Solas grabbed her sister's hand and laced their fingers together. "You'll make a better mother than I ever would have."

She met Loki's gaze as he leaned over them and placed a hand on both their stomachs. Those godly eyes met hers for a heartbeat. A soft, but surprised chuckle departed his lips, and she palmed his cheek and trailed her thumb along his lips.

Loki explained his humor. "He's resisting the transfer. He doesn't want to leave you, wife. Seems he already loves you too."

Too?

She jerked her gaze to his, but he closed his eyes hiding from her inquisition as a slight frown lined his forehead and he focused on saving their son. *My little miracle, I've no idea how you were possible.* With a sharp, squall of protest rebounding in her head, he left her for the safety of her sister's womb. Solas almost wept when she felt the little one shift.

Realizing feathers littered the mattress, she dropped her hand from Loki's face.

It is done. He is safe. Seeing to his wellbeing was all on Loki now. He had more than enough clout to see it done.

"Thank you, Suriel." She squeezed her sister's hand before shifting to lie down beside her on the bed, ignoring the alarming quantity of feathers on either side of her body.

She draped an almost feather-less wing over her sister's stomach. *I love you, my sweet boy.*

Fingers sliding into her hair at the back of her head startled her. She opened her eyes in time to catch Loki's dark head behind her. "Put your wings away, angel." His solid chest nestled against her back, and he curled his arms around her waist once she complied with his request. "Bly, take Suriel to rest. Everyone else, get the fuck out."

Vy shoved Elyon toward the door as Bly lifted Suriel into his arms.

"I can walk," her sister argued.

The rest of their argument left with them. Loki repositioned her so she lay on her back, with him propped up on his side and his hand on her empty belly. "You miss him already?"

She nodded. "I didn't realize how much I felt him until he's gone." Weird since she hadn't known he existed a few hours ago. "I know nothing about children born of creatures like us, Loki." She'd never even seen a pregnant angel, much less an expectant god. "But either touching Soki with our magic bonded us or he grows faster than a human."

He shrugged as if he classified their child's development as an inconsequential event.

"Trust me, this matters. If he progressed similar to a human his heart wouldn't be beating yet, but he's already thinking and feeling if he knew you were moving him to a safer womb." His fingers tightened just enough in her hair for her scalp to protest. "Not twelve hours passed, and Father *knew* he'd been conceived and sent His minions for me. In human terms that's impossible." She'd witnessed enough human pregnancies during her term as watcher to know their rate of progression, and she could sense their development in the mother's womb. "The speed of Soki's progression is relevant."

Loki's eyes fired up with purple, coupled with the hard set of his jaw, let her know he considered her words, but he dismissed her theory with a, "Maybe."

"If you're to protect him, you must be aware of everything related to him."

"Speaking of protecting him, I want you to help me create a new child from the holy relics you gifted me." She opened her mouth to reply, but he settled a finger over her lips. "I'll offer your dad a trade, the creation if He releases you from your soul oath."

"No."

"You promised anything."

"It's wrong. It's innocent like our son. It's—"

"Have you killed children before?"

When she'd been ordered by her father to take their lives, yes. "I didn't enjoy killing them."

"But you did it." She nodded, and he said, "You never balked about slaying them? Not even once?"

"Only with you have I ever refused a command to reap."

"Then why the moral high ground with something that's not even human?"

"I don't know." And she didn't, just knew her knee-jerk reaction was to decline his plan.

"Good thing I secured your promise before you knew my plan." He dragged his hand upward between her breasts to capture her chin in his palm. "You will do this, Solas, and you won't argue with me."

"I can't imagine Father will fall for this trickery. He'll be able to tell it's not our child."

"Have a little faith, angel."

Solas gasped as heat poured from his palm into her chin and slithered along her body.

"Yeah, I realized you liked the way my magic felt when I allowed you to use it to connect with our son."

That'd been a special moment. She'd just learned their child existed, and she'd seeded her magic with his, threading it into her womb in hopes of connecting with their offspring. That's when they'd learned they had a son. But for a heartbeat, the taste of his magic had been so good, she'd almost been distracted by it. "It tastes really good, Loki."

His hold shifted and buried in her hair. "I also realized it's what defeated your father when He attacked. Without it, He would've won. I also know Elyon tried to heal you with his." She gasped when his fingers tightened in her hair. "He ever tries to get intimate with you like that again, I'll pluck all his goddamn feathers."

Loki settled his mouth over hers discharging his magic into her as his tongue met hers. Solas arched against him, grasping at his shoulders as implausible pleasure turned her into a gasping mess of ecstasy. Manna had never tasted this good.

"Shit, woman." He tore his mouth from hers as he moved over her and settled between her thighs. "Sharing my magic with you is more intoxicating than I imagined."

She didn't know how he was intoxicated when she was the one getting the magic infusion. Seriously, she'd been roughly two breaths from climaxing just off his mojo.

Her clothes vanished—he seemed to always be undressing her—and he clutched her hips with his hands. The leather of his pants caused a multitude of contrasts... naked and clothed, vulnerable and powerful, god and reaper, free man and condemned woman.

"Are you my wife? My woman?" His thumbs swirled over her hipbones, and she looked at his face. The magic of his godhood was reflected in his eyes, proof the heat slithering through her body wasn't just lust.

"Yes. I'll only ever be yours."

"Because you think you're dying?"

"Because I love you, Loki."

Loki's gaze crashed into hers. His nostrils flared, and his lips parted, a slight hiss seeping from between them.

She hadn't expected a declaration back, but she'd anticipated something more than *that* reaction. *Knowing him, he thinks I have some trickery up my sleeve.*

Solas lifted her arm from the mattress and settled her hand between her legs, drawing his gaze. Dampening her fingers in her arousal the way he'd shown her, she drew her fingers to her clitoris and circled the nub. "Fuck me, Loki."

"You need to rest." But his gaze remained locked between her legs.

"I'd rather die with you inside me than go out without *living* my last few hours."

"Do you trust me, angel?"

Curious where that question came from, she hesitated a moment. "Yes. More than I've ever trusted anyone."

I don't trust I'll approve of his method in warring against my father.

Loki removed her hand from between her legs and kissed her wet fingertips. He lowered over her, using his weight to press her into the bed, but he remained clothed, so she knew he rejected her request to fuck her. Dissatisfaction burned through her as his other hand went into her hair again, as if to immobilize her, while the one holding her hand laced their fingers together. His next kiss deluged her with magic.

Bliss slammed into her, and she arched to get closer to him. Solas climaxed, and Loki swallowed her cry, his mouth never leaving hers as she crashed with pleasure, his eyes locked tight on hers.

Loki lifted his head, severing the kiss, all the while his power continued to enter her. A connection blossomed between them. Another orgasm approached, and she dug her nails into his shoulders.

He dragged his lips along her cheek and whispered against her ear. "With *this* you're forever mine."

Why'd that sound more like a pledge than a claim of ownership? Like a commitment that'd—

Solas shattered so hard her vision darkened, and she forgot about the vow-sounding words.

"Stop fighting me." His power came faster, harder, as if he fucked her with firm, solid strokes. "Open and let me in."

Was he crazy? She wasn't fighting him. He was forcing her to take his power, and she hadn't thought to reject him once. She'd asked him to fuck her, so he could come into her anytime he wanted.

Solas went over again, forgetting to breathe. He drove her higher, and the fourth climax was sharper, almost painful... but she felt a piece of herself give way, as if she opened the door to something magical.

"That one put the color back in your cheeks." The whisper touch of his fingertips trailed across her cheeks. "One more, Solas."

She thought she shook her head, to tell him she didn't have it in her, but her limbs were heavy with too much indulgence, and she couldn't be sure she'd managed to move. He rolled to his back, catching her thighs in the process, and drawing her over him. With her face mashed against his neck, she curled her fingers in his hair and pulled until he hissed. He quickly arranged her posture and forced her to straddle his pelvis. His fingers tightened on her hips, and he thrust into her.

"*Loki.*" His penetration amid his power circulating her system, it was too much and not enough.

"Let's finish it."

"Finish what?" *Dying?* Because she was sure she was one climax away from being done for. *Best way ever to go out.*

He chuckled, and she knew he'd heard her thoughts. As he thrust into her, his movements slow, his power fast, he said, "I give you *me*, Solas. It's the only thing of real value I have."

Heat bloomed between her breasts, and she could feel his emotion. Startled by that new connection, she took a moment to filter through his emotions, but fear that she'd reject him and what he offered her with this joining batted at her heart. Fear that she'd uttered words of love only to betray him later. Someone had done a real number on him. *Or a lot of self-righteous bastard gods to be exact.*

Breath catching, she inhaled. *He joins us in matrimony the way the old gods did it.* It would blend their souls, while giving her a conduit to power. *His* power would be accessible to her. That's why she already felt more energetic and less weak. He truly was giving her a piece of him. And yet he gave her this while doubting her.

Agitated by his distrust, she lifted her head. His eyes were closed as if he concentrated on thrusting into her. She yanked on his hair again, snagging his attention enough he opened his eyes. "I love you, Loki. If you ever doubt it again, I'll stab you with my feathers until you believe me."

His eyes darkened a touch, his magic spiking. "You're promising bloodshed. I know you're feeling better now." Ignoring her declaration, he gave her shoulders a little nudge. "I shouldn't have to do all the work. Ride me."

His doubt plagued her, but she rode him, movements unhurried even when he attempted to speed her up, she was intent on drawing out their pleasure.

"More," she said, indulging in the taste of his magic as she *took it* from him… and he let her.

"Feeling you is intoxicating."

Solas knew he meant her emotions, her feelings, and the experience of him inside her because she could feel a touch of what he felt too. She struggled to block his sensations before she collapsed in one non-stop orgasm. His magic-infused thumb slid over her clit, and she shattered. Loki pulled her beneath him, pounding into her until he released inside her, wrenching another climax from her.

Once she was able to move, she clasped his face between her palms and kissed him, leaning up a little. She felt her wings droop from their position inside her, but ignored the slight sting in favor of what she had to say.

Against Loki's lips she said, "I do, husband. All that you are is mine, all that is mine is yours."

TWENTY-TWO

"*M*otherfucker!" Loki growled and rolled out of bed. The moment Solas lifted enough for her wings to be exposed, he caught the way they tore away from her back. Fury slashed through him, and agony for the suffering she would experience at their imminent loss. Trying to contain his emotions and not disrupt the planet was like trying to swim out of an undertow.

"What's wrong?" When Solas pushed up further, she flinched in pain, her discomfort obvious as she attempted to peer over her shoulder.

"Don't look, angel." He could barely look himself. Her flesh opened where her wings attached to her body, the gaping wound sickening him. "Bly!" Loki paced the floor at the end of the bed, stabbing his fingers through his hair.

"Y-yes?" Bly stammered at the sight of Solas' back turned in his direction.

She clutched the sheet against her breasts, and Loki commanded, "Bring Suriel."

Bly reappeared with Suriel in a snap, and Loki swung around to meet his first in command's gaze. Suriel must have seen or sensed her sister's condition because she ran to the bed. Thinking on her feet, Suriel tore the purple silk material into an Egyptian style sari similar to what the ancients wore in scriptures and wrapped the base of Solas' wings and flesh. The softness of the silk would be gentle against his angel's skin, and the length of the material provided enough cloth to cover the open wound. Even with the horrid sight of Solas' wings detaching wrapped and concealed from his view, he could still see the image in his head and feel his angel's sorrow.

The room vibrated with Loki's power, the walls bulging out and pulling inward as if mimicking his breathing. "That motherfucker dared touch her wings!" With his words, his power expanded with a jolt, shattering the glass around the room and throwing the furniture against the walls. The bed his angel lay on was the only piece untouched by his rage. "*I* made those wings—not *Him*. And He dares to rip them from her body? God will be dammed for this."

"Loki..." Solas' voice sounded far away. So far away, he knew his rage threatened to overtake his rational side. "*Loki*."

Turning a tilted glare her way, he noticed Suriel clutched Solas' waist while his angel consoled her, patting her sibling's back. He hadn't meant to scare the woman temporarily carrying his child, but he wouldn't apologize for his fury either, even though Solas gawped at him with what he interpreted as indecision and incredulity. Despite his lack of verbal remorse, he experienced guilt for putting Solas through more than she already dealt with.

"We move on with our plans. *Now!*" He held out his hand to silence Solas when she opened her mouth to speak. "Now is when you do as I say."

Storming from the room, he felt Bly at his heels. "I don't want to hear—"

"Loki, you're also my friend."

"Friends don't stand in the way, Bly."

His first in command had the balls to place his palm on Loki's shoulder and halt his movements just inside the ritual room. "I'm not standing in your way. I've always been on your side." Bly avoided his gaze and removed his hold from Loki. "I just want you to slow down for a minute and collect yourself. Your woman is losing her wings, the foundation of her identity."

"With them goes her magic." And he knew her life would leave her soon afterward.

"Losing them cannot be easy to endure even if she knew it was coming." Bly scratched the back of his head. "Being strong for her and presenting a calm manner, even if you don't feel it, will go a long way in soothing her, supporting her, Loki."

"I'm— " Loki moved further into the room, running his finger along the marble altar in the center of the room, thankful for his friend's logic and willingness to go toe to toe with him and talk him down from his rage. "I can't kill Him, Bly."

Bly shook his head in agreement but held his tongue.

"Being unable to protect her pisses me off." That failure had him feeling powerless, and he wasn't comfortable with that diminished capacity.

In his silence, Loki accepted Bly's loyalty and reflected on the words Bly hadn't said, but he knew his first waited for him to acknowledge. No, he couldn't kill the most powerful god in the universe, and that revelation made his gut sink. The only way to *Him* was through His people—to overthrow Him. If he could turn His followers against Him, have them rage against their maker, he'd have a chance, but that would take centuries. He'd thought they'd had a certain kind of truce for a long while. In lieu of outright war, God would send someone to kill him, Loki'd defeat them, and then a couple decades later He'd try again.

Until Solas. Until his child.

"I heard Solas speak of this sword Michael carries, the god-killer. What if—"

Loki cut him off. "God crafts everything with a safety imprinted in its creation. Solas' blade can't cut her, so I'd assume the god-killer can't kill Michael or its creator."

"But Suriel told me Solas used her blade to cut her hand, drawing her blood to mark Sephora."

Loki's gaze snapped to Bly. "Indeed." The difference came down to intent, and during the marking of Sephora the intent had not been to harm but to craft a spell. "Maybe we've found a loophole."

"I can research the sword, ask around."

"We need to move forward with my plans to save Solas."

"Your child is safe, Loki."

"My wife isn't!"

"You'd risk your life, your throne, for Solas?" Bly palmed the back of his neck, reservation in his gaze. "I understand the risks in saving your son, but your wife..." His first looked away, as if embarrassed by his distrust of Loki's motives when it came to Solas.

"You think I'm acting out of ego." The revelation didn't surprise him. Why wouldn't Bly question his reasoning when his ego often ruled his emotions? Never had Loki protected another that wasn't part of his Naglfar, nor had he ever put another before his own safety. Many had been sacrificed to ensure his survival. Sure, he'd saved Bly's life a couple times, but that had been in the middle of battle. He'd never invited unnecessary trouble into his life. No, his first in command had only seen him take what he wanted and manipulate others to do his bidding, but he'd never demonstrated love.

"I'm in love with her, Bly. I'd die for her." Bly's gaze snapped to Loki's. A mixture of unspoken emotion ran through Bly's expression, but Loki thought he saw hope in his eyes. But hope for what? There was no time to delve into his first's reaction though. "Gather the fallen outside the perimeter of this room. Tell no one of our plans."

When Bly disappeared, Loki walked the circular chamber. The shape of the room provided magical protection, keeping things out during a ritual and enhancing magical power. The sphere form was also in the tradition that everything comes full circle. The past ceremonies Loki had performed in this room all benefitted him. But something about the one he'd do momentarily didn't sit well with him. The seer had stated his plan had a price, and as much as Loki tried to bury those words, they ticked inside him like a countdown to something unknown.

"The fallen are assembled."

"Very good. You know what to do."

"Yes. They'll use their magic around the outside of the room as an added protection for you. All their wings will touch to form a circle as you instructed."

Loki clasped his hands behind his back, a slight hesitation at the thought of what he was about to do. Even if he was known as a heartless bastard on top of being a trickster, what would happen next was a decision he hadn't made lightly. "I'll go collect my wife."

Appearing in his room, his eyes landed on Solas. Her back was to him as she stood in front of the mirror staring at herself, an expression of sorrow reflected from the jagged fragment of glass that remained in the frame. Wrapped in lose, purple silk, his angel was breathtaking even when she frowned.

"It's time." Loki cupped her elbow, but she avoided his gaze.

"I know." Solas stared at his chin not meeting his gaze, and it tore at him that she still wasn't fully on board with his plan.

Would she ever be able to fully trust him?

Before he changed his mind and let her cripple his will, he relocated them into the ritual room. Solas spun, taking in her surroundings. When her black eyes turned to him, she silently pleaded with him to alter his plan. He wanted to do nothing more than give her the world and every little thing she desired, and her unspoken plea threatened to soften his resolve.

"Loki—"

Knowing she'd argue his plot to trick her father, he cut her off. "You promised."

"I know."

She still tried to uphold the will of her father. This is what weighed on her? Not her life. Smoothing the tips of his fingers over the marble in an attempt to soothe his jagged mood, Loki tilted his head and met her imploring gaze. "How could you still be so goddamn faithful to *Him?*"

"It's a life, Loki. It will breathe and have a heartbeat. It's an innocent." Wings trembling as if a sudden chill blew over her, Solas embraced herself in a manner that he interpreted as her attempting to soothe away her doubt of what was about to happen. "What if we're wrong about this?"

"There isn't anything wrong in protecting what's mine!" He slammed his fist against the stone, the room shaking with his fury.

Solas swallowed hard, her eyes glazing with a watery shine. "Father's Word says, *do nothing, and know that I am.*"

How could her life mean so little to her? She would break him if she continued to resign herself to *His* will. He'd stop everything just to remove the moisture from her eyes. He'd have to harden himself so they could move forward and he could save her life. "The contradicting bastard also says He helps those who help themselves." Loki flipped his hand in the air, the Chalice and Seeds appeared in his palm. "I'm helping myself."

"He'll feel you move them." Solas stared at the objects with wide eyes.

"The room protects us, and I have the fallen outside blocking any probe in, or magic out." He kissed her nose before putting the cup in the center of the marble. "Call your blade, angel." At her hesitation, he growled, "*Now*, wife."

Solas called for the weapon. She squeezed the hilt of her blade and held it tightly between her breasts.

Loki ran his fingers through the seeds he'd spilled in his palm. "They look like colorful gems, should we pick a certain color?"

"I don't know what the colors mean." Solas pulled her hand away as if afraid she'd accidentally touch the seeds.

"Elyon has blue tips to his wings." Loki pushed the color that matched Elyon's wings to the side and then fingered the black seed. "Your color, angel."

Solas cupped her hand under his and leaned in to look at the seeds, her curiosity filtering into his mind. With ease, he discerned from her that she'd never seen the seeds before, not even from a distance. They were beautiful, and a handful of treasure a pirate would be envious of, the reds, greens, and the purest of white crystal. This is how God created Solas and so many of Loki's warriors.

"I can't pick, Loki, please don't ask this of me."

"Fuck." *Why can't she see this is best for our family?* Her guilt grated on his last nerve. "Don't worry, angel. I'll take on the sin." Loki closed his eyes and selected a second seed. Not looking at the color, he palmed it tight. "Ready your blade to spill your blood."

A shiver raked through Solas as she gripped the handle tight enough her knuckles turned white. Loki grabbed her hand and pried her fingers open. The black seed was as black as her hair and without looking at the seed in his palm he overlapped their hands, making sure her blade rested between them along with the two seeds. "What I do now I do to protect you and our child. And I vow with every feather that has fallen from your wings that I will conquer your attacker." With his words, he pulled the blade through their palms to spill their blood. Once their blood mingled and dripped into the chalice, Loki opened their hands, dropping the blood-soaked seeds inside the chalice. The seeds glowed instantly with a blue and white halo. The light throbbed as if it had a heartbeat. Loki took the pulsations as a sign that the seeds had formed a creature.

"Ready, angel?"

"No."

Ignoring her trembling lips, Loki levitated the glowing seeds, hovering it just above Solas' stomach. His pause was enough time to make his gut sick with his actions, but he reminded himself why he was doing this. Why he was impregnating his wife with a creature crafted from his blood, but not by his seed. No, he wouldn't feel bad about his choice. For once, he tried to save someone other than himself. Although one could argue his actions were still selfish. He couldn't live without this woman by his side.

I'm dying.

Her words in his head served as the catalyst that pushed his hands forward until the seeds vanished through her flesh. Her stomach glowed with the creation. A blue light enveloped her belly, fading into a white hue until it disappeared inside her, expanded her stomach and then settled into silence.

"It's done." Loki touched the Chalice and Seeds, making them vanish. A somber mood filled the room, but he didn't dare look at Solas. He should have done this before he shared a piece of himself with her because feeling her emotions now wasn't sitting well with him.

"Can I go now?" Even her tone raked over him like nails on a chalkboard.

"You have guilt over this—*still*?"

"Why shouldn't I, Loki? We've created a life that will be destroyed. All life is precious."

"Unless the fucked-up ideology of your father deems it not—then you'd kill this precious life. Right?"

"That's not fair!"

"Is it not? Do you think my decision to do this wasn't hard?" He shoved his fingers through his hair and pinned her with a stare. "I do not feel bad about what we did. I did it to save you."

"I take the consequences of my actions with honor. I don't need saving, Loki. I damn sure don't require an innocent life dying to *save me*!"

In the face of her anger, rage engulfed him once more. Her father was more of a master at manipulation than Loki had ever been. "You feel so guilty you think you need to be punished." He shook his head in disbelief as her emotions passed through him. When she would've walked away from him, Loki grabbed her arm and spun her to meet his gaze. "That's it, isn't it?" Staring at her in disbelief, he searched her eyes and hoped he was wrong, but the truth wasn't only in her gaze, he felt it through their connection. "You believe your punishment is death. That it's a justified penance. And you've resigned to it." He pushed her away as if she burned him. "*Fucking Christ.*" He could only shake his head, stunned by the revelation.

"No, fuck you, Loki! Stay out of my head and out of my emotions." She spun to flee, and he grabbed her, pinning her to the wall. "Just save my son."

"*Our* son," he growled. Her guilt pissed him off beyond his control. She cared nothing for her own life, while securing everyone else's, even his. He'd had enough of this bullshit. Bending to her ear, he bit the lobe. The anger in his tone made his voice vibrate as he spoke. "You feel you need to be punished, angel, I've got just the thing for you, but your death is out of the question."

Loki relocated them to the dungeon, using his magic to immediately bind her. Solas yanked her shackled hands the moment she realized the restraints held her captive. With her arms secured high above her head, there wasn't much movement to allow for a struggle.

"*Loki.*" His name served as a warning through teeth clinched so hard he feared they'd shatter.

"Oh, no, angel. I'll no longer tolerate your guilt. This will end now."

"You've no authority over my guilt." She glared at him, eyes narrowed as she tugged on the cuffs, a subtle hint that she demanded immediate freedom.

Mocking her claim, he elevated an eyebrow. "I'm your husband. You're the mother of our son. Your mental health is *very much* within my authority."

"Release me."

"No."

"I've killed too many; someone has to pay for those sins."

"Your father ordered the hits. Payment for those sins is on *His* shoulders, not yours." He slid his fingers along her cheek and tucked hair behind her ear. "Your fall redeemed your soul of those transgressions."

"Please understand, Loki, I'm a killer, not a mother, not a wife, but a monster who *loves* to kill." Her tone pleaded with him to understand. "I bring nothing of value to the table. You both deserve better than me, would be better off without me."

"You're wrong." That she even believed this staggered him. She had awakened him, brought laughter to his life, and given him unconditional love and a son—two things no one had ever given him. Not even his mother. Solas made him stronger, but she undervalued her role in his life.

"You're letting your dick talk. When I'm gone, you'll find another willing pussy to fuck, and you'll forget all about me."

She has no idea I love her. How could she not feel their connection?

Holding her steely-eyed gaze, he stripped them both with the snap of his fingers, leaving her injured wings wrapped in the purple silk. He tugged the material down just enough her ample breasts spilled out, and the fabric worked in his favor anchoring the globes high. Were this moment about their pleasure, he would've shown her how much he appreciated the positioning of her breasts.

Sliding his hand across her stomach, caused her muscles to flex beneath his caress as Loki walked around her, and halted behind her. A white tube materialized in Loki's palm, the shiny lube inside coated his fingers when he squeezed it. "You will expunge that Christian guilt your father has brainwashed you with since your creation."

"I am warning you, Loki." Solas might've growled, but he detected the excitement in her tone. "Release me."

"And I am warning you, angel." Circling his finger around her dark entrance, Loki grappled with his emotions. A part of him wanted to punish her until she forgot her guilt, but she was the only one who could release her self-reproach. A task he could only assist her in doing. The tip of his finger nudged against the tight muscle refusing him entrance. "It will hurt if you deny me, a pain I think you want, angel. Isn't that what punishment is all about?" One wet digit entered her snug channel, and she tensed against his intrusion while her body lit with excitement.

"Goddamn it, Loki!"

"Ah, thou Father's name in vain. That's a start." He brought his palm down on her ass, the abrupt slap stung his palm, and she squealed in surprise. He hit her again as he pumped his finger inside her ass. As much as he wanted to play with her clit, trail kisses down her spine, he knew this wasn't for him, not fully, but was about punishing her for her perceived sins so she could accept life.

Every one of her offenses against her parent came with pain. The loss of her wings, kicked out of her homeland, her crash to earth, alone, afraid, wholly unprepared to live as a human. And those were the reprimands he knew about.

Am I the only one who has ever shown her compassion?

Loki added another finger and pushed fast and deep. A sharp hiss erupted from her lips, and gooseflesh paraded across her skin. Any other time he'd have penetrated her slow, given her body time to adjust to enjoy the dark pleasures of anal sex, but she required more than a seduction, so he pumped his digits vigorously until sweat beaded on her skin. Beautiful beads his tongue ached to lick away.

Thrusting his fingers into her, he kept the pace steady as he cracked his palm on her bottom over and over again, admiring the way her flesh grew rosy beneath his punishment. After she'd taken his fingers for a good thirty minutes, although she warmed to his invasion and his whacks, she still fought him emotionally. Rebellious, taut muscles in her arms made him proud of her because she was a fighter and he'd expect no less from her. Her defiance cracked his intent because he never wanted to break her character, and he loved her spirit. "My strong angel. Beautiful in every way."

His palm came down on her ass cheek again, harder, the need to plunge his dick deep, fast, and hard inside her built in him until he struggled to control his base desires. But then he thought of her willingness to give up, to die because she believed she was unworthy, and he rained smacks against her bottom until she no longer tensed before each blow, but welcomed the sting.

He needed her to have the will to live, to fight for *their* future. He wouldn't allow her to die. He'd punish her until she believed she deserved happiness.

"Are you done playing, husband?" The tenor of her voice sounded mocking to someone who didn't know her, but he heard the false bravado in the pitch.

"Not quite, angel." Loki slid his fingers from inside her and rubbed the head of his cock against her readied entrance.

"You will not take me there, Loki."

"No, angel, I won't." Threading his fingers through her hair, he pulled her head back, kissed along her neck to her ear. "*You* are going to take me in your sweet ass and embrace the punishment you think you need."

Seeing the hesitation burning from her eyes, Loki bucked his hips just enough to threaten her with penetration. The air in the room thickened as he felt her emotions battle him. A war brewed inside her. His deviant cock swelled to a painful thickness at being this close to her ass. He'd threatened her

with anal several times. The urge to take her sweetly there had \
stopped him each time, and now he used it as therapeutic
healing. Maybe he needed this just as much as she did. "Arch
your ass back and take me, angel."

He expected a denial as his rapid breaths matched hers, but
she surprised him by curving her hips backward and the head
of his cock slipped past the tight ring of muscles.

"*Ow!*" Solas screeched and would've jerked away if he
hadn't caught her hips and halted her retreat.

"That's it, angel... feel the burn. Take more of me."
Rubbing circles over her lush, rounded globe with one hand,
his fingers dug into her flesh with the other. "More, wife."

Even as she shook her head, Solas arched back and took
more of his length, lifting on her toes, only to slide his cock
out and lose the inch she'd just gained. Loki palmed the dip in
her back and pushed her downward. "Feet flat, angel, and take
it... take my cock."

"Loki." Her tone had changed, a crack in her voice left an
ache inside his chest. Sliding his hand up her skin, over the
silky feel of her back, across her shoulder, and to her face, he
brushed his thumb across her cheek. Wetness coated his digit.

"No more guilt, Solas." His palm cracked across her ass,
and she bucked backward, swallowing the full length of his
cock. "*Fuck.*" Loki shuddered. The tight channel choking his
dick had his seed rushing to the head of his shaft. He fought
his immediate release as he stilled them both. "How does that
feel, angel?"

"It burns."

"That's what you do to me, Solas." Kissing her shoulder,
he pulled her head back to press a kiss against her lips. "Daily.
I burn inside for you. Obsessed with having you, not just in
my bed but in my darkened heart."

Why? She didn't speak the question, and even if he hadn't
heard the thought in her head, he'd have seen the question in
her eyes.

"I'm in love with you, angel. Can't you feel it?" Her eyes widened at his confession, but he didn't give her time to process the admission. Instead, he continued his lesson and moved inside her, drawing forth another sharp hiss from her. "How do you think it makes me feel when you have guilt for wanting to live?" The thought had his hands grasping her hips and plunging deep into her. She cried out at his brutality, but he was connected with her so he knew the pain was more of a stinging pleasure now. Ignoring her response, he smacked her ass hard, adding to the burn in his palm and her cheek. "That you have guilt for loving me?" Another thrust of his hips ripped a scream from her lips, but the sound was much different from the first one. This cry was infused with something different, deeper, and much darker—pleasure in pain—and he felt her response all the way to his balls.

"I'm bound to you in every conceivable way. Take my cock, wife, take my emotions, feel the sinful burn of *me* inside of you, and punish yourself for loving me." Did his voice crack on the last word? His guard was down, and Solas' feelings rushed into him, evidence that she could also feel his deepest emotions.

With her head thrown against his shoulder, their cheeks scrubbed against one another. Her panting was heavy as Solas pumped back against him fucking his cock with a violence only she could yield. Loki felt her tears on his cheek—heard her internal cries, and it shattered him that she endured such guilt.

"Don't you dare come."

"Can't... stop."

Loki gripped her throat, his fingers digging hard into her chin. She continued to punish herself with his cock, impaling herself in a mindless fashion, her brain a warm buzz along his, as she fought to achieve the pinnacle of pleasure.

He dropped his other hand to her abdomen, stopping the rough backward jerking of her hips. With him buried deep inside her, she gave a frustrated groan at his halting touch. He smacked her pussy, and her eyes jerked open on a startled gasp. Their gazes locked.

"Punishment doesn't come with pleasure." He dragged his thumb along her bottom lip and gave her another swat, this one directly over her clit. Solas flinched, her mouth parted on a scandalized gulp, eyes wide as if shocked by his abuse... and wondrous over her indulgence in the reprimand. His girl *liked* the pain. He wouldn't call her a pain-slut, but it was obvious she found enjoyment in the chastisement. Next time he was inside her ass, he'd fuck her pussy with his fingers and give her the sensation of double penetration. Watching her come undone with both holes filled... he shook the thoughts aside before he forgot to finish his lesson.

Despite having halted her movements, he could feel her desire as if it were his own. Unless he did something soon she'd come regardless what he commanded, and it wouldn't matter that he'd smacked her pussy to stop her climax. So... he used his magic and eliminated her approaching orgasm.

She whimpered her frustration, the word "*please*," falling from her lips as a raspy moan.

It killed him to punish her this way. Loki loved making her come, and it didn't help that he was left with a throbbing cock in the tightest ass he'd ever had the pleasure of fucking and a wife begging him with her eyes to let her shatter. But pleasure didn't play a role in discipline.

"You'll leave your guilt in this room."

"Yes," she whispered. "Anything you want." She was so far gone she'd have said whatever he wanted in that moment.

"For the next day every time you move, or sit, you'll feel the ache of my cock and the burn of my palm on your ass. You'll remember that there is *no* guilt in love."

Solas blinked, tears shimmering in her eyes, and he felt the weight of her guilt drop away, relieving him. "No guilt in loving you, Loki."

"No guilt in being gifted a husband and son that loves you. No guilt in being gifted *life*." Because she'd not lived before her fall, just been a pet for her father to order about.

I want that, she didn't say the words but her thoughts slithered into his mind. *Want to hold my son, want to kill by my husband's side.*

A grin twitched at his lips as relief surged through him. Loki released his tight hold on her. She could hide behind words, but not her thoughts.

Sliding his palms up her arms, he used his magic to briefly open the shackles and placed his hands over hers, laced their fingers, and bound them body, mind and soul. "Then fuck me until you shatter."

He'd expected her to take him a little slower, but as she held his gaze she moved her hips, fucking him like a nymphomaniac deprived of cock for far too long. With his dick nursing her tight ass, Loki didn't last long. When he came with a savage yell he pushed his power inside her, infusing her with strength. His angel shattered in his arms, crying out as their climaxes mixed and jerked them along a turbulent river of bliss.

It took a while for his body to stop humming with pleasure. The discomfort in his shoulders jerked him from the hedonism. Loki removed them from bondage and slumped to the floor with her wrapped in his arms.

Nuzzling her nose with his, he said, "I can live with you feeling guilty for loving me, but please don't feel guilty for wanting to live."

Avoiding his gaze, she pulled at the hair on his forearm. "I feel guilty for being a weakness that will get you and our son hurt. If I can't be strong for you, then I don't deserve either one of you."

He cursed under his breath and repositioned her in his lap, drawing her against his chest, tucking her head beneath his chin. "You are *not* a weakness. I am a god, Solas, I would never have a weak woman by my side. We have a dilemma. It's made you weak, yes, but you have to want to fight, angel, not resign to dying. Do we have a deal?"

"On one condition." She tilted her head back as she slid a finger along his cheek and smiled. "I get a daily Loki-gasm"

"Are you sure you're not part succubus?" Her smile at his teasing faded, and she grabbed her head, pain rolling across her features. "What is it?"

"The baby!" She clutched closed fists against her head.

"Do you want it out?" He placed his hands over her stomach, and she shook her head violently.

"Not that one. Ours!" The fingers of her fisted hand by her temples eased, and the color came back to her tips. "He's communicated that there is something coming."

With a snap of his fingers, they were fully clothed and ready for battle, just in time for Bly, Suriel, Vy, and Elyon to appear in the room.

"We've got hostile company incoming." Bly had already drawn his sword.

No one knew the whereabouts of Loki's cavern except for a few of his chosen warriors. "The Naglfar have come?"

"No." Bly shook his head. "Michael."

TWENTY-THREE

*J*ust the utterance of Michael's name had Solas kicking into combat mode. Her brother would kill everyone before he departed. Her sibling never left witnesses behind. Innocence made no difference when the bystander could be used to confess his tactics. But Solas knew everything about him, how he fought, how he cheated, but worst of all... she'd not ever watched him lose.

All Solas could think about was the safety of her family. She'd advise Loki to run, but she knew that suggestion would court disaster. But if she couldn't save her husband, she could protect her child. Looking Bly straight in the eyes, she said, "Get Suriel to safety."

"We need him to win this," Loki argued.

"If we fail"—'and die' remained unsaid—"*our son* will need him more."

"Take her." Loki didn't so much as blink in Bly's direction but maintained his entire focus on Solas. She could read so much in his gaze. Would these be their last moments together? Could they win the battle to come? He loved her, and he'd die to defend her. She had to figure out how to keep him on the breathing side of things.

"But, Loki—"

"*Do it.*" Her husband cut Bly off, his tone not open to argument.

The squeak of Vy's shoes as she shuffled her stance was like the blare of a siren in the silent room. Solas snagged the hesitant glance Elyon flicked between Loki and Bly.

The tension in the near noiseless room was strong enough to ring Solas' ears, while Bly's bitterness felt like a tangible imprint on her skin.

"Only answer *my* call." Loki softened his voice. "Assume everyone else is your enemy."

At Bly's hesitation, she broke Loki's gaze and peered at his man. The need to argue burned in the other man's eyes.

"Bly," she said drawing his attention. "Our child is heir to the Naglfar, he'll need you as much as he'll need Suriel. Sending you with her to protect him is a bigger honor than fighting at Loki's side."

Bly's chin jutted at a challenging angle. "My place has always been at his side."

"It's my time to be at his side."

"But can you get the job done, little reaper? I've yet to see anything but failure from you."

"*Bly.*" Loki barked, his glare hostile. "Disrespecting her is disrespecting me."

"It's okay, Loki. Let him speak his mind." Bly was right. She weakened them all. Why couldn't Loki see that? Solas shook her head, and answered his first in command's challenge. "I honestly don't know. But if we all die today who will take care of Suriel and our son? She's a guardian, a protector, but she's not a fighter." *That makes her better mother material than me.* "Who will teach our child the ways of your people? How to survive? How to fight?" She could've gone on, but it'd have to be enough to win his compliance.

They stared at one another for a long moment, tension thick between them, but she understood his anger. Because of her request, Loki had clipped his wings, and forced him to cower instead of fight at his master's side. Bly handled the moment far better than she would have. Finally, he nodded, and she knew it was the only form of consent she'd receive from him.

Suriel stepped to Solas and offered her dagger. "You know what it'll do. I gift you the power over it. Use it to defeat

Michael and come back to us." Her sister shot Loki a reticent glance. His temper tantrum had hindered his relationship with Suriel. "*Both* of you come back to us."

Solas hesitated, trying to figure out how to refuse the gift without hurting her sister's feelings. If she died, Michael would come for her, and Suriel would need the weapon's aid.

"It'll come back to me when you no longer need it," her sister said as if she could discern Solas' thoughts. Maybe she could. As a guardian, it was her job to predict her charge's next move.

Solas accepted the gold blade, the base of the handle dotted with heavenly crystals, and the metal fiery hot in her palm. "I love you, Suriel. I'm sorry I never told you before today."

"Oh, Sol..." Suriel hugged her tight and whispered in her ear, "I've always known."

With a frustrated scowl, Bly draped his arm around Suriel's shoulders and disappeared with her.

With no time to waste, she tucked Suriel's blade in the waistband of her leather pants. As she stripped out of her shirt and the bindings Suriel had put around her wings to hold them in place, she caught Loki's frown right before she offered him her back. "Remove my wings."

"Fuck no."

She turned just enough to face him, catching the horror of her request in his gaze. "I keep trying to move them. In battle, they'll slow me down, handicap me."

"Gone, they'll handicap you worse." He pummeled his hair with his hands, one right after the other sliding through the thick, dark strands. "Don't ask this of me. I won't. I cannot."

"If you want me to fight to live, then you *have* to do this."

"Is she always this intense?" she heard Vy ask someone, but everyone ignored the woman.

"I cannot maim you like that, angel. I'd rather die."

"They're already crippling me, Loki." This connection between them allowed her to fully comprehend his denial. To shear off her identity would hurt him way more than it'd ever hurt her. "Elyon, you're up."

Loki pointed a finger at Elyon and growled, "I'll pluck all your feathers if you fucking touch her."

Her trickster cupped her face between his palms. "If your wings are gone, so is your magic."

"They're falling off because my power's almost depleted anyway. I'll have a little left, but I can utilize your infinite magic instead." She fisted his shirt and yanked, desperation driving her hard. Her wings hindered her, and they were unusable. Michael would exploit the disadvantage to his advantage. "When they fall off, I'm dead either way. Losing my feathers, losing my wings, it's the ultimate disgrace for my betrayal against Father because they're everything to me. But the joke's on Him. For the first time in my life, you and Soki are *my everything*. He can take my wings, he can take my power, and it won't matter because I've found something more valuable. *You. Soki.* And my emancipation. You two are my *only* reason to live, but in order to have that opportunity I need to be on equal footing with Michael."

Not that she'd ever be on equal footing with Michael. Regardless that she was ranked second right below the *Sword of God* and all angeldom feared her, she couldn't compete with his skills.

"I'm taking that motherfucker on, not you."

"He'll cut us off and engage me alone. I won't stand a chance against him with these." She wiggled her wings and winced at their looseness. "That's how he operates. Taking me down first will weaken you. Trust me, he'll find a way to separate us."

Loki closed his eyes and leaned his forehead against hers, as one of his arms tucked about her shoulders and pulled her against his chest. "When I get my hands on Michael's god-killer, I'll drive it straight through your father's blackened heart."

"It won't kill Father."

"I don't care. I'll have it."

"To possess the god-killer you'll have to kill Michael. It goes to the person who takes his life."

"If I have it, won't that put a kink in His strategy to kill all the gods since I don't follow His bidding?"

Yeah, she couldn't see Loki taking orders from anyone. And losing the weapon would agitate her father.

"Okay." One way or another, she'd make sure the battle ended with Loki in possession of the god-killer. "Take them *now*, Elyon."

A slight sting was all she felt, and then Loki's magic punched her in the chest, drowning out the pain of Elyon's sword slicing through what remained of her wings. The thud of their weight hit the floor. She'd cried the first time, and attempted to crawl from her sibling before he could take the other one. This time, she embraced their loss because it meant she stood half a chance of making a difference for her family.

Loki kissed her lips, a soft, non-sexual kiss. *His* pain over the loss of her wings bothered him a lot more than it did her. She'd meant it when she said she valued Loki and their child above everything. The loss of her wings meant nothing to her when compared to the value of her family.

As his palms ran along the severed lines of her wings, the heat of his healing touch warmed her but not as much as the grit in his eyes. And his love, *Jesus his love,* was a physical touch, a caress, a wall of protection around her heart, repentance for her sins... and a reason to live.

"I'll return them to you when this is over," he said against her lips, "and *no one* will ever remove them again."

I'm in the demi-god's throne room, little sister, if you'd care to join me. Michael's unwanted presence slithered into her mind, ruining her sweet moment with Loki.

"I heard him," Loki said before she could speak. "I don't have a throne room, but let's go kick his teeth in anyway."

Solas took stock of their mini-army. Eleven fallen, along with Vy, Loki, and herself. It wouldn't be enough with the reaper attendance she felt supporting Michael. Identifying them by their imprint, she'd trained most of them. She wasn't just their teacher, but their advisor, and they'd come to take her down. Killing them would hurt, but not as much as having her husband injured would.

Loki called forth her weapon and handed it to her as they strode along the hallway. "Didn't want you expending your magic to retrieve it."

Out of the corner of her eye, she caught Vy doing a double take. Thinking of others must be a novelty for him if his action surprised his second in command.

The purity of his consideration swelled her heart, and she smiled. "Thanks, husband."

Loki surprised her when he allowed her to enter the room first, with him at her back. Inside the circular room, she noted the red-stained floor and walls splattered with the same color. *Blood.*

Her husband's emotions had gone quiet, unnerving her with his ability to block them from her. *At least fifty of my reapers are present.* All efficient at killing, but not skilled enough to defeat her or Loki. Their nervous glances and their indecisiveness told her they all weren't on board with this mission. Certainly, Michael felt their tension? He couldn't be that arrogant, could he?

"Your throne-room décor lacks ambience, trickster." Michael perched on a stone slab, one leg hanging over the ledge, the other bent and his foot anchored on the edge, with his wrist resting on his knee. In his grip was *his* sword, the blade so sharp it was a milky translucent color. The tip pointed toward his foot that swung back and forth.

"Only the pompous—"

"Or dickless," Vy added, and Michael sent her a sharp, irritated glance.

"—require a throne room. This"—Loki made a circular motion with his hand indicating the space, and she felt something lock into place—"is a sacrificial chamber, dumbass."

Michael's foot slid off the slab, and he hopped to his feet, his grip tightening on the hilt of his sword as he glanced about the room. Uncertainty flashed in his gaze, but she doubted anyone but her noticed.

"The room is sealed. *My* command is the key." Loki smirked. "Want to take bets on the *only* way you're getting out of here?"

"Father will open it for me." Her sibling seemed too confident, like he had all the answers, and even knew the outcome.

"He cannot manipulate *my* magic any more than I can His."

"As the one true God, master of the universe, His magic out maneuvers any demi—"

"I'm a god." The grit in Loki's voice resulted in a disdainful grin tugging at her brother's lips.

"Father lied to us, Michael." *He also deceived me about Loki's moral character.* "Ask yourself what else he lied about?"

"It's blasphemous, little sister, to appoint the trickster a higher status than he warrants."

"Believe it. Don't. I don't give a fuck. You'll *know* it soon enough." Why'd she find her trickster's arrogance so sexy?

Michael dismissed Loki and turned his attention to Solas. "No one but you has to die today, Solas."

"You're the only one dying today." Loki palmed the small of her back, his agitation apparent in the swishing of his thumb. She gave him a sidelong glance and spied him gauging the other reapers in the room. "Are you going to talk us to death or engage us?"

"So eager to die, trickster?" Michael lifted his arm, fisted his hand, and executed a twisting motion.

His magic jerked Solas forward straight into his sword. She cried out as the blade penetrated her chest, not stopping until the hilt slammed against her ribs. Movement behind her, feathers shifting and raining about them. A battle had begun. Just as she'd predicted, he'd separated them.

The smell of blood hit her nostrils as Michael elevated his eyebrows. He slowly peeled her fingers from the handle of her weapon, allowing the blade to drop to the floor with a loud clang. "Too easy."

"Telekinesis. That's a new trick."

"Picked it up from a demi-god." Michael smirked. "He was easy pickings too, just like your trickster will be once you're dead."

"Dream on." Inhaling hurt, and she struggled to speak. "He'll bathe in your blood."

Loki's battle-yell echoed in the room, ramming all the reapers against the stone walls and caging them there with ease. For once his magic was under control, and no earthquake rocked them about.

Michael's eyes widened just a fraction. Loki's power obviously surprised him. A mere demi-god didn't have that type of magic. Sure, some demi-gods possessed strength enough to move things with their mind like Michael had just used, but only a god could tame this many reapers at once and with such ease.

Her brother slapped a dagger to her neck, forcing her head to tilt backward. Still believing he had the upper hand, he smiled. "Move another inch closer, trickster, and I'll slice her throat."

Take my magic and live, wife. It was the first time Loki had ever spoken to her mentally. She hadn't even been sure they could speak telepathically. In this moment, she realized he'd simply blocked that avenue of communication.

Solas remained silent, drawing her thoughts and emotions as close to her as she could so they wouldn't distract Loki. She focused on staring into the cold, calculating eyes of her brother, as she curled the fingers of one hand around his holding the base of his sword. As her blood spilled over her hand, she attempted to draw strength from Loki's magic, but Michael's weapon prevented her from chugging the only source of power that'd keep her alive. If Loki realized that, she feared he'd make a reckless move that resulted in his death.

Right now, only her life was on the line. And if she died, she'd make sure Michael went down with her. She still had a thing or two up her sleeve, and she wasn't to ever be dismissed. Her brother knew this better than anyone.

"You've a choice, Loki." Michael twisted the sword, wrenching a scream from her, the move extracting the last of her magic. As she panted through the pain and the sudden debilitating weakness, her brother said, "Your life for hers." The blade against her throat vanished, replaced by the god-killer. "You'll lie down on the slab and let me shove my sword through your black heart."

Don't make the deal. He'll kill me once you're gone either way.

The infant inside her must've recognized its imminent death because it fought back, funneling electricity from Solas' fingertips into Michael's hand. He jigged, scraping her neck with the god-killer, and nicking her enough a small line of blood oozed down her throat. That one scratch sealed her fate... *but not Loki's.*

Lifting a trembling hand, she drove Suriel's dagger into Michael's heart. The weapon froze her brother with her still pinned on his sword. She felt his panic, and she could sense the magic he funneled at the dagger in an effort to break the spell.

"Move fast." She dragged in a ragged breath, fighting to breathe. *It hurts to breathe.* "Suriel's magic won't last, Loki. Kill him, and the god-killer is yours."

You're all that matters, he said into her mind. And then he was there at her side. His eyes found hers before his gaze slid over the position of the sword evaluating her injuries.

"It won't end until he's dead. Kill him for me, Loki." At her request, her brother jerked, proof the magic in Suriel's blade faded.

"As you wish, angel." Her sword elevated from the floor and went into Loki's palm. He used it to stab Michael in the neck. He yanked the steel free and jabbed it beneath Michael's chin, driving the sword upward until the tip exited the top of his head. Loki twisted the same way her brother had. "Die, motherfucker." Her husband didn't stop there. Oh, no. With an, "I'm sorry," against her ear, he pulled her off her brother's sword. Solas whimpered at the new pain lancing through her chest as Loki slashed her blade horizontally to severe Michael's head, then he punted the skull across the room as her sibling's body hit the ground. Michael's sword and the god-killer clattered to the floor, and a whoosh of breath came from her reapers. Surprise. Loki had won. Fear. What would Loki do to them?

"What will your next move be?"

Saving you. His mental voice was all business. *Then putting your fucked-in-the-head father through an eternity of hell.*

"Detain the reapers in the dungeon." Loki commanded as he swung her into his arms and settled her on the slab Michael had been sitting on earlier. "They'll swear allegiance to Solas or die." He pressed his palm against the wound in her chest. A purple aura surrounded him as he shoved his power into her, but she was so numb she felt nothing.

"It won't work. The magic in the god-killer..." she coughed. The movement wrenched a cry from her, and something wet trickled from her mouth. Horror slid across Loki's face as he thumbed the cut on her neck. She could feel the panic edging into him, but somehow he managed to blank his features. Didn't do much good when she could *feel* him.

"Don't give Him our creation. Innocent. Save it." She struggled to inhale. Fuck, but it hurt to breathe. "Used electricity to—"

"That's my magic."

"Has your magic." Solas lifted a hand and trailed bloody fingers along his cheek.

"It shouldn't be capable of any magic this young."

It has a god as a... father. She would've went with 'creator' instead of 'father', but if she stood a chance in hell of Loki viewing it as anything other than a bargaining chip, she must engage his protective instincts.

"You're not fucking dying, angel. You prom...*ised*..." He choked on the last syllable. Despondency burned in his eyes, and his mojo struck her hard and fast, causing her to bow off the table. Once again, she felt nothing. Not even a spark of tingling to hint his attempt to heal her would succeed.

If she could make her death easier for him she would. She loved him, wanted nothing but happiness for him. Watching him suffer thickened her throat, and she wanted to cry for him.

Give Soki a good name. A strong name. Something that'll strike fear in the hearts of his enemies.

"You're helping me with that, wife."

My reapers are his inheritance. She stuck with mental communication because it hurt to talk, and she could form coherent words with her mind.

"You're not dying, goddamn it."

Only one person could halt her death, and He wasn't in a forgiving state of mind where she was concerned. Tears fell from Loki's eyes and flowed along his cheeks.

He jerked her against him, pressing his face to her neck, and wept, his grief wetting her skin and breaking her heart. Funny that she could feel his heartache, but nothing else.

She slid her fingers through the strands of his hair and tilted her head so their cheeks brushed together. *Love you, Loki.*

"Keep breathing, angel." His lips moved against her skin. *"Live for me."*

She wanted to, oh, how she wanted to, but the dice had been thrown, and the fates had cut her strings.

Before Loki, she'd been nothing but a robot, a slave to her father's will. In the beginning, she'd been ashamed of her failure to kill Loki, but because of him she'd known passion, love, and the gift of a child.

He alone taught me what it meant to live. She'd fallen at his feet, and he'd shown her more kindness than her father. Loki had been a gift to her, a blessing.

As Grigori, she'd watched humanity through jaded eyes, while fascinated with their freewill, even their freedom to reject a loving Father. *He loved me only as long as I obeyed.* Humanity's choices were emotional at best and irrational at their worst. She'd believed herself above them, and reaped them because she devalued the beauty and purity of their choices.

Until Loki.

The moment she'd set eyes on him, she'd known he wasn't the monster Father made him out to be. And then her husband had shown *her* the beauty and purity of her choices.

If she had it all to do over again, she'd make the same decisions.

"No regrets, hus—" Exhaling, a strange rattle escaped her throat.

Loki was my salvation.

Pain lanced through her at her slow, ragged inhale.

Loki lifted his head and shook her by her shoulders. The terror in his eyes and voice, nearly undid her. "Fucking breathe, Solas, or you won't like what I do."

His eyes were the first I looked on after my fall, and they're the last before my death. Poetic justice. Fitting.

I love him. Thank you, Father, for forcing my fall.

Tears ran unchecked down his cheeks, and he bellowed as he struck her chest with his fist. She didn't feel the smack. He struck her again as if he thought the blows would force air into her lungs. "Your punishment will be worse this time."

I liked his punishment.

His arms went around her, and he crushed her against his chest. "Breathe. Don't leave me. P-p-lease, angel, please b-breathe."

Another exhale rattled from her chest. Suddenly Vy loomed behind him, and she placed her hand on his shoulder. "Loki, I—"

He shrugged her off with a snarl, and she stumbled away.

"He can't win. Can't have you." Loki pressed his lips against hers, their foreheads met, and he held her eyes. "C-can't live," he sniffled, "w-without y-you."

Her lungs refused to inflate and draw another breath. He attempted to blow air into her mouth, but the effort was futile, and her chest refused to rise.

Honor my memory by living, husband.

Wetness hit her cheeks, and he broke down, sobbing as his salty tears hit her tongue.

My last taste of him.

Darkness narrowed her vision, but she stared into Loki's purple eyes, thankful for him even in her last moments of life. Loki dissolved behind a gray haze and—

On her knees, hands bound behind her back, something snug encircled her neck, pinching into her skin. She blinked at her brother, Gabriel, as he circled her. His expression was severe, angry, and his eyes narrowed, icy, there'd be no mercy from his hand.

"How shall we begin, sister?"

TWENTY-FOUR

$\mathcal{I}$n the silence of the room Loki realized the howling sound of pain, a sound he'd heard from many of his enemies before their final breath, came from him. Lifting his head from his angel's chest, he held her tighter against him. An electric shock to his fingers lying over Solas' stomach pulled him back from the darkness threatening to consume him. Another pulse of electricity had his wife's lifeless body bowing.

"Stop!" Loki hovered his palm over her stomach and sent a small charge of voltage back to the creature inside her. Did the little one attempt to make her heart beat? How something so small knew the anatomy enough to try to jump-start her heart, Loki didn't know. The creature he swore to protect with a simple nod of his head at Solas' last wish thumped against his palm as if demanding attention. Loki squeezed his angel's hand, slipping in the blood covering her skin. Unchecked tears spilled onto the back of her hand, making clean strips over her skin like raindrops on a dirty window.

The clean patches of skin were an odd thing to focus on, but he felt numb. This couldn't be real. He didn't lose. She'd promised to fight to live. The scene replayed in his mind like a movie. Had she sacrificed herself for him? She'd have known her brother well enough to predict his move, his plan of attack.

Gritting his teeth as anger stirred inside him, Loki called to her, shaking her gently. "Angel."

When her head lolled back against the crook of his arm, the slice on her neck from the god-killer taunted him for his failure to protect her. At the sight of the cut, the floor beneath him rumbled as a sign of the simmering rage he felt. Soon his fury would boil over and cause natural disasters. It was just a matter of time.

"My Lord." Vy's voice called behind him.

"Shh." Something in the distance sounded, inside Solas' head as if her mind still lingered with life. *Shall we begin, sister?* Angling his body so he could face Vy while still holding his angel tight to his chest, Loki glared at Elyon beside her. "Who's with her?"

"That's what he's here to tell you."

Loki stared at the fallen angel. Elyon's head tilted as he stared at Solas. The sadness in his eyes, matched the graveled pain in his tone when he answered, "Gabriel."

"She's not dead." The elation he felt quickly faded when the realization of where she was hit him. Limbo. Was her suffering and painful death not enough to absolve her father's need for revenge?

"Her blood touched the god-killer." Elyon approached, but Loki held his free hand out to halt him. "Let me take her from you. I can prepare her body."

"Don't come any closer." Loki's body vibrated with the need to kill his wife's fallen brother. "You think I'd allow you to prepare her body for death when I know she lives?" His anger rocked the room with a sizeable quake. Vy stumbled, clutching the wall as she reached to pull Elyon away from Loki.

The feeling of flames licking across his skin from his right shoulder to his fingertips made him twist his hand to check for burns he knew would be there. *What the fuck?* He palmed the god-killer, the sword sitting way too comfortably in his grip as if it'd been custom made for him. Tossing it to the floor, his gaze snapped to Elyon's. "Don't say a fucking word."

"But I must, Loki."

"Bly!" Ignoring Elyon, Loki called to his first in command.

"I thought you needed some time, that's why I didn't return after the fight ended." Loki noted the look of disapproval Bly shot at Vy, but this wasn't the time to deal with disgruntlement in the ranks. They'd been in an ongoing pissing match for years.

"Is my child safe?"

"Of course." Bly's tone sounded agitated at the question.

"Yet you were here before I summoned you, when you were clearly instructed to stay with my child."

"I came when I felt the earthquake. Your son is safe, but don't be angry with me for looking out for your safety as well. It's been my job since we were young. A habit hard to break, *my lord*." Hidden beneath his first's words were many emotions ranging from admiration to fear. Loki couldn't be angry. Bly had never failed him, and deep down Loki knew Bly would ensure the safety of his child before Bly came to him.

"If I don't return, I give all that I am and all that I have to him."

"Return from where?"

"I'm going to claim my wife."

"Let me go with you."

"No. Your place is with my child."

"This is suicide," Elyon said.

"Suicide would be taking a step closer toward my wife, *fallen*." No one would touch her. After lifting Solas into his arms, Loki kicked the god-killer further away from him. That damn sword had been nothing but trouble since Michael had first threatened him with it. "We follow the same plan as before. It's just modified a bit." Modified a fucking lot if he was honest with himself.

"Loki." Elyon stared at him, his face crinkled with what appeared to be confusion.

"What, Elyon?"

"She was cut with the god-killer."

"This means what to me?"

"It means Gabriel can't touch her yet. She awaits judgment from Father."

Loki spun, Solas snug in his arms, as he battled the rage inside him. His vision darkened, and his muddled thoughts couldn't make the association of what this meant. Did his little minx intend to get cut, knowing the sword would place her in judgment? "What of the soul oath?"

"The god-killer cut delayed her soul oath death, but it's still a valid oath."

If he'd learned one thing in the time his beautiful angel had been in his life, it was to never underestimate her intentions. Waiting for her to make a move, if she even had one, wasn't an option. The dead weight of her body in his arms remained a solid reminder of the depth of this situation. No, he had to act now. "He will *not* judge my wife."

Loki closed his eyes enjoying his connection with the earth as the energy rumbled through him. When he opened his eyes, he stood one mile from the tip of the world's tallest mountain, Mauna Kea. The volcano had been inactive for many years, but the feelings inside him threatened to make the core heat and erupt. Adjusting his angel in his arms, he started walking up the mountain. With each step, the mountain seemed to grow taller. After fifteen minutes, he was sure the elevation had grown, making his path to the top never-ending.

Loki sighed and shook his head. "I can do this all day," he shouted toward the top.

"So can I, Loki." The familiar baritone vibration of God's voice boomed around him.

Cursing under his breath, Loki continued his journey to the mountain's summit. After another fifteen minutes, he'd gained little ground. "Seriously?"

"Go back, Loki. You're not welcome on my mountain."

"If that's what you desire, but I've come to negotiate a trade with you. I have something you may want."

"Unless it's the abomination your tainted seed impregnated *my* reaper with, there is nothing to discuss."

Fuck.

He'd tainted two seeds, the one inside Solas now and his son. Guarding the creation through the chalice had been done with the utmost security. There was no way God had found out.

"We have much to discuss then." Loki felt his body separating, stretching, and moving through the air without his permission. When his feet hit solid ground once more, he felt disoriented. Looking around, he realized he stood at the tip of the mountain. In a panic, he tightened his arms, relieved when he felt his wife still in his embrace and snuggled against his chest.

"Remove your shoes, for you are on sacred ground." The powerful voice, almost as painful as the light beginning to shine in the distance, sounded so loud Loki fought to keep standing.

"Fuck off."

"I have eternity to wait, Loki, do you?"

No, he didn't. Because this asshole could be in many places at once, which meant he could judge Solas, release Gabriel on her, and stand here arguing with him at the same time. He'd never removed his shoes during their past meetings! So why now? Just to see him jump through hoops? *Goddamn it!*

"Your ego gets the best of you again." A chuckle from the almighty had Loki biting the inside of his mouth. Many words piled to the front of his mind like a mad dash of shoppers on black Friday.

Looking down at Solas, Loki cursed and toed the heel of his boot. Maybe he'd throw it at the fucker for good measure. With his boots off, he walked toward the light, staring straight into its center. The blaze would burn the retina of any mortal, and some demi-gods. But Loki defied it, glared at the light even. Never once had he seen God, just a silhouette inside the light.

"That wasn't hard, was it?" The outline moved and changed shapes when God talked.

"I've come to collect my wife. Negotiate for her soul oath."

"Why would I agree to this when I know you'll give her a chance to live?"

"For fuck's sake, if she was one of your precious humans you would have already forgiven her." Loki's anger would get the best of him if he wasn't careful, but the more he tried to cork his rage, the more it brewed with uneven bursts of hostility.

Spotting a flat, long rock the height of his knees, Loki moved a couple feet to lay Solas along the slab. After adjusting her body and cupping her hands over her belly, Loki returned his attention to his enemy. Fear tugged at his gut. The irrational thought that breaking contact with Solas' skin would somehow be a permanent separation had him keeping one hand over his angel's. "You want my child. You've sent many to kill Solas for that purpose."

"And it seems I've won." The orb flickered with a burst of blue and white light. "The child will soon die inside her womb."

Fuck! The feeling of being cornered was new to Loki. Frustration set his feet in motion, and he paced in front of Solas, blocking her from her father's view to shield her from His victory, as if somehow Solas would feel her fall all over again if she knew her father saw her defeat. If he had found a loophole with the sword, he'd have it rammed through His heart by now. At the thought of the sword, a familiar burn started in his shoulder, shooting down to his palm. The god-killer made a sound unlike any sword he'd known, almost singing when he held it. With a quick motion, he moved his free hand over his angel's stomach, encasing the little creation in a protective ball of electricity. Loki waved his hand again and pulled an orb pulsing with power from her womb, but left the infant nestled safely in her womb. "Give me her soul oath before it's too late."

He knew her father would think he bargained Solas' life for the child's.

"One more thing."

The smug sound in God's voice had Loki growling, "We had a deal."

"That was before you killed Michael." The reminder of the almighty's original ultimatum to bring Him their unborn child caused Loki to grind his teeth, while He went on in His self-righteous tenor, as if He'd already won. "And now you have the sword."

"What do you want? The sword?" Loki tossed it toward Him.

"No. I want you to finish Michael's job."

"You want me to kill myself?"

"I want you to kill all the others who claim to be gods, with the god-killer, and restore the balance."

Loki grimaced. "You want me to wield a sword in your name?"

"Or she dies."

Motherfucker. Wield a sword in the name of God? And people called Loki merciless. God held all the cards at the moment, or did He? Loki could agree. The sword would make it easier for him to gain more control in his world. When he was done, he would tell the almighty prick to go fuck Himself or kill Him with His own sword. By then they may have found the loophole Bly spoke about. Without further consideration Loki said, "I agree. Give me her soul oath."

A bright beam of white light expanded toward Loki faster than he could move. Searing hot pain encased his right forearm. Tears hit the back of his eyes at the feeling of a thousand hot needles moving in and out of his flesh as if something was being sewn into his skin. Loki fell to his knees, the pain too intense for him to defy a moment longer. In this moment, he knew the power of God, and it was much stronger than his own.

Once the light vanished, Loki twisted his arm to look at his skin. Seared into his flesh were words from an ancient language he couldn't understand.

"You have her soul oath, *Sword of God.*"

Goosebumps protested his new title, but Loki shook it off as he pushed to his feet. The muscles in his legs protested with unexplained weakness, and he wobbled like a newly born calf as he gained his footing. Pride had him squaring his shoulders and glaring in God's direction as he sent a mental message to Solas. *You are reborn, angel. I give you life. Your wings will regenerate once you're in the safety of our bedroom. Call on my power so there is no pain. And this time, angel, your wings can never be taken from you.* He waved a hand over his wife, and she disappeared.

"We're done here."

"Not quite, *My Sword.*" Loki loathed the unwanted title because it was a reminder of his defeat against his enemy. But the silhouette inside the light grew more defined as if energized by His victory. "The child." The light reached out toward the electric ball floating between them.

Loki snapped his fingers, the electric bands wrapped around the ball faded, leaving an empty clear bubble floating between them.

"Loki!" The sky thundered with God's anger.

"Now, now... you didn't actually *ask* for the child. You said the child would die inside Solas' womb." Loki stepped back as the white light pulsed, turning black around the edges like a stormy sky. "The agreement was for me to swing your stupid sword a couple times."

"Trickster till the end, Loki. You will pay for your deceit."

"Don't be a sore loser. You know you didn't ask for the child in the agreement but relinquished that part of the agreement when you assumed you'd won and it would die in her womb." The sky grew dark, rumbling with His anger as a clash of lightning struck the mountaintop a little too close for Loki's comfort. With Solas and the creation safe, Loki felt cockier about his deception. He may have to wield this damn sword, but his angel lived. Calling the god-killer to his grasp, Loki stepped back. "I'm surprised the almighty didn't see that coming."

"*Loki!*" The sky opened, and hail rained down in massive chunks.

Loki winked at the silhouette before closing his eyes to relocate to his wife.

TWENTY-FIVE

$\mathcal{F}$alling from limbo to earth came with a soft landing. Solas bounced when she landed on the mattress in the chamber she'd shared with Loki, the cave bedroom, not the penthouse he'd first taken her to in the beginning. The magic here felt stronger, interlaced with ancient mojo she could feel but not identify.

The tickle on her back caused her to leap off the bed and turn her back toward the body-length mirror Loki shattered during his temper tantrum. She yanked her shirt off and peered over her shoulder to catch sight of the tips of wings that sprouted from the scars on her flesh. Loki's mental speak came back to her: *You are reborn, angel. I give you life. Your wings will regenerate once you're in the safety of our bedroom. Call on my power so there is no pain. And this time, angel, your wings can never be taken from you.*

No pain emerged from their regeneration, but only a slight tingle like a tickle or an itch. Either his magic aided her without her awareness because of their connection, or it was because where they were severed hadn't been cauterized like when the Lamb of God took them. Instead they'd been healed by Loki's loving touch.

Loki remains with Father.

Terror slammed into her. Her parent outgunned him with magic and an army of angels. If He wanted Loki dead, nothing would stop Him so long as Loki remained in His domain.

The sudden appearance of Suriel and Bly startled her, but only for a moment. She dug a tank top out of a drawer, a ridiculously pink thing that sported the word 'princess' in rhinestones. Dismissing the inanity of the garment, she tugged it on, the fabric settling into place between her reforming wings. "Bly, I require your assistance to aid Loki."

"He sent word to keep you out of trouble. *Here*."

She narrowed her gaze on Loki's first in command, ready to tear into him. He did *not* want to go toe to toe with her on this.

Suriel snagged her attention by hugging her. The moment their belly's touched, an electrical discharge arched between them. Her sister jumped back, gaping at Solas' belly. "What was that?"

She sent the creature inside her a mental scold. *Back off.* At the assault, her son inside Suriel gave off a frightened vibe. In an effort to soothe him, Solas settled her palm against Suriel's stomach. *So long as I live, sweet boy, no one will harm you. You are safe. You are loved.*

"I don't have time to explain what that was, Suriel, but I promise I will later. Bly, your help is expected. *Now*."

"I have my orders." Bly shook his head and crossed his arms over his chest, guaranteeing she'd have to kick his ass.

Suriel gave one of Solas' feathers a sharp tug. "Sol, your wings... they're *stunning*."

She didn't have time to discuss her wings until Loki was safe. Staring at Bly, she said to Suriel, "If your guard dog doesn't help me, he's going to experience firsthand how one of them feels slicing *his throat wide open*."

"Classic reason why you need anger management classes," Loki said from behind her. The sneaky bastard, she hadn't heard him enter. "Although you're likely to murder the therapist before you get the help you need."

"*Loki*," she breathed in relief and would've turned to face him, but he palmed her nape and tangled his fingers in the sensitive strands at the base of her neck. The fingers of his other hand trailed across the line where her wings rejuvenated. Solas shivered at his touch and thanks to the heightened sensation of her wings, his wing-caress spread across her body. Even her clit pulsed in reaction.

"Leave us." The air of the words puffed against the side of her face. Bly and Suriel exited without so much as a goodbye.

"Let me see you, Loki, so I know you're unharmed."

Instead of releasing her, he used his grip on her hair to tilt her head back at a slant so their gazes could collide. The purple overshadowing his green irises attested to his godhood and that his magic, possibly his emotions too, remained elevated. He gave the top line of her wing a heavy-handed stroke, and she whispered his name again as gooseflesh buzzed along her skin.

"Do you like your new wings?"

"Of co—" His fingers slid through the feathers, and heat punched her in the gut, forcing her core to clench with need. "*Loki*. They're more sensitive than before."

"I could make you come from doing just this."

Yes.

"I should make you come this way as punishment for not even taking the time to look at the new wings *I* gave you." Loki *tsked* her as if she'd been naughty.

"Thank you for returning them," she whispered, her focus locked on his mouth as he lowered his head toward her, and his strokes continued through the network of her quills.

Her scalp lit up, protesting the constriction of his fingers in her hair, while her breathing escalated, and her pussy vibrated.

"Thanks for fighting to live like you fucking *promised*, wife." Loki smashed their lips together, a punishing connection as their teeth knocked together.

His tongue tackled hers, and she could taste his drive for violence in his kiss. That only excited her more regardless that she could feel his thin grip on control. She gasped at the unexpected sting when he yanked a feather free. Solas kissed him back with all her emotion, but sent him a silent thought…

I did fight to live for us, for our son.

Lie. You knew how Michael fought. You should've expected he'd impale you on his sword that way.

Solas opened her eyes. Prisms of purple sparkled, drowning out his green. In the face of his anger, he continued to kiss her, but his rage couldn't be dismissed from the passionate way he smooched her.

Loki... she sent a mental image of her stroking his cheek with her palm. *I've fought with Michael more than ten thousand years, and I've never seen him execute that move. I didn't even know he could move people or objects like that.*

Loki jerked free of her mouth and stared at her as if he calculated the validity of her words. The hand that'd been stroking her wings, curled around her stomach, and the moment his palm touched her belly the creature inside jolted him with static electricity.

"It did that to Suriel too when our stomachs touched. We might have a problem on our hands." *Told you we shouldn't have created it, Loki.*

I can spank you for your insolence, wife.

As far as threats went, that one sucked ass. She'd enjoyed the last time he spanked her and fucked her anally. His eyes darkened to a deeper purple, verifying he'd read her mind.

"Brat, don't bully the god that gave you life and that particular power. I can take your life as easily as I gave it." He thumped her abdomen, and the being inside her settled down. His arm moved higher across her torso until the feather he'd plucked moved into her vision. "See... I marked you as mine. Even your fucking father cannot deny who you belong to now."

Black remained the dominant color, but purple shimmered as he rolled the quill between his fingers. Stunning, just like Suriel had said. And they'd been gifted to her. Swallowing down the weird emotional burn in her throat, she gave him a teasing smile. "Does the purple spell out 'Loki's property' across the span of my wings?"

"Why didn't I think of that?"

Solas snagged the feather from his grasp, and he released his hold on her. She trailed her fingernail along the spindles, producing a purple metallic shimmer against the inky foundation. "I'm at a loss for words, and saying thank you doesn't seem to be enough."

"You can thank me by not dying again. A blow job is always appreciated too."

She laughed, realizing she felt free, as if the weight of the world had been removed from her shoulders.

He pinched the bridge of his nose. "I'm serious, Solas, don't die on me again. I came close to decimating the world with my sorrow." Needing to touch her again, he brushed his knuckles across her cheek. "You have a distinctive scent when your emotions are high with *love*. It took me until your heart beat its last rhythm to figure out where I'd smelled the scent before. It was you, angel. All these years watching over me. I felt your love within the shadows but didn't know what it was. When I smelled you that first time you fell at my feet, it filled me with such need that it scared the hell out of me."

Solas hugged him, wrapping her arms tight around his waist, and she settled her ear against his chest finding solace in the sound of his heartbeat. A second later she cocooned him with her wings. He hugged her back and kissed the top of her head. The smell of him engulfed her, reminded her all remained well in her world.

"How'd you escape Father?"

"We made a deal. I received your soul oath in exchange for picking up the mantle of *Sword of God*."

"Loki, no!"

"It is done, angel."

Irritated by his calm tone, Solas shoved out of his embrace. "That makes you Father's bitch. I'd rather be dead than have that."

"That's melodramatic. I'm a god. I'm no one's bitch." Like always, his cockiness overflowed.

"Never thought I'd see the day the trickster was duped by my parent." They glared at one another while she let that sink in. "You've no idea what you agreed to. He calls, you go. He commands, you do. There is *no* room for denial. The sword will compel you to follow His directives."

Loki got in her personal space, tangled both hands in her hair, and yanked her head back. "I made the deal for your life. What would you have done in a similar situation?"

"My soul for yours was not a sensible deal."

"It was the *only* sensible deal." He gave a little tug, and she gasped at the prickles along her scalp. "Answer the goddamn question, Solas."

"I don't know, Loki!" She blinked a couple of times to eliminate the blur of tears. "How do you think I feel knowing you bartered your soul for mine? How would you feel if I bartered mine for yours and the trade put me in a bad spot?"

Loki's breath caught as if she managed to sucker punch him with the last question. "It'll be fine."

"He'll demand you kill me, our son, your Naglfar—"

"*Our* Naglfar."

"—and probably even the fallen that've aligned with us."

"I'd never harm you or our son."

"You won't have a choice, Loki."

"Your god said he wanted me to only kill the others who claim to be gods so the balance would be restored. He demanded this of me in exchange for your life."

"Is it so hard to believe the legendary trickster could be tricked? What He said wasn't the total truth." His eyes blazed bright with purple, brighter than she'd ever seen, and she could feel his anger like the sting of wasps along her skin. Solas did not back down because he had to understand the severity of his new role. "Your love for either of us won't be enough to save you from the magic in the sword that'll compel you to follow *His command.*"

"You couldn't have shared this information *before* I lopped off Michael's head?"

"Don't turn the blame on me." She placed her palm over his heart. "I gave you the god-killer free and clear. *You* made the unnecessary deal."

"Goddamn it, woman, you drive me crazy with your stubbornness. You know why I agreed to the deal with Him."

"I thought that's why you made this creature in my stomach." Speak of the devil, it protested with another charge, and Solas squealed in surprise at the sharp sting.

"I've had it with your tantrums." Loki lifted Solas into his arms and settled her on the mattress. "Hold still, angel."

He held his palm over her belly. Purple and silver strings of magic, interwoven like a DNA helix, filtered from his hand and filled her womb.

"Why didn't you give it to Father? That's why you made it."

"Your last wish was to save it from Him. Only an ass would ignore a final request."

"I didn't expect you to honor that request." She trailed her fingers across her soul oath stitched into the flesh of his arm. "What'd you do to the baby with your magic?"

"Bound its powers." He caught her hand and kissed her wrist. "Am I missing something here, Solas? I'm unfamiliar with this type of magic. How can it have power this young?"

"I don't know." She shook her head. "It grows faster than Soki, but none of Father's creations had access to their magic this soon. Even after their birth, they were weak, gained their magic slowly, and had to be trained. This seems to understand how to use its power early."

"No one had to teach me. As a child, I brandished my magic with an intrinsic knowledge."

"I'd like to have seen you as a child brandishing your magic." Why'd the idea of him 'brandishing his magic' give her kinky notions?

"I was a bully and flaunted my dominance."

"Not much has changed then?"

"I should swat your ass."

"You should."

"I already restrained you with my magic, angel." Loki's eyes brightened with mischief as he Eskimo kissed her. "I have more tricks up my sleeve. Naughtier tricks I'll happily use on you."

"So then..." That promise made her wetter, and she cleared her throat to pick up the conversation. "Maybe the creation's ability to manage its power has something to do with your magic, mixing our blood... I don't know. You *are* its creator, its father for lack of a better term."

"I'm only Soki's father. We need to decide on a real name before you grow attached to that ridiculous one."

Solas smiled, not because he hated the name Soki but because Loki ignored what could be a problem and focused on their family instead. "Since you don't like Soki or Loki Junior, I'm guessing 'sweet boy' isn't an option."

"Fuck no." Loki moved with such speed she almost lost the ability to track him with her eyes, reminding her of the significance of his power. She still had no idea what all he could do, or how powerful he was. Had she engaged him in a real death match, there was no question who would've been the victor.

He moved over her, shoving her legs apart with his knees as his fingers dove back into her hair and anchored her to the mattress. Once settled between her thighs, he said, "He needs a stronger name. I want what you want." She elevated her eyebrows, questioning him because her body died for something else other than a name. "His name alone should strike fear in the hearts of his enemies."

Yes, she definitely wanted that for Soki, but that'd come as he aged and created a *name* for himself.

Loki rocked his hips, teasing her with a hard scrub of his cock against her pussy. Her core melted for him. "I'm already wet for you, husband."

"I know." The smugness of his smirk teased a grin from her.

"Conceited bastard."

"The hazards of being a god well-versed in satisfying sexual appetites."

Solas laughed as she wrapped a leg around his waist and swayed her core along the line of his hard-on, drawing a groan from him. Adding to the sensation, she dragged her nails down his back and buried them into his leather-clad ass. "Then why aren't you inside me?"

"You've other thoughts on your mind. I want all worries out in the open before I make you come."

Solas stopped her hip thrusting as fear frizzled along her spine.

"I'm afraid speaking my fears aloud will jinx us." And what was the point in saying them if he already heard them?

"We're going to find a loophole to get out of the *Sword of God* bullshit. Bly's already on it. Tell me your other fears. I want to hear them. *Need* to hear you state them."

She wished she could believe they'd find a loophole, but her doubts morphed into a life of their own. "I can't stop thinking since Father's omniscient—"

"I swear to you, He's *not*."

"For the sake of argument, pretend for me that He is omniscient."

"Go on."

"I can't stop thinking He knew when He put me on you how everything would pan out." The purple in Loki's eyes faded a little, letting the green shine through. "He knew I'd fall for you, knew we'd conceive, knew Michael would nick me with the god-killer, knew you'd kill Michael and bargain for my soul oath. He saw it all. *Knew* it all would come to pass."

Loki shook his head. "He was furious I didn't give Him our child. He didn't see that trickery coming."

"Are you sure?" The slight narrowing at the corners of his eyes, testified to his doubt.

A brief glimpse of Loki's memory on Mauna Kea flashed through her mind. God thought He'd obtain their infant, and Loki tricked Him instead. If she received the recollection accurately, her parent hadn't specifically asked for their son, but He *had* haggled for Loki being the *Sword of God*.

We are fucked.

"You're the ultimate weapon, a rogue god, wielding the god-killer. Father has plausible deniability so long as you're swinging the sword. You're known as a loose cannon. When you start killing in His name, none will believe it's for Him, but will be certain you seek your own purpose." Worry settled in her gut, and despite Loki binding the creature's powers inside her, she felt its anxiety too. "Your powers will magnify the weapon. The more death you deal, the more powerful you'll become."

"How so?"

"The god-killer is nothing more than an extension of your hand. Your power will be amplified through it." *He'll be unstoppable while he manipulates it, and Father knew that.* She was certain of it. "You gain the power of the gods you kill."

"If Michael had killed me that day at the chop shop, he'd have gained my power."

"Yes," she said even though he wasn't really asking, just working it out in his head. "You think the blade suits your needs, but I'm afraid He's played you because He's already seen it all. So..."

Biting her cheek, she shook her head afraid to breathe life into the question lingering on her tongue.

"Say it, Solas. Just say it."

"Did Father sacrifice me to gain control of *you*?"

TO BE CONTINUED

ABOUT THE AUTHORS

GRACEN MILLER is a hopeless daydreamer masquerading as a "normal" person in southern society. When not writing, she's a full-time lacrosse mom for her two sons and a devoted wife to her real-life hero-husband of over twenty-five years. She has an unusual relationship with her muse, Dom, but credits all her creative success to his brilliant mind. She's addicted to writing, paranormal romance novels, horror movies, Alabama football, and coffee... addictions are not necessarily in order of priority. She's convinced coffee is nectar from the gods and when blending coffee and writing together it generates the perfect creative merger. Many of her creative worlds are spawned from coffee highs and Dom's aggressive demands. Gracen writes in multiple genres—paranormal romance, paranormal erotic romance, rock star contemporary romance, and dystopian romance. To learn more about Gracen or to leave her a comment, visit her website at www.gracen-miller.com.

Amazon Author Page:http://amazon.com/author/gracenmiller

TINA CARREIRO is a multi-published author who resides in South Florida with her family. At the young age of 15, Tina started working to help her family and became a jack-of-all-trades, working in many different areas from managing an automotive shop, to putting her computer programming degree to use. In 2010, she retired from her office job to live her dream and write. Her addiction to romance novels began at a young age when she started sneaking her mom's Gray Eagle series by Janelle Taylor, and it was then her love for writing began. Her paranormal romance series, Power of the Moon, has gained popularity amongst the fans of this genre. Tina is married to her best friend and the love of her life, and is a full-time gaming/cosplaying mom for her son and daughter. When not writing, Tina enjoys reading romance novels, zombie movies, restoring classic cars, cats, crafting, graphic design work, and coffee with caramel macchiato creamer. Poking fun at herself, and everything in between is her key to laughter and a long and healthy life.

To learn more about Tina or to leave her a comment, visit her at http://tinacarreiro.com

Amazon Author Page: http://amzn.com/e/B0057FRXL2

OTHER BOOKS BY GRACEN MILLER

Road to Hell series
Madison's Life Lessons (novella)
Pandora's Box (#1)
Hell's Phoenix (#2)
Genesis Queen (#3)
Royal Partnerships (#4)
King Eliel (#5)

Stand alone erotica books
Taboo Kisses (ménage)
Elfin Blood
Demon Spelled (dark gothic ménage)
Fairy Casanova (*1Night Stand Story*)
Celia's Connection (Twin Flame series #1)

Dystopian Romance
Lie to Me

Hot Wired series
Rockin' the Heart
Lost in the Beat

You can easily find all of Gracen's books on Amazon:
http://amazon.com/author/gracenmiller

OTHER BOOKS BY TINA CARREIRO

Power of the Moon series
Power of the Moon (#1)
Covet the Moon (#2)

Darker Side of Blue series
Assume the Position (#1)

Double D Ranch series
Rearranged (#1)

Stand alone short story
The Plan

You can easily find all of Tina's books on Amazon:
http://amzn.com/e/B0057FRXL2